THAT IRON STRING

JACK KOHL

The Pauktaug Press
Pauktaug, New York

ISBN: 978-0-69234-445-3

Cover design/cover photo: Al Jarnow
Interior design: Gary A. Rosenberg • www.thebookcouple.com

Printed in the United States of America

Contents

CHAPTER I

IMMINENCE

It is likely that nearly everyone has heard, at one time or another, the many arguments offered to young people against a career in music. Let one say that a young person fixes upon a career as a classical pianist—a solo concert artist, perhaps. Legions of professionals and laymen—even those who generally support him and want for him what he wants for himself—will point out tirelessly that the odds are stacked against his success. Even if one starts out with an excess of the requisite talent and enthusiasm, innumerable obstacles can be cited that stand in the young pianist's way—vast amounts of competition, a lifetime of dependence upon the lonely art of practicing, an itinerant existence, general financial insecurity, the dwindling demands of the public for an increasingly inapplicable art form, and the likely fickleness of that same public if by chance it does embrace a young pianist.

But based upon the events of last year, and the autumn before that, may I venture to add yet another consideration that should be taken under advisement—the risk, the physical threat posed by the piano itself? One has been made aware, of late, of the many pianists who over-practice themselves into debilitating states of tendonitis and carpal-tunnel syndrome. But I refer to something much more extreme. It is easy to become complacent about the piano's great but generally stationary bulk—which, when conspiring with gravity, can become one of the most crushing objects in man's domain. I do not mean the threat posed by the keyboard lid. That danger is often the feature of slapstick comedy. A straight man plays away while a cruel jokester lingers over the player, ready to smash the lid down on the unsuspecting pianist and his vulnerable fingers. No, I refer to the threat posed by the great weight of the grand piano as a whole. Few common things place so much weight above the ground and a cozy little space beneath the object. And man puts this on wheels, too—making it ever so dangerous on an incline. Clips from old silent films often exploit the gag of pianos falling from the sides of city buildings as they are being raised into apartments via ropes and pulleys. But last year, and the autumn before that, gravity and other circumstances conspired to make falling pianos offer new grist for cinematic farce. Perhaps someone will exploit the tragedies that way quite soon—as people do not wait as long as they once did before doing such things. Yet beyond the benefits of good taste, the makers of the pianos involved would certainly like a quieting down concerning the recent chain of terrible disasters—because the high-profile venues where the tragedies occurred have brought scrutiny upon the piano making industry. And there has been a rather foolish cry from the public about something being done to grand piano design so as to help prevent such disasters in the future.

But like all the other warnings given to young people about careers in the concert world, I think this newest one will have little effect. Undoubtedly such disasters will continue to occur, so long as man is dependent upon music. There is nothing to be done about it, really. In fact, I think it may only draw more young people to the art—now that the piano has an added element of imminent danger to its already seductive, romantic, threatening aspects. This new trend hasn't kept me away, I must confess.

Last summer, I read yet another article about the string of strange disasters—more so because it had material about my cousin, Boston, in it—as I rode the train into New York City so that I could finish my move out of Manhattan.

Over the course of the preceding day, in my aunt and uncle's hearse, I had moved my belongings from my Manhattan apartment back to Pauktaug Village, on the north shore of Long Island. As I did not have too many things, and as the hearse was rather large, I was able to make my move with only one trip. Most of my furniture—including a bed, a set of drawers, and a small couch—went to my roommate, a trumpet player. He was so pleased to have them, that he hardly realized the pleasure was all mine in not having to transport these items ever again. He and I had gotten along rather well, as roommates go—for most of our schoolwork, as music students, was practicing that went on outside of the apartment. We both practiced at school. His trumpet would have been too loud for our building, and I did not have a piano in the city. So we rarely saw each other.

When I did see him, all things conspired to render him a bit red in the face. The playing of his instrument left him a bit ruddy cheeked at school. His drinking left him red at other times. And when we said our goodbyes, he was so eager to take possession of the furniture that my last view of him was of his crimson brow during efforts to test-lift his new property for moving. I left him and my Manhattan apartment behind with good-natured forgetfulness.

I had learned to enjoy my time in the city, but I was glad to return home for my forthcoming final stretch as a student. I had gone to undergraduate music school out of state, in the Midwest, but I took my master's degree in New York City. Now I was to continue at the same city school. But I opted to try commuting back and forth from Long Island so that I could work on my final performance degree while living at home in my native town. There I had a piano, the house of childhood and youth, and my Aunt Elizabeth and Uncle Harry.

My cousin was returning, as well. He was the same age as I was (twenty-nine), but he had only just finished his bachelor's degree. My cousin, Boston Gourd, had done well as an undergraduate pianist—remarkably well (supernaturally well, really)—but he began to compete frequently during his second or third year of school. He became so involved in that process, and so successful for a spate of nearly seven or eight years, that he deferred finishing his degree in favor of playing competitions. They led to innumerable festivals and concerts for a time, yet these results ultimately began to dissipate until he was playing only near his school in Los Angeles again. He registered for his remaining courses and worked toward finishing his degree. During that time he also entered two more highly-publicized competitions—one of which was in San Francisco, the other in Maryland.

In a letter of last spring, my aunt had suggested that he live with us in Pauktaug and that he go on to graduate school, as I had, in New York City. My cousin was as much a child of that Long Island village as I was, yet his guardians had passed on during our last year of high school, and he never returned after that. And despite my aunt's efforts, we never heard from him—save for a few times just after he left. And we never saw him again. Yet Boston and I grew up on the same dead-end street, and we were rarely more than one hundred yards apart for almost eighteen years. We had always been a close pair, and somehow the intensity of our mutual interests spared us a destructive rivalry.

Yet there could never be any question—and this I do not venture as affected modesty, but as an undeniable fact born of honest observation—that my cousin was the superior pianist in every measurable respect. Somehow I persisted in my own endeavors at the piano, notwithstanding the constant closeness of such a superior standard. And somehow we escaped comparing ourselves technically—perhaps because comparisons were obviated so early on—and we discussed instead, even in the midst of outdoor play, what it was that we had seen, so to speak, through our practicing.

It should be understood that Boston's disappearance from Pauktaug was not characterized so much by a desire to escape his home ground, it seemed, as it was by a calling that carried him into an escalating density of activity and travel. He seemed to follow this calling with all the will and heart at his command. And it should be understood that the will and heart he brought to bear came in tandem with a spirit that was deemed, with almost no notable exceptions, as intrepidly kind and affable. That is why we were puzzled by his complete silence after he left. My aunt would write to him once or twice a year for over a decade, but there was never an answer.

When he was close to finishing his bachelor's degree, in his inimitable manner he went on a whim to auditions held in Los Angeles for several of the large and notable New York music schools. On hearing of his acceptance to all the graduate programs to which he applied, he mentioned the possibility of school to my aunt—starting in the first of the surprise letters he wrote in response to hers of last spring. He was going to return to Pauktaug, if he could. Did the offer of the room on the third floor that could be his at anytime still stand? Of course it did, wrote back my aunt in a little note. And she telephoned him several times to tell him the same thing but never reached him. For quite some time, we (my aunt, my uncle, and I) thought this might be a whim of his. Yet soon after the telephone call, materials from the music school of his choice (which was the one I was attending) began to arrive in Pauktaug—letters concerning the orientation and immunization of new students and new teaching assistants. My cousin had easily won for himself an assistantship in accompaniment, a commodity not as easily secured in the dense and competitive world of Manhattan's music schools as it may be from time to time in less celebrated spots. I had tried several times for such an assistantship myself, but I was never successful at getting one in New York. Soon, more pragmatic signs would appear of my cousin's intimated return.

Both Boston and I held leases that ended in July, so it happened that we were both to make the move into my aunt's house in Pauktaug by the first of August. On that final July afternoon of an almost humorously hot day in Manhattan, I returned to my apartment, put a few last things into my backpack, and took leave of my roommate.

Not having to return to the city for another three weeks—for the fall semester did not start until mid-August—I took the opportunity to pick up a packet I had been told my teacher had left for me in the school office.

The packet contained acceptance forms and materials for a new a tri-annual piano competition to be held in New York, the Manhattoes Competition. It was to draw contenders from around the world. I had sent in a tape for it, in a rather indifferent frame of mind, at the suggestion of my teacher. Usually, I balked at the notion of competitions. I rarely felt eager to learn the extra material sometimes required for the entry tapes, and I always disliked the inconvenience of making recordings. I had learned to do without the world of competitions—though I had been in a few—but this competition's repertoire requirements curiously paralleled many of the works that I already knew (and for which I already had reasonably good recital recordings). This factor, coupled with the newness of the contest, made the Manhattoes Competition seem unthreatening. My unwittingly cavalier attitude somehow worked in my favor—or to my disfavor, if I am honest, considering my usual diffidence about testing myself in such arenas. My teacher's note informed me of my acceptance to the competition.

I was one of thirty people chosen, and because of my teacher's political power in the intricate and ancient music machine of New York, he had been privy to an early list of the contest's selected participants. He was also one of the founders of the Manhattoes Competition.

I quickly resolved to go through with this new prospect. Leaving an affirmative reply for my teacher in his box, I left the school behind. Complaining of the inequities, iniquities, and destructive influences of piano competitions had become a cliché, I resolved. Refusing to participate in this contest would seem only a yielding to fear. I felt happy in my decision.

I took the subway to the Long Island Rail Road, and soon I was coursing under the river and then surfacing on the head of the fish-shaped island that has always been my home. At least some think it looks fish-shaped. I have always thought it looks like a concert grand piano viewed from the bass string side—the North Fork suggesting the raising of the piano lid's front flap. Sometimes it appears to me like a lithe young woman lying on her side, facing me—raising, thrusting her left leg into the air during an exercise routine.

Even when I lived in the city, and even when I went to undergraduate school in Ohio, I always returned home whenever I could, so that my stays away seemed more like trips than resettlement. My love for Long Island always made me wonder how Boston could stay away for so long. Though he had lost both his guardians there in quick succession, it seemed that if he retained even a fraction of the affection that I maintained for Pauktaug, then it would call him back. Yet, as I have observed, he remained a ghost there for over a decade.

As I considered my own transparent reflection in the car's window—as the other rail lines and the backs of houses and schools seemed to pass across the features of my face—I thought of my cousin's return. He had decided, he told my aunt, to return by car on a quick but scenic road trip across the United States. My aunt had suggested to him that perhaps I should fly out to California and drive back with him. But he replied strongly that he was nearly ready to leave by the time my aunt proposed this plan, and that he was looking forward to the silence of the drive. He planned to arrive on the first or second of August.

My room had remained where it had nearly always been on the third floor of our very large house (the first floor and basement being occupied by my family's funeral home business). My aunt's room was on the second floor. My uncle lived in a small house that was the nearest one to my aunt's. Our funeral business had once been a palatial home at the end of its own long driveway, just off one of the parallel streets to Main Street, Pauktaug. In the early twentieth-century, two sets of three frame houses were built along both sides of the drive, making it a street. When the old main house itself was finally sold to my grandfather and converted, he also added another small house between the funeral home and the first of the three houses on the south side of the street—that little house ultimately becoming my Uncle Harry's.

On the third floor of the main house were two very large rooms, one used for storage, the other mine. The first of those two we planned to give to Boston, if we could get his piano up there. His instrument—a fine seven-foot grand—he had shipped. It was to travel by piano moving truck with other instruments across country and arrive on the sixth of August.

The train ride east unfolded from the city to the north shore Long Island of my affections—which is a suggestively dark roll of streets and older trees forming an enfabling barrier to the still, rippled brine of sheltered harbors. And soon, near where the dorsal fin would be if one holds to the idea of a fish's shape for Long Island, I left the train. I had been wearing headphones during the ride—so that I could review a recording I had made of myself. An old man on the platform asked me what I had been listening to.

"Piano music," I answered.

"Yeah, that's relaxing," he answered.

I took off my headphones and began to walk home in the darkness.

As I made my way from the station and north into Pauktaug, and upon crossing the last of the more frequented boulevards, my favorite stretch of ground in all the world unfolded before me. On both sides of the rough, sidewalk-lined, road are nothing but wooded, dark slopes—the outer fringes of land that belong to unseen houses that have their entries from the south along the busy county route 25A.

I moved along out of this little valley—the incline of my course descending slowly, for I was moving toward town and sea level—and soon the elementary school came into view.

I made a right onto the road that runs north and parallel to Main Street, and ultimately leads to the ascent of the hill to home. As I made my way up the slope, the lights of the main house were running bright with business, for there was a viewing in progress. The lights in my uncle's were out. He was at work with my aunt in the office. Yet the rest of the street had its usual low glow of living—porch lights and porch floors shining in the haze. One could feel—or I could feel, surely—that this July thirty-first was going to be a true August Eve, though the air had not changed yet. I looked to the west for signs from Main Street and the trees beyond it, and to the north where the Long Island Sound lay, and to the east where the woods stretched into an aboriginal blackness. All was still, notwithstanding my suspicions of imminence. The small gravel lot, obliquely in front of and to the right of our house, if one were looking from the front door, where mourners—where the "still-living," as we called them—parked, was full, and cars lined the street.

I knew the main customer in this case—"the main customer" being the term we used for the deceased.

I worked my way discreetly to the right and along the gravel drive that my uncle's house shared with my aunt's, and was soon in the back of the business and in the front of my home.

The lights in the kitchen shone above the brightness of the porch lights, and I climbed the stairs and entered amidst a wave of moths. Then I went downstairs to the business.

My aunt and uncle were both in the office. The still-living and the main customer, Mrs. Rhodes, were doing well. My uncle took a pause so as to permanently welcome me back into the house again, but soon he left to resume his post as monitor and host for the mourners. My aunt hugged me for her welcome and smiled, and then told me about the delivery. The piano movers had arrived days early. They had called just before my return and reported that they would be in Pauktaug within a half-hour. My aunt had asked them if they could not make another of their stops first or wait until morning. They in turn asked if there was not any possibility that the piano could be delivered right away, for our house was their last stop of a transcontinental run. They could leave the truck at the New York yard in the morning and fly home the same day if they could complete their business tonight. My aunt's only objection was that it might cause trouble with the mourners. But the driver said he was confident he could work rather quietly and that he could pull the truck into the back of the yard, since my aunt mentioned there was a driveway that led to the back of the house.

I interjected the news of my teacher's note and my good fortune, and my aunt pledged a little tea celebration while we awaited the piano's arrival. She reported the news to my uncle, and then my aunt and I went upstairs to the kitchen. Our dog, Sarah, was there.

In contrast to the tiny frame and silver hair of my aunt of nearly eighty, our dog of only three had the build of a laborer and hair of sable blackness. It was hard to keep her in as I went outside to sit down. Our giant back porch—again, front porch when considered from the point of view of daily living—wrapped around the length of the house's rear and embraced its two sides and most of the front. I planted myself at the southwest corner and looked out and down our street for the approach of the piano. Sarah somehow joined me anyway. Soon my Aunt Elizabeth was there as well, with tea and cake. We discreetly watched the departures of mourners and whispered a review of my day's most exciting news.

Aunt Elizabeth asked to see the materials my teacher had forwarded to me—the new prospectus, forms, and the list of accepted contestants. I retrieved it from my backpack, and she strained to read it by the blue glow of the limelight moon. I continued to speak of my day, when my endearingly cloudy-minded old aunt (she was out of tune with things in general) interrupted me.

"It's funny that Boston didn't mention this—"

"He probably didn't know about this one," I broke in.

"Oh, he knew. He's on this list, too!" she said with excitement as she passed the paper on to me.

Boston's presence on the roster came as a relief. Lingering in the back of my mind was the idea that the others on the list were probably of that caliber that approximates infallibility. Boston's being on the list confirmed this. And his presence alleviated my fear that I should train with the ambition of winning. This was no maudlin bit of self-deprecation—but rather a confession of raw fact. There were those of a level that I simply could not approximate. Occasionally, I could err against my average in favor of an illusion of higher quality. Yet those occasions were as accidental as the evenings on which I misrepresented myself by extremely poor playing. A great expectation can fall upon those who accidentally prove themselves in combat one too many times by mere chance and fortuity. I had made a series of such benign mistakes, and the ante had been raised to a level where my best could only just match the failures of those who would be knocked out in the early rounds of such a contest as the Manhattoes Competition.

Sometimes I played better than I am able as a pianist. Yet the grist that would be afforded by the process seemed irresistible to me—in as much a non-musical respect as it would be musical—and so I confessed as much to my aunt. And I told her that I was going to go through with it.

Of course, Aunt Elizabeth judged me by the nights of chance and the sounds of practice and by the knowledge of the personal intentions that sounded behind the sound of my playing. I knew better—concerning my actual skills—as many a pianist must know better than a myriad of relatives and a thousand admiring laymen. Yet sometimes, unfortunately, a pianist is just good enough—as I was—to be unable to justify to anyone, even himself, a decision to put the endeavor aside once and for all.

The competition was scheduled for the last two weeks in October. Three months notice was short, I thought. But the new competition was already so confident of likely prestige, it seemed to presume that all who applied would naturally quarantine the latter half of October for the possibility of such a trip to New York. I, of course, did not have to worry about the aspect of travel in this case. Yet I had never even suspected that I would be admitted to the competition.

Even my acceptance to graduate school had struck me as only a misfortune of my occasionally excellent performances, and I was sure that probability and averages would eventually lead me out of the conservatory world of New York. Yet I survived my master's with the praise of my teachers and a clear conscience. And let me say again that I do not affect modesty when I speak of these things. I merely attempt to share a truth of which I am confident—that my brain, soul, and heart were never specifically configured for success in music or at the piano. There are those, of course, with such a configuration, and though they oftentimes must work as adamantly as those who do not have it, they are attended as if by a certain shield in battle—a shield that I can never raise. I joust without armor, and too many times I have won by chance and have never had to take the spear of the other rider in my bare chest. But who is the other rider? Sometimes, I think that it is some vague but nevertheless palpable being that one might style as Music itself. Sometimes, I just think it is fear and plain self-disgust.

In the deepening night, I could look down on the front lawn and see my Uncle Harry leading two old women to a car. The main group of the mourners was just then appearing on the walk and the grass and heading to the gravel lot and the street. Some of the nervous vigilance that was distracting my aunt from excitement about the contest and my permanent return to Pauktaug was then abating. She retained, even after years of connection with the funeral business, a fear that some inadvertent aspect of our daily lives might accidentally aggrieve one of the mourners. My aunt was not overly solicitous of the chronically lachrymose, but she was always keen to avoid inflicting casual wounds upon them. The mourners for this final viewing of the day were nearly gone. Still, the piano movers were not in sight.

We were a small funeral parlor—only able to admit two main customers at a time. We survived more on the community's desire to preserve an illusion of rural quaintness than on any practical competitiveness. There was not enough space in our floor plan to admit of the turnover that even a place like Pauktaug could provide. We prospered on the remembered effectiveness of another time.

The viewing of that night was for Mrs. Rhodes, my first piano teacher. But the funeral for Mrs. Rhodes was not until ten-thirty the next morning, and as we had no one in preparation, a respite then came upon my aunt. She turned the last of her day's energies upon me.

"Port, did you think about it again?"

"About what?"

"About playing for the service tomorrow. It would be nice. She was your first teacher—and Boston's. She was so proud of that. Everyone who'll be there knows that."

"No, I thought about it. I'm sorry, Aunt Elizabeth. I can't turn this into a concert. No matter what, it will look like I'm showing off."

"Portsmouth! No, it won't. And it won't look like a concert. I told you that already. Just pick the right piece and all it will say to people is that she lives on through her students—that music lives on forever."

I was just coming out of a quiet period that had made me feel a bit blasé about all sentimental obligations, and I was resolved not to do it—to be the organ grinder's monkey at the next morning's funeral. But I was spared saying anything more about it. At that moment, the piano moving truck appeared at the end of the street.

My uncle emerged from the front of the business and quickly hobbled (like my aunt, he was almost eighty) to the back of his little house and went inside. He was eager to prepare for watching the delivery. Oftentimes, as well, our other neighbors would watch the delivery vans ascend our street and roll to the north side of the house where the access to the basement had been built long ago by my grandfather. Many times I had watched innocently fascinated eyes observe the van get as far as that doorway and then turn away their attentions during the moment when the main customer in his container would pass over the last bit of ground between truck and door. There are times when a fascinated child will watch the transfer for a spell, yet that fascination usually gives way to some instinct to look away after a time. Whether this impulse is intuitive or gained from admonishments from elders I cannot entirely say.

On this July night, however, the delivery seemed larger than any our neighbors usually saw approaching the main house. The truck passed the very last of the still-living (who were just then getting in their cars), and it was sure to have offended the easily offended among them as it groaned in low gear up the gradual slope to our house. Sarah was cast over with joy—a full text of which was written in the almost black-mercury fluidness of her eyes—and my aunt put her fingers in Sarah's collar.

Deliveries were always shielded from Sarah, but she seemed to sense a difference in this event. Generally, she was quarantined a half-hour before the delivery of a body. But as this was a very different kind of delivery, we were, of course, willing to grant Sarah a little more liberty.

My aunt and I tried to wave the truck forward—for we could see them leaning hard to the left and looking through the blackness and across the covering glow of porch lights in search of house numbers. They came to a full stop in front of the Paws'. The Paws, theirs the first house on the north side of the street, had a guest who must have been left on the porch and isolated for a moment, for he could not say what house number the truck was in front of when asked. He took to looking with them for the number. They could not find it.

"Do you have a piano coming?" shouted the taller and the seemingly more agent of the two truck men.

"I'll ask," called back the guest.

My uncle emerged at this time from the front of his house. He had changed already from his suit for the business to his jeans and shirt for the business at hand, and he began to walk down the sloping street to the truck.

The guest emerged from the Paws' house and pointed up the street. My uncle reached them then to confirm this. Soon the truck was pulling around the south side of the main house. The Paws and their guest ambled up the street just a bit after the truck. Two of our other neighbors from the side opposite the Paws began to watch from their porches. None of them could see very much once the truck rounded the south side of our house. They all seemed interested since it seemed that the delivery was not one of our usual customers. But they soon went back into their houses. It was getting dark.

The taller of the two truck men jumped from the cab when they pulled in, and asked loudly over the running engine, "Elizabeth Gourd?" My uncle pointed out Elizabeth Gourd, my aunt, descending the stairs of the back porch.

"B & T Piano Movers," said the taller man as he leaped back up into the cab and turned off the engine—at the same time pointing blindly to the company name on the side of the trailer. "But I'm not B and this isn't T," he said with as much speed as he moved—so as to show, I think, that the late hour of delivery would not have an effect on the speed and wakefulness with which he would perform his task. "I'm R and this is R. I'm Rich, and this is Rick," he said, and he pointed out the latter fellow, who was equally lanky as his leader.

They soon fell to the opening of the truck's back doors. I ran down from the porch at this point, for I was eager to see the emergence of Boston's piano from the shell of its transcontinental crossing.

I placed myself squarely behind the open doors and stood a few yards back. Rich and Rick threw aside a thick padding from the lone crate and tossed the shroud into a pile in the trailer's corner.

For a fascinated moment I considered how this instrument had only just then passed before the house that had contained it for so long, Boston's old home. My cousin had lived in the first house on the south side of the block with our Aunt Maryland and Uncle William nearly all the days of his young life. But after his departure for college, he took his piano with him.

It rested now in the wooden casing, and I could not see its polished blackness. The case was covered with old stenciled addresses and the torn remains of decals, but our address and name were prominently evident on a sheet, taped to the crate's side and covered over with lamination. The instrument was on its side and resting, locked in place, against the left interior wall of the deep trailer. Rich unbelted and unhooked the silent, heavy crate from its secure position. Both men moved the crate toward the ramp, and then down slowly on twin dollies.

Being out in the night air during that scene of intense labor and practical informality reminded me of the time (when I was in high school) when my Uncle Harry had let me accompany him during his supervision of an exhumation. There was something fascinating about seeing the box raised out of the earth—to see where it had corroded; to see where it was intact. It was somehow a wonderful and an irresistible sight.

Rich wished to take a survey of the terrain at that point. He studied the porch stairs and the screen door, and then looked over the daunting terrain of the interior flights of stairs. Rich said he thought that it was going to be a challenge to make some of the interior turns. He began to jog down the porch stairs when my aunt asked him whether he and Rick would not like to have anything to eat or drink before they got started.

Well able and willing to carry out the task she proposed, but hardly expecting, at the same time, to have to perform it, my aunt was surprised, I know, when Rich paused seriously then and answered without any levity, "That's probably the best thing right now."

Thus ensued a curious lull spent in the company of strangers, who took to sitting on the gravel at the base of the porch steps. Sarah was down in the yard by this time, and the two fellows instinctively closed the back gate so as to keep her within bounds of the enclosed back lawn. Sarah and Rick and Rich seemed to take quickly to mutual admiration—based, perhaps, on a shared interest in eating and drinking (in silence) at ground level, in being handed things there from my aunt, and in taking satisfaction in unshaven, whiskered chins.

Uncle Harry talked with them about their trip for a bit, and I listened—all the while fascinated by the piano that still lay in its crate below the back of the truck.

"I guess we know now for sure that Boston's coming," my aunt said to me after she finished serving sandwiches and drinks to the movers.

"Yes, I think he's coming, too."

Then, with a speed that alleviated my uncle's latent fears that the two fellows may not stand up again for the night, the piano movers raised themselves and resumed their task with creditable speed.

They adjourned to the driveway once more to begin the difficult task of attending to the large instrument.

All the night, then, seemed poised on the great shift from summer to the most delicate hint of incipient autumn. Yet the air at that moment remained still. Somewhere lingered the trigger—whether in Nature or in my perception I could not yet say.

It had not occurred to me that the movers would remove the crating before moving the piano. At the moment they began that process, I kneeled down with an absorbed fascination and waited to see the emergence. My interest at that point was not toward any artifact of my cousin's, for my interest in him then—despite our years of fraternal boyhood adventures, despite his subsequent decade of mysterious absence, despite his wild success on the competition and festival circuit—was governed by my indifference to any former brother who could vanish with such ease from my confidence. Yet my resentments for him as a relative had succeeded to enough indifference that I could look forward to his protracted and indefinite visit as I might for any interesting stranger.

My interest in the piano was as in an artifact of my own past. I myself had spent many hours at this large instrument when it was in my Aunt Maryland and Uncle William Gourd's house down the block. Boston and I often shared this piano when we started to play. Aunt Elizabeth did not then have a piano in the main house that was not in the area of the business, and it was often too late for a little boy to practice when the business was finally done for the day. And my aunt did not like for me to have to practice within those surroundings.

I crouched in closer to the piano movers as they carefully applied crowbars to the crating. A place was hidden within the box, you see—a place that had been to other places now itself, but was still its own same place. The crate's lid came off, and a brown, thick, quilt-like covering—similar to those that were heaped in the interior corner of the truck—was visible. Yet the familiar shape was before me now—there lying like a massive, filled-in silhouette of the letter *P*. The keyboard end was now distinguishable from the pointed end. With a well-rehearsed gesture, the two fellows were able to verticalize the piano on a large handtruck, and they began the slow process of wheeling the piano through the gate and toward the porch steps.

Sarah lost interest in the piano rather quickly after it came into the yard. She now seemed totally absorbed in an exploration of the fence's perimeter. My aunt went to retrieve the piano's bench from the truck. Trying to carry it from its two height-adjusting knobs, she gave up on the task instantly because of the bench's weight. I took over her effort—and then bypassed the movers before the entrance was blocked momentarily by the piano. The bench was the first item of Boston's to return officially to Pauktaug.

My uncle—in an inscrutable, silent way—somehow seemed to gain admittance not as an unwanted advisor to the move, nor as an assistant to be tolerated, but as an intermittently able-bodied member of the crew that faced a massive ascent with the shrouded piano. Though, again, he was nearly eighty years old, like my aunt, he was still of a youthful slenderness that did not yet suggest brittleness. He was an even six feet tall and strong—and he was bald save for a neat ring of gray and white hair that was close-cropped on the side of his head and at the back of his neck.

This trio negotiated the porch steps, the porch, the doorway, and the kitchen with a surprising speed. I took part in the great moments of heaving, yet would back away during the moments of consultation between Rich and Rick.

My aunt went out into the yard and into the growing lateness to chasten Sarah for suspiciously pacing the length of the new fence for a bit too long. Aunt Elizabeth and Sarah could soon be heard conversing in the kitchen as the turn for the first great ascent of interior stairs was about to start.

With some unwitting and perhaps unrepeatable calculations, we managed the turn onto that first stairway. Rick even climbed over the instrument—which looked now like a giant whistle to me—and managed a monkey-like quietness and delicateness in his movements that implied an impunity of weight. It seemed a direct foil to the consequence-laden ponderousness of the cargo in hand—a threat to itself and anything on which it might fall. As we began the push up that first flight of stairs, Rick seemed again a sort of monkey to me—pulling an elephantine prize of carrion far above its proper place of disintegration on the forest floor.

When the middle landing of third floor stairs was reached, I could hear the screen door downstairs open and slam shut, and then I could hear my aunt open the door, as well, and pursue Sarah out into the yard at an easy pace.

I looked out the screened window near the stairs. During the last great push and pull, the sweet cool wind of baby autumn was born. If there are Indian Summers—incongruous, late, spans inserted in the midst of other times—might there be said to be an entire host of Indian Seasons yet unnamed? I looked out the window as I dried my forehead (and my back; by pressing the back of my own shirt against myself), and watched the tops of the trees yield to the new fat baby, a holy wind infant, a cooing spectral papoose of Indian Spring. Then I heard Aunt Elizabeth and Sarah return to the kitchen.

The next phase would last past midnight, for no matter what the angle—and no matter what horizontal or vertical combination of positions we could conjure for the piano—we could not make the turn in the stairs onto the latter half of the ascent to the third floor. My uncle finally repaired to his house for tools, and Rich and Rick and I went along with him into the air to cool. The wind was such then that odorous, green leaves and twigs were being cast down from the raccoon skyline. Sarah watched our journey with agitation, and she pressed with increasing frequency at the back screen door. My aunt busied herself in some other part of the house, carrying out a general cleaning in anticipation of our imminent familial arrival.

Rich, Rick, and my uncle had to squeeze past Sarah and hold her in with as much vigilance as it took to keep out the moths. Soon, we were all (save for Sarah and my aunt) back on the third floor. My uncle had resolved to remove the banisters entirely from the stairway so that the move could be completed without any more speculative attempts at ascent. Sometime near one in the morning, all the banisters were removed (and left piled in order for the morning's reassembly).

Just as we reached the third floor with the seven foot instrument, and as the summer-scouring wind seemed to be peaking outside, I could hear my aunt yell to Sarah to stop doing something. Then came the sound of the screen door as I had never heard it before—and then my aunt calling out Sarah's name into the windy night.

My aunt came up to what would be Boston's room after we had arrived already with the piano. She asked me with a laugh if I would not mind looking for Sarah after the job with the piano was done.

"I left the screen door unlocked and the gate open?" my uncle asked with disbelief.

"No," my aunt smiled helplessly, "Sarah tore down the door

and leaped the gate. You can take your time starting after Sarah, Port," my aunt said to me. "I just want to make sure she is in before morning because of the service."

I laughed back my yes, acknowledging my memories of Sarah's few disastrous contacts with mourners from the business.

We continued with the piano. Rich and Rick took to raising the piano on its legs. Soon they noticed that the bolts that held the third, far leg of the instrument were just shoddy replacements that did not fit the holes.

"I'll just screw these in anyway, for now. The piano will still rest pretty securely on that leg—unless someone really tries to push against it or something. But I'd order real replacements for that," said Rick.

My uncle looked at the bolts from the front legs and then whispered to me that he thought he had fair approximations for them in the basement. He would look for those tomorrow, and then we could use them for the third leg while waiting for the right ones to arrive.

But soon the piano was standing on its legs, and its full black length was apparent in the palely lighted room. After the pedal assembly was reattached to the bottom of the instrument, Rick played the opening of some popular song for a few seconds and then laughed and closed the keyboard cover. Then Rich and Rick seemed intent on starting their removal immediately. They gathered up the brown covering that had been around the piano for the duration of its ascent and its cross-country voyage, and collected their tools, and soon they went down to the kitchen with my uncle.

I remained before the piano in solitude for a few minutes. My task of retrieving the errant Sarah could be deferred for a time—for morning was the deadline and Sarah never wandered but to three places in the same succession on most of her jaunts anyway.

Curiously, it was not the keyboard that interested me. I do not recall even opening the keyboard cover then to try a note on the piano. I left that part undisturbed. Somehow, the main lid interested me. In the windy blackness that came through the screened windows, I opened the lid to peer down on the long frame, the strings, and the army files of tuning pins that stood at attention near the label end of the piano. At first, as I slowly opened the top, I recalled with levity my own images of the piano seeming like a giant letter *P*.

I lifted the piano's lid all the way open in the dark room, and felt the temperature that had been trapped within it. It rose from the ribs of the copper strings. This was a place—the inside of the piano—where something had happened, in a way. Yet I could not discern what that something could possibly be. Someone had not done something over these strings so much as had come to some thought over them. Something had been concluded over them as they shook and were dampened, as they were hammered and stifled.

I thought to find a nostalgia lingering in the strings. Here was something else. Here might be a grief borne to exult a witness not to admiration or pity but to a clandestine sympathy. I closed the lid for the time being.

It was a curious sensation that peering into Boston Gourd's piano had given me. It was not something that could be reported, really, to people like my aunt and uncle, so I did not speak of it. I left the instrument in its new place before the western window of the third floor. I looked about the room briefly and gave my first bit of attention to the other objects in the room. On the wall my aunt had hung a few prints of Western scenes—one was of sun-swept Indians listening to the inexorable growth of the humming wires on the Plains.

I went downstairs. At the kitchen table sat my aunt, Rich, and Rick. The latter two were preoccupied in telling my aunt about their cross-country trek, the growing circles below their eyes and the grizzle about their cheeks and chins belied by the energy and pride of their descriptions.

I waved to Rich and Rick—enough to imply that we might not meet again should I be long in my search for Sarah—and they waved back, smiled, and continued to eat and talk. My uncle had offered to let them stay in the spare rooms he had in his house. Yet they declined the rooms. Perhaps they were afraid to sleep so close to the house where a lot of dead bodies might be, for all they knew. I had trouble arranging sleepovers in the main house because of that when I was little. But they said they often slept on the top of the trailer in sleeping bags. They must have been sure about the rooms, for in the early morning light, when I would ultimately return to the house from my search, Rich and Rick could be heard snoring at opposite corners on the top of the piano moving truck's trailer.

Thus, with much labor and heat behind me, I took laughing leave of everyone and proceeded on an unavoidable but beautiful journey after Sarah.

I probed for the lucubrating walker-hound in the woods behind the main house. I cannot venture how many times it probably was that I passed very close to Sarah and did not see her—she taking joy in her coal-black pelt and muscle to temper her panting breath, so as to watch me silently with her heart-big, oil-well eyes, on that night when Boston's piano returned to Pauktaug.

CHAPTER II

ANACRUSIS

I awoke to a bright-lighted, cool morning of dry air and sun. It had finally rained before the darkness was through, but not before I had returned home with Sarah in tow. After waking, I went into the hall and looked out the south window to see that the truck had vanished. They must have pulled away with a certain amount of finesse and discretion, for I never heard anything from them or their truck after I went to bed.

The banisters and railings from the stairway that led from the second to the third floor still lay in neat piles in the hallway, waiting for my uncle to put them back in place.

It was nearing nine in the morning as I went down into the kitchen. My uncle was there, but my aunt was still upstairs dressing for the service that was to take place at ten-thirty that morning.

My uncle was finishing breakfast—and attending to the broken screen door—and I ate a bit. There would be only light work in the business today, as there was only one main customer, Mrs. Rhodes, downstairs—and, somewhat unusually, no one on the schedule for the other viewing space or in preparation in the basement. Yet my uncle asked me—for my aunt employed two others

for the business (and they were both away that day)—if I would
not mind helping a bit downstairs toward the end of the service. I
did not mind at all, and I went upstairs as nine o'clock approached
to change into my business clothes—a suit that I even used for
recitals sometimes when I was out of things to wear. I was pretty
sure that my aunt's campaign to have me play at the service was
over.

Soon, I had changed into my shirt of white and my suit and
tie of black. I took a look into Boston's room. I marveled at that
moment at the remarkable degree to which the black finish of his
piano had remained relatively free of scratches and marks of wear.
Save for a few nearly imperceptible marks along the left side and
a white scratch of about a foot's length on the top's folding lid, I
could see very little damage on the instrument. In fact, the white
scratch had been there when the piano was over in Boston's boyhood home down the street—when it was in my Aunt Maryland's
and Uncle William's house. I remember how the white scratch
came to be there.

In late junior high and early high school, Boston and I went
through our first phases of extended practice days. Though
Boston's piano was excellent, it was rather aggressive in its tone
and volume. My Aunt Maryland and Uncle William did not have
neighbors who were bothered by the sound of practicing. It was
Boston who was keen on muffling the piano during practice. Very
early in life, my cousin complained of being so close to a source of
unremitting sound. To start, he began altering his practice routine
by not playing with the large piano's lid all the way up. Because
there are two supporting sticks of wood for the lid in the piano—
one long, the other rather short—using the piano with the lid all
the way up is often referred to as playing at full-stick. Perhaps this
is not a universal term, but I have heard it often enough. Boston
soon abandoned playing at full-stick—practicing at full-stick not
only being too loud for a regular sized room but also somewhat of

an affectation—and he was soon fatigued by half-stick, as well. In place of playing a grand piano at half-stick, some will place a pliable, soft, item in between the lid of the piano and the piano's rim, in the same place where the sticks function. I have seen phone books used in this case, and magazines rolled into tubes or just folded in half. And I have even seen just a flat magazine used for creating the smallest of spaces, making the piano appear like an amateur ventriloquist, its mouth slightly open though it would like to appear closed while the sound comes out.

Then, of course, one may play with the lid entirely closed. Yet the top is still open in a way, for the folding portion of the top, which is immediately adjacent to the keyboard, is folded back to admit use of the music stand. In extremely aggressive pianos, this exposure of the piano's insides can still be pressing upon the ears of the person working so close at hand.

Not until I had played for some time in my life did I see a further step some take to mitigate the sound of practicing. Such a gesture one rarely saw, save in the studios of those who made their livings through practicing the piano. It is simply that one remove the music stand from out of its sliding, slotted place inside the instrument, close the front flap of the lid (then the piano is entirely closed from the top), and place the music stand on top of the closed front flap. In this step of muffling an instrument, equally short stacks of music are often used to pad the contact points between the music stand and the top of the piano's lid.

Boston got to this step rather quickly, but he soon abandoned the stacks of music in favor of a thick quilt that he folded so as to cover the front flap of the piano. He then placed the music stand on top of the quilt. This achieved something of the effect that Boston was after.

Some experts may ask if voicing a piano would not be a better solution. (Voicing a piano is a labor that alters the volume and tone of an instrument through a series of applications made primarily to the piano's hammers. Among those applications: the softening of the hammers by filing them down or by pricking them many times over with pins; the hardening of the hammers with chemical applications. And there are other approaches, as well.) Boston did have his piano voiced, but its natural character bounced back into place so quickly that Boston put aside the notion of constantly having his piano revoiced in favor of applying his own ideas.

Uncle William and Aunt Maryland objected to the quilt only in that it seemed a sort of sponge for dirt. Thus, the quilts that had a place on the piano were rotated quite often. Once, however, a very tiny particle—almost like a grain of sand—must have become lodged below one of the quilts. When Boston slid this quilt away for cleaning, it left a long, oblique scratch on the right side of the piano's folding lid.

I pondered the scratch for a bit, and then I thought of Boston's trademark equanimity of spirit—exercised upon finding the mark. Though, like anyone, he would have preferred that the mark had never been carved, he did not dwell upon the then indelible white line in his otherwise solidly black piano. It might be said here that whatever irritations I may have felt for Boston's seeming ability to let our entire connection vanish after he moved away from Pauktaug, I have never wavered in my admiration for his seemingly indefatigable good spirits during those years of our youth. He did not strike one as being unduly good-natured, but simply as a likeable fellow who never turned his ire upon the strikes of inevitabilities or chance. This I thought of as I looked at the white scratch that shone so readily in the bright light of the morning.

I adjourned to my room and played a bit on my own instrument. My piano was large and powerful but had a wood finish, unlike Boston's. (Boston's piano had been bought new, and I envied the color and the untouched appearance it bore.) Though my piano was of an excellent quality, I went through a period of vanity in which I thought that grand pianos should all be black like their favored examples on the platforms of the concert world. It was only a coincidence that my piano was of such a fine caliber, really, for my grandfather had come into it with the purchase of the house. The original owner had bought the finest piano he could around the turn of the nineteenth- into the twentieth-century. It was in the house long before it was ever thought it would be used every day. There was another fine grand piano (bought later, in my lifetime) down in the area of the business, but my aunt still preferred that I not practice down there, even when I was older—more for my sake than for any intimation that I was desecrating the silence of the dead. I almost never practiced there—save for a few times in the summer when it was unbearably hot on the upper floors.

My practice was interrupted by my aunt calling me down, and I looked out the window to see that more time must have passed than I had imagined, for the first of the mourners had arrived. I descended into the kitchen and then down the stairs into the office. My uncle was already changed and at the front entrance, admitting people for the service.

I could see in my aunt's eyes that she hoped I might still suddenly volunteer to play at the service. But I said nothing about that.

I asked my aunt what I might do, and she suggested that I join my uncle at the front door. Oftentimes in funeral homes, mourners admit themselves and look with fear for the first faces they will alight upon—which are, at times, to their chagrin, the faces of the directly bereaved. My uncle always felt that even the presence of a disassociated party at the front entrance appeased the trials of the only moderately connected—and he liked (more than this) to watch the mourners park their cars in the gravel lot on the left side of the house and along the length of the block. My uncle was always very solicitous of the parking that went on along the street, for only a keen attentiveness to that affair kept the mourners from presuming upon our neighbors with their cars. Because of the relative ancientness of my family's business in Pauktaug—and because of my aunt and uncle's solicitude toward our neighbors—we escaped many trials that our somewhat peculiar location may quite easily have engendered. A new business on our site, for example, would hardly be permitted the zoning that we enjoyed—they could never win it, in fact. And, again, only the painstaking efforts of my aunt and uncle kept anyone from complaining that we would have to surrender a larger section of our land for parking. Keeping to the very small gravel lot was always a paramount concern of my aunt's.

At one time—when my grandfather still commanded the business—three of the seven smaller houses that line our street were occupied by my family. My Uncle Harry Gull—who is, obviously, not a Gourd and is my uncle only in a euphemistic sense and not by marriage (he never married)—lived even then in the same small house on the south side of the street. He was my grandfather's closest employee after his sons. And then, of course, my Uncle William (a son of my grandfather) and my Aunt Maryland lived in the house three doors down from my Uncle Harry. My Uncle William did not remain in the family business very long after high school. And finally, my Aunt Elizabeth and Uncle James lived in the center house (on the north side of the street) for a time before they moved into the main house.

But even as the four-sevenths majority of the past yielded to the two-sevenths minority of the present, Aunt Elizabeth and Uncle Harry were able to maintain a vigilance that prevented any neighbor from going to the Village Board.

Uncle Harry and I each leaned against the outside banister of the two opposite stairways that led up to the second floor's wrap-around porch. After the first few mourners arrived, there was a long lull.

"I wonder how far Boston is by now?" my uncle speculated.

"He could be anywhere, really," I said. "Aunt Elizabeth said he was supposed to arrive on either the first or second of August. But if he doesn't come by then, do you think he'll feel obliged to warn us that he's late?"

"Probably not. Can I see the stuff about the competition?" my uncle asked, after suddenly brightening at the remembrance of something.

"I'll run up and get it!" I ventured, and I ran up the porch steps to the back entrance. Soon I returned with the envelope. The lull in arrivals continued for nearly ten minutes, during which time my uncle read over the pamphlet for the contest.

"All of the finals are going to be live on television and radio?"

"Yes," I answered, trying to intimate how daunting that sounded.

Then my uncle indulged in his habit of slowly reading aloud. "'The cash prizes match the highest of those awarded by the world's leading competitions, and the new competition offers contestants the widest live broadcast exposure in finals competition in the United States.'"

"Yeah, I can't believe that I'm even in this," I said.

My uncle only grimaced with disdain for my comment without even looking up.

"Is this the list of the participants?" he asked, and he held up a blue sheet with the names that my teacher had purloined.

"That's it. There's me—and there's Boston."

"That's something that you're both in it. You think that Boston knows about this? You know, I bet he doesn't even know yet. Hey, it would be something if it comes down to the two of you!"

Tired of the endearing yet implausible praise, I said nothing to directly counter this.

"Is everything all right with your piano?" he asked. My uncle had undertaken to apply his labors to the insides of my piano, when he and I became fatigued with the personalities of the local piano technicians.

"It could stand a few things. But mainly a tuning."

"Yeah, we'll do it soon." He paused—and then, having inventoried his concerns for me, the idea of pianos also made him turn against me a bit and inventory a concern for my Aunt Elizabeth.

"Port, are you going to play this morning? Your aunt really wants you to do that."

"No, I'm not," I said resolutely.

"Does she know?"

"Yes, we already discussed it Everything is fine with that. I'm not playing."

My uncle softened again.

"So long as your aunt is satisfied."

He handed me the competition literature then, and shuffled down the street to advise a mourner not to park half of his car on the Paws' lawn. My poor uncle—as my aunt's hazy mind continued to fade with age and efforts to remember, my Uncle Harry compensated in our family by intensifying applications of his mere capableness. But he was no more penetrating than he had ever been, even though his attempts at heightened agency fooled me from time to time.

Soon we were monitoring a full arrival of mourners, and when it seemed that the last of them had arrived, we directed the last few elderly drivers to the gravel lot and walked back to the house.

There was to be a small Catholic service. I had never seen the priest before, and as I took a place near the doorway to the office, my aunt told me that he was a substitute. One can tell very quickly —even if the qualification is not made by the speaker—whether the deceased was known personally by the officiating priest or minister. This was one of the many cases where I suspect that little or nearly nothing definite was known of the exact subject, so the material he delivered was very familiar.

At first my attention was moderate, and then it grew as I had hopes that the priest seemed to be set for taking a few risks in the biographical line. But then I removed my attentions altogether—for he took no risks. With all the flowers about him, he looked like a conductor turning to his public to say a few words of thanks. His hall was packed—filled with folding chairs, like the overflow seating they sometimes place on stage for popular performers.

I closed my eyes, and half-dreamed of my first meeting with Mrs. Rhodes.

My Aunt Maryland had found for us a teacher who lived on the west side of Main Street, in the streets that ran into the high hills above the harbor. Rather, she had asked Mrs. Paw from whom her daughter, Lana, was taking lessons. Lana was the same age as Boston and I.

On a late summer day, when I was six, Aunt Elizabeth and Aunt Maryland gathered us all at the end of the street in front of Boston's house. My two aunts, Boston, Lana Paw, and myself were assembled to make a walking trek across town to Lana's piano teacher—for the first piano lessons for Boston and me. Mrs. Rhodes was willing to give half-hour lessons to the very young for two dollars. If one moved along, there was an hour lesson for four dollars. In light of what my aunts later would pay for our lessons, these fees now seem difficult for me to comprehend. But such was the case.

Lana Paw, who lived in the house across from Boston's, was a slender girl with brassy hair. Even her child's face was not enough to conceal the chiseled attractiveness that would expand into a woman's.

As Lana found that Boston and I had a limited interest in the prospect of piano lessons, she took to walking with the vanguard of our group—telling my aunts what it was that we would need for our lessons and how we would need to practice each day. And, then, with equal suddenness, she broke off that topic and received a general interview from my aunts with equal pleasure.

Both of my aunts had married Gourds. My Aunt Elizabeth

had met my Uncle James in high school. She was widowed within three years of marriage. After my grandfather surrendered the business to his second son, James, my Aunt Elizabeth and Uncle James moved into the main house with my grandfather. My grandfather and Uncle James died—both of heart attacks (perhaps somehow sympathetic demises)—at nearly the same time. Yet my aunt stayed on and continued the labor of running the business. My Uncle James's friend and primary employee—almost a sort of partner after my grandfather retired—was Harry Gull. For almost three quarters of a century, Harry Gull maintained a touching devotion to my aunt and the establishment that equaled—or perhaps exceeded—my aunt's own allegiances. And there was a beautiful, never realized, but perpetually incipient sense of romance between my Uncle Harry and Aunt Elizabeth—such that it was the source of my appellation of Uncle for Mr. Gull.

My grandfather was said to have been a kind man notwithstanding his prosperity. He was, himself, descended from a line of New England undertakers, and after apprenticing to his father for a time and seeing that Massachusetts business pass primarily to his elder brother, he struck south for crops of his own expirees. My grandfather successfully established himself on two shores of Long Island Sound, for he had a business on the Long Island side and on the Connecticut side of the water.

My grandfather's oldest son, William, showed no interest in continuing on in the business, and though he happily lived in a house in the shadow of the family enterprise, he preferred the life that his calling to the law allowed him in the village routines of Pauktaug. My grandfather's second oldest boy was my Aunt Elizabeth's husband, James. He took to the business with cheerfulness, and his thoughts did not seem to carry him away from Pauktaug. My father, Brentford Gourd—who was not only the youngest of the three brothers, but freakishly the youngest (twenty-five years younger than William)—upon the death of my grandfather, became the ward of my Uncle William. He was only four years old when his father and the middle brother, James, passed away.

My Uncle James and my grandfather died quite suddenly, as was observed above, and Aunt Elizabeth and Uncle Harry, moved by twin powers (by love, and by shock from the inevitabilities), maintained control over the two funeral homes. But my father, Brentford Gourd, took on the running of the Connecticut business in the early 1960s, and there he met his wife, my mother, and I was born (in 1969) in sight of the water and in distant sight of old Long Island.

This was something of the disposition of my family's history as I knew it when Boston and I marched off in the tow of our aunts and Lana Paw on the day of our first lesson. I had resisted the idea of piano lessons for quite some time. And Boston also balked at the notion. Yet my Uncle William had bought a fine new instrument that year, and Aunt Elizabeth had the grand piano moved upstairs in our house—the piano that came with the main house when my grandfather bought and converted it into a business. Thus, two large pianos had been put into position for use, and the eternal belief that children might be at hand who could be taught to play them was raised in earnestness.

Boston and I had both liked to play *with* the pianos if not to play them. I well recall the time that I first poked about the large piano that was in the business area of the main house. For years— far longer than most who go on to become proficient piano players—I retained an indifference for the piano as a musical instrument and preserved my original perception that it was a sort of place that I would go to for mechanical and aural experimentation. The notion that the keys were only so many controls of a maritime helm or cockpit was my paramount concern when going to the piano. I took pleasure in making it sound without an application of technique or a connection to music. I had an affection for it outside of its history.

And Boston seemed to take equal pleasure in going to the piano as an object of play that yielded curious sounds when equally curious twists of fists and fingers permutated upon the keys. My aunt would occasionally yield to our requests—these times being before the grand piano was moved and before Boston's family bought their piano—and she would go into the business area and close off the doorways where some poor main customer lay, and allow us to play with the piano. If we kept our experiments to a limit, she would let us remain there indefinitely. But if we transgressed some inner limit that pertained to her sense of proper volume and force, as much in view to the nearness of the dead as to the living, she would reappear and send us to the woods—for not only could there be two mummified old Pauktaugers in range of our poundings, but my uncle was quite often below us creating new mummies in the basement workroom.

We pounded on the keys as if we were knocking on ancient doorways. We formed our fingers into different shapes—we splayed them out and kept them flat (such that our hands looked like the skeleton shapes of fishes' pectoral fins); we brought the fingers into a slightly curved shape from that form (and our hands were like the talons of hawks and eagles and other birds); we re-flattened our fingers and brought them together so that our pounding hands were as the pectoral flukes of whales; we parted the fingers from this position and had the cloven hooves of deer; we curled the fingers tightly so that they formed neat little squares, but we kept the hand flat and tried to expose a bit of space and webbing between the fingers (thus we had the paws of dogs and wolves and large cats upon the keys); then we made true fists and we were the apes, man's nearest brothers; and then we would occasionally unfold our fingers unto human hands, and drape them across the keys with an untrained indifference, bringing nothing but the power of the human form to the depressions, and nothing of a trained attack upon the well-historied keys. We kept the ivory coasts a mystery—though we traversed them in evolutionary patterns.

The little boy, Boston, who walked with me at the rear of the column that was making its way toward Mrs. Rhodes' house on the west side of the village, was the same fellow in appearance and spirit who had played with me at playing with the pianos on the first floor of the main house. Boston was a hale, stout (but not paunchy) little fellow with jet black hair and sharp face. He was a child that could only be characterized as aloof when left alone—by which one means that he could survive and divert himself and ponder some unreported deep for as long as his solitude went uninvestigated. But if one were to call upon his isolation, he would cheerfully break it for any invitation to return to the world. And when some misfortune struck us when we realized such invitations—if, say, perchance, Boston should cut himself severely in the woods when taking a jump at my suggestion upon his bicycle along the trail—then he seemed to recover with an admirable speed. He was not a weepy sort. And he was not of the kind that would lay blame for any misfortunes that befell him. He seemed to admirably take all misfortune upon himself as either the blow of chance or humorous self-failing.

But he was not, at times, without the common fears of boys his age. I have mentioned that it was difficult to orchestrate sleepovers when I was very young. Boston was among the children who felt ill at ease in the main house after the sun went down. So, when he and I would plan a sleepover, it was generally for his house. Though I did not care for it very much, Boston was always eager to share the ritual of Aunt Maryland reading aloud—just before the lights were turned out for us to sleep. I heard long fragments from Victorian novels during these times. But most often I heard readings from an old literary anthology that was a favorite of my Aunt Maryland's. This book was a large, wearing, deep green, cloth-bound volume: *Bay State Greatness, From the Mayflower Compact to*

Concord. I thought Boston seemed indifferent to what was being read. He always seemed removed and distant, contemplating his deeps before deep sleep. And after Boston and I were very still for a long time, my aunt would often put the book down after reading on to herself for awhile—and then work late into the night on long letters to a cousin of hers in Maine.

There was something in Boston's family training—the life instruction that came from his adoptive aunt and uncle (especially my Aunt Maryland)—which augmented the inner sense of unsounded deeps that have been only alluded to so far. That unsounded deep was as a palpable sense of intellect—emanated even from an affable, modest child—that seemed when at play to be searching for some object or way or process to conjoin with its jolly immensity.

Once more, Boston's deeps were warmed unto the very bottom by an amiable yet powerful pair of people who were somehow slightly distant to me, but only because I placed them at a distance out of a primitive reverence. They were of that stock of being that I worshipped as the makers of the second waves of ghosts for the land I loved. And when they passed, they seemed to me to be as one of the last of that second wave. There were the Indians. Then there were the Yankees. My Aunt Maryland and Uncle William were of that tribe that were the Yankees. Not the tribe defined by the term that embraced all Americans in the World Wars; not the tribe that defined any man from the Northern States in the American Civil War; not the tribe, even, that filled New England proper between the passing of the Puritans and the blooming of the cities and their kick-line canyons. They were as examples to me of that tribe that was new indigenous— not of mixed blood but so mixed with the new spots of the New World that I have never seen the sense of saying that the Indians were altogether gone.

They were not aloof Yankees, my Uncle William and Aunt Maryland. They were silent from such an immense implication of busyness that I am sure they would have deferred their labors for an affable pause had you asked them for it—for no laborer could have finished working the field they seemed to toil over and lucubrate upon. A hiatus is not begrudged over an eternal project. I cannot say for sure what their labor was. Aside from an impeccable neatness of home and grounds and personal conduct, their labor could never have been defined by association with commerce-laden terms like *Yankee Dollar* or *Yankee Clipper*. It might better have been appended to a phrase like *Yankee Searcher* had there been such a title in the American language.

They were figures of an almost hoary whiteness to me. And their craggy, aquiline, features had achieved such an equality of definition that the couple bore out the oft-cited notion that ageing married pairs often come to resemble one another physically. Their paleness did not leave them with an unhealthy pallor. It was their hair, rather, and the pale blue and gray of their eyes that gave them a dune-dusted strength of appearance.

My Uncle William was known to me as a figure in the village of Pauktaug—a sort of ubiquitous man. No matter where I went in the village in my youth—and this did not exclude odd hours of the evening and morning—my Uncle William could likely be seen fulfilling some aspect of his ubiquity. He was, if not always engaged in some conversation on sidewalk, in store, or diner, then on his way somewhere—or walking about incessantly (for walking was an earnest avocation of his). One was always welcome on his walks, yet they very often led to one of his unplanned conversations somewhere in the village. Thus, a child or young person was often inclined to drift off from the walks and go his own way after, say, a zoning discussion became entrenched at the end of one of the docks on the west side of the village.

This walking seemed to be a march, otherwise, toward that inscrutable goal of unmanifest destiny that my aunt and uncle were driven to. Their vague ambition formed the core of their mutual affection, and it burned warm till the close of their lives. The inability of this drive to fix upon an object or reflection in the material universe did not produce irascible people. Rather, it seemed to produce immensely patient beings who were content to wait with their drive, and use it only should some fitting reflection of their mutual inner vision take form in the compromised clays of the earth.

They had no children born to them, yet such a fertile union of a mutually fired pair was slated, it seemed, to come by a child unavoidably. This was not because it seemed vaguely fated. But because the unspoken churnings of their interior could not fix upon some art or manner in which to settle their restive drive, it seemed inevitable that only another being could be entrusted with that unresolved cause which they could neither take up nor put aside. Their drive, their pull to some magnetism yet unnamed, was lovingly fixed upon the little coal-haired baby that became theirs in 1970—at the exact same time that I was given over to my Aunt Elizabeth. Boston looked more than coal-haired in relief against his new parents; he looked altogether like a coal at rest between two fields of snow. The latent wandering that fostered the epic busyness that reeled behind the eyes of my Uncle William and Aunt Maryland seemed then content to wonder what fossil mystery would be released from the old, old, earth should this little coal be lighted and allowed to burn. I do not mean to say that they made an object of this boy or channeled frustrations into him. They merely kept him dry with their love. They kept him high and dry on an island of mild and intelligent guardianship—kept him dry should he be ready to spark and burn. They kept the figurative matches near. They kept him bone dry for the figurative pyromania that is the due of some fated, speculative, little souls. He was no wanderer like they. He came up from the ground and would light fire should only the local sun beat down long enough. The happy, local, sun of removed yet extremely comfortable Pauktaug was theirs to let through. And he sat still in it as he played.

The late summer day that we began our march to Mrs. Rhodes's house was magnificently foggy, however. The village was steeped in mist and clouds. My aunts and Lana Paw were still in the lead as we made our way off of Main Street and into the hills west of the village.

"You still don't want to take piano lessons, do you?" asked Boston of me.

"Not really," I answered.

"I don't want to either," grunted Boston, and we continued through the fog.

Lana Paw drifted back and accosted us with the future.

"You'll have to practice an hour or a half-hour each day! And you'll have to do theory papers and copy theory things into the back of your assignment notebook!" she admonished. Boston said nothing to Lana. I was more easily angered and teased by her—for I was sure then that I loved her very much.

Soon we were before Mrs. Rhodes's house, and Lana led us into the vestibule, which smelled of apples and newsprint and rain.

Aunt Elizabeth was enamored of the scene. My Aunt Maryland, however, knew more than the scene was before her then, and she looked about the inner room and toward the yellow-lighted parlor to our right, from whence came the sound of a piano—and she displayed a small, aggressive smile of recognition through her hawk-like features and aged whiteness of vestigial femininity, which slightly denied the tiny crags and creases of her features. This was not a palpable aggressiveness that marked the measure of incipient ambitions for her nephew. This was a benign face of salubrious warring instinct, a bellicose expression that faced some definite but impalpable foe. This was a front shown by horded confidence to the powers of external expectation. This was power shown back in the face of power—a non-goring rut that can mysteriously appear during moments of great health.

Lana Paw ordered her music books as she walked into the lighted room from whence came the reports of a piano lesson. Boston studied his Aunt Maryland for a time, and seemed transfixed as if by a power that was, notwithstanding his sympathy to it, not directed to him just then. But he gathered something from it all the same—a sort of misunderstood permission to follow some latent beam of confidence that also possessed him to front this scene with a sudden and seemingly unaccountable surge of health. He ceased to borrow very quickly from furtive looks to his aunt, and began fronting the scene with an unmitigated independence that required no audience or league.

"Do you want to take piano lessons?" I asked Boston, then.

"Yes, I think I'd like to," he said to my surprise and my slight sense of betrayal.

Mrs. Rhodes appeared and offered us seats in the living room. A little boy made his way out of the next room, where the piano was, and Lana went in after Mrs. Rhodes to take his place.

Boston and I were left with our aunts for the next half-hour.

Aunt Elizabeth suddenly looked to my Aunt Maryland after a long stretch of quiet and the distant sound of Lana's fragile playing.

"What is it, Maryland? What's wrong?"

Aunt Maryland looked to Boston, then.

"I just may want more for him. I think there should be something more for him."

Soon my cousin had his lesson, and then Mrs. Rhodes emerged with the happy news that Boston had already taught himself how to read and play.

CHAPTER III

KEY SIGNATURE

I awoke from my remembrances—and awoke literally, as well. Uncle Harry put his hand on my shoulder, and I stood up to join him outside. There is a general routine that follows in which one instructs the attendees as to the driving order. And then I climbed into the limousine driver's seat after the priest and the widower and his nephew entered—and then one other person, an old woman, bustled into the car just before I pulled the car out into second place in the cortege. The priest said little, and the next of kin were rather quiet, controlled, resigned, amenable fellows. As I pulled into the wooded, tree-lined hills and streets on the other side of the village—and drove past the site of my first piano lesson—I looked into the mirror to take a second glimpse of my fourth passenger. She smiled at me in the mirror, changed her position, and leaned over to touch me on the shoulder.

"You don't remember me, Portsmouth, I'm—"

"Mrs. Paw! Of course I know you, Mrs. Paw. I just didn't get a good look at you when you got in. I didn't know it was you back there."

Mrs. Paw was Lana Paw's paternal grandmother. She lived in an area far on the other side of the woods that met the back of the main house.

"I hope you're awake now!" she whispered as a joke.

"I didn't fall asleep back in the house, did I? You didn't see that? Did a lot of people see that?"

"No!" she laughed. "But I saw you nod a bit for just a little while. I could only see you because I was near the front and on the left. No one else noticed. Don't worry."

Old Mrs. Paw continued: "I was just worried that you might fall out of your chair or tip it over and hurt your piano-playing hands! Elizabeth told me you are going to be in the really big new city competition. You must be so excited. Practicing hard?"

"Not yet. I really have to start, though. It's in October, and I just finished my move, and—"

"And Boston, he's coming home, too, and he's in it, too. That's really something," Mrs. Paw interjected. "Have both of you ever been in a competition at the same time?"

"Not since high school. And never such a big one. I could never beat him—I can't ever beat him—but it will be fun even just to have to get ready for such a thing, and to watch so closely as Boston will probably, easily—"

"But, now, Boston hasn't been his old self of late, I hear."

I was a bit irritated, as always, to find that someone else—and, in this case, someone that I felt was rather peripheralized from the Gourd field at the moment—knew as much, if not more, about my soon-to-return cousin's recent biography as I did.

I tried to beat her to an annotation of her last statement. "Of the last three he has been in—"

Mrs. Paw either did not hear me or she could not wait to cite the morbid oddity that characterized the last international competition in which Boston had played.

"In the last competition, I think they should have cancelled it when they learned there was trouble making selections for the finals. That's what I think they should do—jus cancel it when they can't make up their minds easily! And then that pair of jurists passed away so tragically! Those were sad, terrible, deaths. And Boston was knocked out because the jury was no longer divided after they were gone. That didn't sound fair to me. And, oh, those jurists—they were really famous, weren't they?"

"Yes, they were."

"Those were horrible deaths. How did they die again?"

"Mrs. Paw!" I rasped.

"Ooh! Sorry!" whispered Mrs. Paw. "We'll talk later!" She patted me on the shoulder, leaned back, and then invested the priest with a bit of talk until we reached the cemetery gates.

There, after the cars finished lining up and parking, I performed my last duty for the day—as a stand-in pallbearer. Soon, I drifted away quietly from the last part of the priest's service and ascended the ridge at the north end of the cemetery, where one can command a good northeasterly view of Pauktaug harbor, the Sound, and distant Connecticut.

It is quite something to be able to find so many of one's forebears interred in such a bucolic spot. Though the north slope of the cemetery houses the truly ancient dead of Pauktaug—Dutch and English settlers from the colonial period, and even some of the names that made Pauktaug briefly powerful until the first decade of the twentieth-century in the whalebone corset and stays industry (including a man of that line from whom my grandfather bought the main house)—the south slope contains many names that are personally well-known to me. My grandfather, Lawrence Gourd (1880–1944) and his wife, Anne (1896–1940); my Aunt Maryland (1914–1988) and my Uncle William (1915–1988); and even the vague figures that were my mother and father rest rather high up on the west side of the southern slope of the Rural Cemetery. I have found that I sometimes ponder the stones of my Aunt

Maryland and Uncle William—and even my grandfather's and his wife's, perhaps because my grandfather was responsible for so much of the environment of my early existence and the house and the lay of the land on which I learned to play. But I rarely, if ever, thought much when I looked at the stones of my grandfather's youngest son, my father, Brentford Gourd (1940–1970) and his wife, my mother, Laramie Eaton Gourd (1943–1970). They are buried next to my Uncle William and Aunt Maryland, as it was the latter pair who took Brentford in as a son, upon the death of my grandfather, when my father was only four years old. Brentford's mother, Anne Gourd, had died from the complications of labor, shortly after his birth.

Also in this line of headstones is one for the brief romantic marriage of my Aunt Elizabeth's youth—a stone for James Gourd (1920–1944). I hovered before his marker, at times, for somehow I was grateful that his spirit never aggresively lingered over my existence with Elizabeth Gourd and Harry Gull. As this Uncle James and my grandfather both passed away in the same year, and as my Uncle William had no interest in the undertaker's business (as has been observed before), my Aunt Elizabeth and Uncle Harry assumed responsibility for the Gourd funeral businesses in Pauktaug and on the Connecticut side of Long Island Sound. My Aunt Elizabeth had come into her romantic marriage with a reluctance founded only on the nature of her husband's calling—and the lifestyle she would be obliged to lead because of it. And yet, even after the death of James Gourd, she elected to stay in the shadow of the pall that had hovered over the happiness that had been their brief union. She kept certain things living—mainly for personal memory's sake; yet somewhat for legacy's sake, as well— by learning to minister to the dead. And thus the pall became a keepsake. There was no fortune in her eye, for my Uncle Harry and she ran a business for the dead with a rather terminal approach to business. They did not expand the main house with the growth of the communities peripheral to Pauktaug. But we did pretty well just the same.

My Aunt Elizabeth and Uncle Harry took the business under care, and my Uncle William and Aunt Maryland took the four-year-old Brentford under theirs.

From the little that I have been able to gather, my father was a rational but rather distant child. Yet he seemed to brighten with early maturity, and after finishing college he enthusiastically accepted my Aunt Elizabeth's offer of the Connecticut business. For eight years, I believe, my father worked on the Connecticut side with relative ease. He resumed an old habit of my grandfather's, as well—he bought himself a grand-sized motor boat with a large interior cabin and took to ferrying back and forth across the Sound for visits and consultations with my aunts and uncles.

I have mentioned that I rarely linger with much thought before the graves of Brentford Gourd and Laramie Gourd. But I often-times think of them as I take to the summit of the cemetery when I can slip away from a service—as was my liberty on the day I describe.

The priest continued—and one could tell from his tone that he was only near the center of his eulogy. Even though I knew he was making the signs of the cross, from a distance he looked like he was conducting a choir.

I ascended the slope and reached its peak. I was in a little city of stones at the top of the hill. But more than as a city of little skyscrapers, the area in which I stood seemed a rolling prospect of giant piano tuning pegs. The older stones seemed pegs that had been scored and scratched as if by the insatiably precise ear of some giant, perpetually unsatisfied phantom tuner.

From the height of that coign of vantage, I could see across the village to the east slope of trees that concealed our dead-end street. Beyond that lay the Sound. At a little jetty on the Sound beach that is contiguous with the grounds of our business and main

house—but out of view from anywhere but in spots very near it—
are the more suggestive tuning pegs for Brentford and Laramie
Gourd. The piles of the jetty are more apt stones for them.

As I have observed, Brentford Gourd took to the habit of
motoring across the Sound for his visits between Pauktaug and
Connecticut. He would moor the boat at this jetty—the same that
my grandfather had used and had restored from the original
owner's construction—and then march up the steep path that led
to the main house. In the early months of 1970, Brentford Gourd
and his new bride and newer baby crossed the Sound for Pauktaug.
They traveled with a female guest. She had an infant with her, as
well. This baby was Boston, they say. The other was I, they say.

When Brentford Gourd met my Massachusetts-born mother
in 1968, she had already formed a friendship with the woman who
was thought to be Boston's mother. My Pauktaug relatives met this
woman once, but little was known of her. And despite the seeming impossibility of such a case in the late twentieth-century, she
left this world with Boston as her only mark. Remarkably, later on,
authorities could trace her to no living relative. Indeed, her full
identity was never known. She was simply my mother's friend, Jessica—that is all I ever heard her called. None of the friends of the
Gourds on the Connecticut side of the water had ever heard of her
or seen her, and no one reported her missing later on. She remains
a total mystery. Even her name, Jessica, was diffidently recalled for
her by the Pauktaug Gourds who had met her only once. She
was vague.

I have heard it speculated that Brentford and Laramie may
have been planning to adopt the child of the mysterious Jessica.
That was one theory. I have heard many, actually. But this seems
the only one worth soberly venturing—as it holds some shreds of
possibility, despite it being nothing but a guess. Some think that
she may have been only a nearly friendless friend of Lara Gourd,
and that she was something of a subject of the largesse of the new

Connecticut Gourds. Yet the most significant speculation that came (dismissively yet somehow seriously, as well, at the close of the only lengthy inquiry that Boston and I ever made about the subject before the assembly of all our aunts and uncles) was that no one could swear that the parentage was not really the other way around—that is to say, that I may have been the son of this Jessica, and Boston the son of Brentford and Lara. It was also suggested that as no one saw Lara during her ostensible pregnancy, it was possible, as well, that Boston and I were brothers. Brothers by Jessica—or maybe, even, brothers by Lara. I have seen pictures of Lara and Brentford Gourd. I think the evidence is clear enough even from the photographs from whence my cells did spring. I was never as sure about Boston. Yet there is a paucity of other evidence, and a singular lack of paperwork. Boston and I both, somehow, came out of our infant situations with no birth certificates or hospital records to be found. This may sound incredible, but such was the case. Needless to say, the transfer of guardianship to my uncle and aunts was a long, arduous, tenuous, and often painful process for them.

It also seems incredible to me that Aunt Maryland and Uncle William—or, even, Aunt Elizabeth or Uncle Harry—did not once see the new Connecticut Gourds during the time when all things could have been made clear by observation. But Brentford and Lara Gourd sincerely cloistered themselves or affectedly sequestered themselves after the style of certain, private, pioneering newlyweds and extended invitations to no one as the imminence of my physical self—or Boston's (or both or neither)—crept upon the form of Lara Gourd in 1969.

And besides the photographs, there was the physical comparison one could make between Boston and me as we aged. As has been observed before, Boston was of a hale complexion, a certain strength of frame, and with truly jet black hair that had a hint of surf to it when it was not beaten into a placid calm by comb or

brush. I had differed from all these qualities with enough significance to rule out, I always thought, the possibility of our being
siblings—my hair a sandy lightness; my nose a little more rounded
and less sharp; my overall frame a bit leaner and angular. Yet was
it impossible from looking at us to conclude that we were brothers by blood? Perhaps not.

It was mainly my Uncle Harry that did the answering for
Boston and me when we asked after the story one last time during
our late teens. All my aunts and uncles had been having dinner at
the main house, and after a dignified review of the story and the
speculations that emerged from it, Uncle Harry, Boston and I
took a turn about the woods that begin just beyond the back of the
business.

We took up the story again as we walked the path of the old
baseball diamond. The ballfield emerged amidst a surrounding of
thick second-growth trees, and its diamond was preserved solely
by use. Its green was filled in by golden, wheat-like grasses, and
beyond the outfield, where the woods continued and were even
darker, was an old gravel drive that led to the ruins of a farmhouse
foundation.

Usually, a walk with Boston and Uncle Harry through the
woods took a turn about the old house's grounds. But we went
down to the beach that night. When the jetty came into sight,
Uncle Harry retold the story—

After a long, odd period of silence, Brentford Gourd had called
his brother, William, and his sister-in-law, Elizabeth, and told
them he was bringing across his wife, a friend of his wife's, and
"two surprises." He called impetuously on the same morning that
he wished to ferry over. My Aunt Elizabeth had been called first,
for some reason, and she ventured right away that they could stay
on the third floor of the main house if Maryland and William
Gourd were not ready for guests. Brentford Gourd accepted right
away. I would think that something of a slight to the man and

woman who had played the role of mother and father so willingly to Brentford, but I do not know exactly what the subtleties and rhythms were of all those relationships.

Brentford Gourd did make the pledge that he would call just before setting out, so that Aunt Elizabeth could suspect something was wrong if they did not appear after a certain time. My father granted this promise grudgingly, and it would not be surprising if he felt that he had made the pledge with enough equivocal language to justify his pretending not to recall having made it. He never made the telephone call, but sometime in the very late afternoon of a cold March day, their boat left the Connecticut shore and plied its way into the lobster blanket of the Sound.

When night fell and no call came, Aunt Elizabeth and Aunt Maryland met for a bit and then, of course, took to calling Brentford Gourd's number at intervals. There was no answer. Aunt Elizabeth was considering placing a call to the Coast Guard at the Eatons Neck Light House, but Uncle Harry and Uncle William thought that was a premature gesture. They thought they should wait another hour—until, say, nine at night—and then call the Coast Guard or the police on both sides of the state line that nebulously ripples across the Sound.

Uncle Harry went down to monitor a viewing that went on until ten that night, and when that was over and he returned to the second floor of the main house, he found Aunt Elizabeth and Uncle William sitting quietly at the kitchen table, listening to Aunt Maryland as she spoke to the Pauktaug Harbor Master on the telephone.

While she continued with her call, Aunt Elizabeth and Uncle William told Uncle Harry in hushed voices that the Coast Guard would take a quick look along the probable line of crossing since they already had someone out in that area for the evening. Uncle Harry whispered back that he was going to walk down to the jetty for his own satisfaction and look out onto the Sound with his binoculars, though he knew that he would probably accomplish very little.

Striking north toward the water through the backyard and into the leafless trees of early March, my Uncle Harry could see the stars wavering in the black ice night through the shivering tips of the bare branches. And as he crested before the descent to the beach, the lights of Connecticut's distant shore came into view like a current of incandescent sea life stretched into a narrow, confined band—like the rings of galaxies, dependent upon a mighty gravity.

He could hear an engine sounding in the distance, yet as he finished his descent of the slope, approached the jetty, and reached the level sand, he could only see two unknown boats tethered to the end of the little pier. The cabins of both boats were unlighted and still, and the moon shone, slowly bending—a reflection in the glass of the windows as the two boats drifted at their moorings.

My Uncle Harry walked along the sand and looked out across the seeming emptiness of the Sound. All looked clear and quiet—save for the sound of the unseen but running engine. Before leaving to return to the main house, he went to the start of the little dock, put his hands in his pockets because of the cold, and walked out slowly onto the salt-iced boards of the jetty. He paused when he realized the sound of the running motor was still evident—even more evident as he ambled slowly out on to the jetty. He thought it might be a sort of acoustic shadow, at first—the sound of a boat in the harbor, coming from a couple hundred yards from the west, the sound bouncing oddly down the alleys of the village and off the quickly climbing slope of land that meets the harbor to the east of the village. Such was his conclusion for a half a minute. He passed the first of the two boats. As he surveyed its empty back deck and its black, empty cabin through its windows, the engine sound passed from his mind again. But as he moved onto the second boat the sound seized him; for there, tethered to the jetty, was Brentford Gourd's boat clearly displaying its name along the stern:

Wampum. And the engine sound he had been hearing since near the beginning of his walk was easily connected to the boat just before him.

My Uncle Harry had to tug at the boat's line. It had not been snuggly moored to the jetty yet—rather, it was held only by a single tether that had been quickly lashed to the dock at the boat's first landing. He had the boat close enough to him quickly so that he could leap on board. The boat was of such a size that it did not seem to give at all when he landed upon it. There was no one to be seen on board, and the cabin had its blinds drawn, but one could make out through the covered window of the cabin doorway, once one was standing on the stern deck, a faint lantern glowing from within. The door would not easily yield, but when Uncle Harry had it open, instinct moved him to secure the door in the open position with a heavy suitcase that sat on the stern deck seats. The cabin coughed forth a thick black smoke. Before probing the interior, my uncle climbed the ladder to the wheel and the ignition. There he found the key still in place, and it turned easily. The sound of the engine quickly passed away, and the smoke seemed to ease a bit.

Inside the cabin he found the bodies of Brentford and Lara Gourd. The latter seemed to be posed in death in the manner in which she left life—aiding her husband before a subsidiary access panel to the inboard. Why he would have opened the access hatch to the motor at that time, or what he had hoped to accomplish was never really learned. The figure that could only be cited speculatively as Jessica lay dead on the seat nearest the exit to the cabin. This dark-haired woman seemed to have entered to investigate the Gourd's excessive absence, and to have been trapped inside on finding that she could not open the door again. There was a radio still on in the cabin. My uncle turned it off.

He reported that he next had the gruesome thought to look for the "two surprises," the suspected babies—expecting, surely, to find but two ashen-hued little bodies somewhere in the cabin or bunk area. However, they were not inside. Upon looking on the stern deck once more, my uncle found what looked like a hastily contrived little tent made from a bedspread—put up to cover something from the wind, perhaps, as the preparations were being made to leave the boat for the jetty. Underneath the bedspread my uncle said that he still expected to find two, small, shocking, cold, white, and gray bodies. But, instead, asleep, lay—not two little gray corpses—but two little rosy fellows, deeply unaware and peaceful, snug in winter suits and still more blankets, both encased in his own little shell of a car seat. My uncle said that I soon began to cry. But Boston was quiet almost the entire night.

Uncle Harry took both seats and put them on the jetty. He freed us from the straps and then hurried with us to the house.

For the first six months, both Boston and I lived in the main house. Soon, after a great deal of investigation and legal labor—which occupied my Uncle William for half of his working day during that entire interval—Boston became a Gourd of William and Maryland Gourd, and I became a Gourd of Elizabeth Gourd. Uncle William and Aunt Maryland had asked my Aunt Elizabeth to take both the babies—as they had had Brentford as a baby and felt this might be Elizabeth's chance to take to Gourd orphans—but my Aunt Elizabeth felt that she could not suddenly have a charge of two. Uncle William and Aunt Maryland said that they would be willing to do their best by the dark, hale little stranger if my Aunt Elizabeth was ready for me (the baby they assumed was Brentford Gourd's). I do not know how the last conclusion was made, and I never asked.

Having no names for us, my aunts settled upon two maritime city names to honor our mysterious, waterbound births and our presumed New England sources—Portsmouth for me; Boston for Boston. Aunt Maryland's name took on its unique spelling because of her mother's place of birth—thus there was a precedent for this manner of naming in our family. And I presume that my mother's parents had dreams of the West and Wyoming when they named their daughter Laramie.

I descended the hill slowly when the priest seemed to be working his way toward the coda of his eulogy. I passed the family plot, but I did not linger there on my way back to the limousine—did not linger about that spot where even the mysterious third adult passenger from that ill-fated Sound crossing is still buried. Her grave is next to Laramie Gourd's and marked simply as *J.,—1970*.

Uncle Harry carried all through the laborious business of the funerals as my Uncle William carried all through the laborious business of the adoptions. The former performed the unusual duty of preparing the familiar and mysterious dead for the ceremonies and burial. Uncle William worked on the prospect that would carry a secret excitement with these passings.

Aunt Elizabeth also had Uncle William sell off the Connecticut business and its property.

Though I rarely thought of it, our waterborne origins had intimations that were far more suggestive to me than any mere Mosaic overtones.

There were times, especially in the summer, when Boston and I might find ourselves playing war on the slope above the jetty—or swimming in the water only a few yards to the east of its piles—and I would think of the dark, smoky boat, running in neutral, and of its passengers, they only yards from completing their journey. And they would suggest to me, the young Gourds of the past and their mysterious friend, the remembrance of the ancient crossings of the Connecticut Indian tribes onto Long Island—more aptly, the descent of Connecticut's powerful tribes upon the more pacific Indians on the south side of the Sound. The bellicose tribes are said to have crossed and demanded tribute from their militarily weaker counterparts on what was called Paumanauk. Some say this name translates as *fish-shaped*. Perhaps. Yet I prefer the other notion—that the word suggests *Land of Tribute* or *Land of Shells* (the latter term suggesting the currency of the tribute).

My father had been an aloof child, and he never quite embraced—or could not intellectually understand—what my Uncle William and Aunt Maryland wanted to offer him. When he took the Connecticut-side business that was given to him by the family, he may have felt he had moved closer to them, at last—that he had lowered a bit of his remove. I cannot say for sure. Yet his taking pleasure in extending himself through the family business as a way to articulate some newfound affection for the family itself was hardly what was wanted of him from Maryland and William. He seemed to believe in a patriarchal pride that would be resurrected in a business that was only run then by Elizabeth and Harry for very different, nearly forgotten, reasons. And what was hoped for from the newest Gourd was not just a trite recognition of nostalgia. Aunt Maryland and Uncle William had cleared the way and were ready to receive—as was my Aunt Elizabeth in her cloudy way, as well—for speculation of a different order. For a family so long connected to that enterprise that emphasized what one cannot take with them, it had readied itself for the accumulation of those things, or that one immense, manifold, yet ineffable thing, that could be.

Thus, when Brentford Gourd came a-warring over the Sound one winter's night to demand tribute with his *Wampum* he was stopped—as, surely, some of the bellicose crossers must have been from time to time in the old pre-Dutch days when all of Long Island's bays boasted the mists of porpoise breath and the hoarse barks of seals. He was stopped, and as payment in mourning war, he and his were killed, and the infants were taken so that they might be offered what he had so long overlooked—they raised on the opposing shore and never to long for the solid continent.

I thought such things when we played by the Sound. Boston rarely seemed to take note of the spot.

I rejoined the funeral at its end and drove my party of four back to the main house. Mrs. Paw did not wish to go to the somber luncheon that was being given by the next of kin in a restaurant in the village—she felt too tired, she said—and so I volunteered to drive her home. On the way over to her house, she recalled Boston's imminent return many times, and she liked to pair off the recollections with the complementary image of how it was that not a few times, when she thought she was all alone in her garden at the edge of the woods, she would turn about to discover two bare-chested, blue-jeaned natives with self-styled bands tied about their heads, crouched low in the weeds on the shore of the forest, like evening rabbits, watching her foreign ways. They would not speak. But she recalled that if she offered the right provisions—sometimes pieces of cake, or drinks of milk, or allowances from a jar that held stray marbles and old buttons—they might be persuaded to rise and enter her cabin. And they could be further persuaded to play to her upon her little upright piano—play to her from the music they had learned that had been brought over from far beyond the eastern bend of the horizon on the single-repertoired roar of the masking ocean.

CHAPTER IV

PRACTICE

After Mrs. Paw was safely inside her house, I drove back to our side of the woods near the village. Uncle Harry, Aunt Elizabeth, and I had lunch, and then I stated that I was going to invoke a schedule for myself starting then—as I really did not have that much time to prepare for the competition. I knew I would have even less time once school began in a few weeks. My aunt then went down into the office to work on the first floor, and my uncle went into the basement to prepare a new arrival for a viewing for the next day. This new main customer had been delivered just before I returned from Mrs. Paw's. All would be quiet as to visitors until the viewing the next evening. We still had heard nothing from Boston. There were no messages. He could be very close or still very far away. But he was expected any day. My aunt said that since he was unreachable, she almost preferred not to speak of it—it worried her to think of him driving so far alone. Uncle Harry did not comment on it, being slightly irritated, as I was, by my cousin's tiresomely secretive movements. Perhaps he was in Ohio by then, we had all said. And we left it at that.

I went up to my room on the third floor and began the process of breaking myself out of a little practice slump. There had been extenuating circumstances, of course, but I still felt that, had I been an ideal soldier, I would have sought means and time to practice when I was in the midst of my move out of Manhattan. Such opportunities did present themselves, yet when they did—and when they still do under similar circumstances—I usually decline them in preference of the time when I will have a standard schedule again (when I can say to myself that I have practiced for a given block of impressive hours). Such is a foolish instinct, yet it is difficult to break. I think such impulses were formed in me early upon hearing of the legendary practice regimens of performers and composers of the past. Yet I am sure the legendary were more capable of adjustment in difficult circumstances than I am.

There is something arduous about beginning practice after a hiatus, for there is a certain amount of basic ground that needs to be resurrected before progress can be made. At least, such is the case for me. Though sometimes one finds the basic ground hard to win back over the first day or two, there is also at times a discovery that certain unwelcome, learned, aspects hovering near the basic ground have been forgotten through lack of practice—a pianist, then, rather like a vacationing runner who returns to his workouts to find himself more winded than usual, yet free of certain quirks or pains that accumulated in his technique before he let his schedule lapse.

I was mulling over just such a discovery in my fingers, when the home line of the phone rang. A minute or two later, my aunt called up to me from the stairs that the call was for me. I went down to the kitchen, and my aunt whispered that she thought it was my piano teacher calling from the city. She was right.

"Portsmouth, this is Neil Silver. You doing all right? Anyway, I think you picked up the materials I left for you, and I just wanted to congratulate you on earning a place in Manhattoes. Listen, I'll be away for awhile—till just before school starts. I'm practicing like a madman so that I can be ready for my engagements in Russia for mid-month. I don't want to murder the pieces, you know. But I'm trying to work out a Thursday or Friday afternoon lesson schedule."

He paused here, not so much for an answer about a prospective lesson time as for an inquiry from me about his "engagements in Russia." After a year as his student, I really could not bear playing that game, so I merely volunteered with civility, and seeming innocence of his real intent for the gap in his speech, that I had nothing planned yet in my school schedule for those days.

"Good, good. I'll put you down, say, for Thursdays at two o'clock? All right? Good. Things have been just crazy for me. You sure you want to try to win a competition like this and get a career? You'll end up with a schedule like mine!" Here he laughed, and I gave as much back as I could—for he had inserted a compliment for me in the midst of more circuitous self-praise.

At times I wonder if my ostensibly natural aversion for nearly everyone I encounter in the world of classical music is nothing but an oblique preparation for myself should I not be able to survive amongst them pianistically. I had picked a career that pulled me, when I worked hard at it, from the company of those with whom I felt most comfortable. Though I do not have a desire to surround myself with an anti-intellectual, affectedly rustic coterie, I do not wish to be trapped in the affected pseudo-intellectual world of the concert platform either. And there seems to be an undue number of the self-confident, yet intellectually deceived in classical music. My professor, Mr. Silver, though ultimately a pleasant and civil person, was just the sort of fellow who ultimately makes me feel regret for the company that most often breaks in upon the solitude of practicing. There is a forced tradition—sometimes it is more than forced; it is totally imagined—that the relationship between consummate teacher and truly advanced student is to develop into a deeply sympathetic bond. Though I suppose I have seen some who claim to have such a relationship—and some who practice its trappings when an audience is present—I doubt that such relationships are very often successful. I am sure that there are exceptions. I only wish to mock the proliferation of a mannerist culture that rarely fulfills itself. In its fulfillment I would find it repellent, as well.

Neil Silver was one of the busiest pianists on Earth—indeed, his success was truly on a planetary scale. Though he was not yet quite old enough, he was expected to take a place as one of the venerable pianistic names of the first half of the twenty-first century if given time and fortuity. He had played with virtually all of the major orchestras, and was already, at the age of about forty, able to cull from his itinerary literally dozens of dates that would be the pride of pianists who still struggle to secure a regular playing career for themselves.

When I returned to New York for my master's, I resolved to audition for the school from which Silver had recently decided to accept a few students. I made this my goal: to practice to the point that I would unquestionably be granted my choice of teachers if admitted to the school. Having such a goal made me sharpen my skills as I had never done before—not even the competitions I had already been to moved me to such a schedule of refinement—and I was successful, to my amazement. I felt so powerful upon this accomplishment, that I thought I might even be slowly catching up to the invincible level of my cousin. Perhaps because I had never been quite as brave and fearless in combat as I knew Boston and his sort must be, having to prepare for a combat that only involved auditioning in a private forum allowed me to achieve a potency that I knew I would not have to sustain. If I had been in an actual competition—the point of which would be to prove a level of mastery through winning that could be offered, presumably, for a career's length of time—I may have sabotaged myself with a half-effort. But I gave all for the audition. Yet I think that the push toward graduate school was certainly an impure gesture. I wished only my vanity satisfied with a place in Silver's class, and I hoped to take my terminal degree in music so that at the very least I could apply for a teaching position in a university.

I confess that actually winning a spot in the Manhattoes Competition made me think of a playing career with an earnestness I had never before entertained. It flattered me, as well, that someone such as Neil Silver assumed that such a thing was my intention—and that such an intention was not in need of checking. Yet in times that were quiet socially for me, I always found communications from him rather irksome. They made me feel somewhat pathetic.

"But how are you doing in general?" continued Mr. Silver.

"Pretty good, I've just finished moving back home, and I'll have it easy as a night practicer from now on."

"Good, good. Listen, you have the repertoire requirements. Unlike the other newer competitions, which are becoming more and more liberal in what they ask the competitors to play (some do not make any but the broadest specifications), this one is a kind of hyper-reversion, you know. Almost all the works are specified. I think there is only an option point in one—maybe two—of the categories."

"It's just one, the commissioned works. There are two of them," I inserted.

"Right, right. Good. You know all the rules and what is ahead of you. This is kind of a ground-covering competition, a literature-learning competition. We hope it will reveal the artists who can reveal themselves even when the circumstances are all dictated to them and on short notice. Oh, hey, you know, I wanted to ask you something. This Boston Gourd—I've seen him at about every competition I've been to, judged, or heard about for, what, the last five years. And I never thought about the names being the same, but someone told me you were cousins."

"Yes, we are."

"I had thought he was from the west coast, but then—yeah, this is how I found out you were cousins—I saw on the sheets for the competition that he gave a forwarding address that was the same as your new one. I knew I saw the same address twice in a short time while looking over all that paperwork. Then—yeah, that is how it went—I asked how you two were related precisely when I was at school last week and saw your roommate. He said you two were cousins. Jeeze, that's going to be a noisy house out there for the next few months. You're going to have to work hard to beat that cousin of yours."

"Yes, I know, but I don't really expect to beat him, he—"

"But he hasn't been doing as well as he was there for awhile. You know, he is amazingly consistent—amazingly consistent. But juries are not. He placed low there for a streak, and didn't even place for awhile. Then he started to come up again in the last couple, I think."

"Yes, that is what I heard, but—"

"You mean you don't hear it from him?"

"No, not really. My aunt has heard from him by letter recently. But I haven't heard him play—or really talked with him—since we were both about eighteen and he went off to school."

"Really, you two just—" I was a bit irritated by this intrusion, but I answered honestly.

"No, he just became more and more independent of the past, I guess—till he almost faded entirely from our sights. But my aunt does hear from him now. I haven't heard him play since he was, say—"

"Well, again he is an infallible technician. Infallible. And I don't use that word lightly. It's the judges who are changeable, fickle. They have to be, really. But if your cousin has another good streak of luck for awhile he is bound to get a secure line of engagements that should carry someone like him to a rather secure playing career. I know he's had a few recordings, but if he just gets another streak of luck from the powers that be, he should be unstoppable. That boy was born to play. Born to music, really. Oh, and wait—I saw his name on the list of incoming master's students at school. I couldn't believe it. Did he audition? Imagine someone like him auditioning! At the west coast auditions, I guess. Where were they, in Los Angeles?"

"I guess that's how he did it. I think my aunt said something about it."

"Amazing to think of someone so close to being free of such things having to go back to school. Heck, I don't know what I can do for him, but I hope he knows he's welcome in my studio."

"I'll tell him for sure when he gets here. I don't know what his plans are. I'm sure he'll appreciate the offer."

"Please do. Again, I don't know what I can do for him. But what can anyone do for him?" Mr. Silver laughed, and I thought he was nearing the end of the call, but then he pitched into a tangent-like coda.

"You know, your cousin just had some ill luck with the juries. They're all for him. But they can't always be for him, maybe, they think. Since he hasn't secured a career yet but keeps coming back to these tiresome contests—I can't believe I'm helping to start another—maybe they just subconsciously raised the standard for him, since he just keeps coming back as strong as ever. It's uncanny, really. I saw the last one he was in. He has a machine-like ability to call upon his technique when the pressure is on. But, then—and I am sure you heard about this—he is also part of what they call the cursed group—this group of the top ten, fifteen, or twenty, or whatever it is, contestants who were at the last two big international competitions and had a judge pass away so awfully at each one. It slowed down the whole thing for awhile. I mean I'm sorry they died and all. They were great colleagues. The loss is irreparable—and the contests were kind of a mess after all this dying. I mean, actually, there was one last December—and, holy smokes—"

"Two in May," I inserted.

"Right! Two at the one in May. I was there. You know, those two were *for* your cousin, in fact. I was forced to vote for two others over your cousin. I mean I had to. They were, are, like him, infallible. And they just struck me as having that little bit of— What? Je ne sais quoi! Don't tell you're cousin! That was dumb of me to say that—to have mentioned anything about the judging. But he'll have it another night, another time. On that level they all do from time to time. Anyway, we were all set to cast all these final votes in May and then all this terrible, terrible tragic mess. We even thought they wouldn't allow us to continue. Everyone had worked so hard. Stopping hardly seemed a fitting tribute to the dead. It was scandalous—scandalous to us all—to lose such artists like that in May. God rest their souls."

I had been quiet for this last stretch, so Mr. Silver suddenly interjected, "Wait, this isn't all news to you?"

"No, I've heard about it all and read about it."

"Well, Portsmouth, I'll see you in late August. Give my regards to your cousin. Tell him to feel welcome to contact me. And, again, I'll see you on that last Thursday this month in my studio at two o'clock. Keep working. You don't have much time left."

I wrote down the time for my lesson. Soon I was back upstairs at the piano. As was the case with my exchange with Mrs. Paw in the limousine earlier that day, there was something that irked me about the peripheral knowledge that Mr. Silver had of Boston.

Nearly anyone might impute a stratified case of rivalry to the falling out between Boston and me—or to his falling away. I even forced myself to consider this as a possibility for a time. But I was soon convinced that such was not the case. Something else was at work. Aunt Elizabeth had suggested that perhaps it was the change that came over most upon moving away from home, or perhaps he had met a girl. I could only suspect something more inscrutable—as if upon living out of range of my ability to call him across the block or yard with my own, living voice had removed my ability to pull Boston from the reveries I had seen him in since we were little boys.

I dismissed my thoughts of Mr. Silver's call and my wayward cousin as best I could, and I applied myself to the two new commissioned pieces that were on the list for the competition. We were only required to play one of the new works. But as they were indeed new, and since there was no recording of either of them to help me make a decision as to which I wanted to commit to and learn for the contest, I set aside the whole afternoon to giving myself the best idea I could get as to what both of the pieces sounded like before settling on one.

As the afternoon ended and six-thirty neared, I settled on my choice. When I rose from the piano to get ready for dinner, I thought again of my call with Mr. Silver. I had mentioned to him—as was my custom when alluding to my social status with my cousin—that my aunt had started a correspondence with Boston. To my amazement, I first realized that I had never before asked if I might see those letters. But I felt too proud and irritated to ask my aunt about them, then.

Aunt Elizabeth, Uncle Harry, and I went into the village for dinner that night, and when we came back I retrieved Sarah for a long walk in the woods behind the main house. Mrs. Rhodes's death had me thinking of the past, and the woods helped set me to recalling the most peculiar piano night of my childhood with Boston—and Lana Paw.

About two years after that first day of lessons for Boston and me, Boston was already a minor celebrity. There was talk of him attending a prestigious pre-college program in the city. His celebrity was spread a bit further one night at a recital Mrs. Rhodes held for all her students at the elementary school. We all played, and Lana's grandmother insisted on hosting a little party for the three of us after the concert. For some reason, we three campaigned to walk to the party on our own after the concert, and with great reluctance from our aunts, Boston and I received permission to do this. Lana's parents did not seem to mind the idea. Everyone else would drive—and probably pass us or follow us on our short walk.

We three marched through the deep summer night and reached Mrs. Paw's house. It was hardly a half-mile from the school. But no one was there. Then it became very unclear to us if the party was not supposed to be at Lana's house—though still given by her grandmother. Boston suggested we cut across the woods and see if anyone was back on the home street.

In blackness engraved with blue lines from the cutting moonlight, we crossed into the woods. We marched slowly and quietly along the trail that led to the rear of left field of the old baseball diamond. This trail branched off to a secondary trail that went further through the woods, tracing the edge of the outfield until it joined the trail from right field's rear that led to the old farmhouse hollow. We reached the branch, and it was then that we first heard the music. It was from a radio, it seemed, sounding from far off, and it was not clear from which direction the sound came—the sound of loud rock music. Boston thought that it might be coming from down the slope on our right, from the beach. Lana thought it was from straight ahead, more or less, near our own street.

I thought it was coming from the left, from the southeast, right from the low clearing where the old stone foundation was. We all stood silent for an instant to reconsider its direction. Boston suddenly changed his mind. It was coming, he thought, just as Lana said, from straight ahead.

"We can't go back that way!" I whispered vigorously. The three of us all started to whisper then.

"Yeah, we should go back! We should go back to my grandma's! Or we should go back and walk along the street the long way back," Lana added.

"Aahh! We can make it this way. It's not much farther. It's not much farther! It's probably just teenagers!" rasped Boston. "I'll go and check out the way around the stone house."

Just as Boston had begun the latter of his last two phrases, Lana had gasped, "The teenagers!" I had almost done the same thing. They were *the teenagers* to me, as well—a small group who sometimes met in the woods and left behind steamy black campfire rings in the dewy mornings. Mrs. Paw (Lana's grandmother) had made calls about them to the police. The teenagers entered the woods through her backyard at times. My uncle and aunt did not want them in the area behind the main house at all, for the teenagers were certainly not using the woods for the observation of Nature or for playing games on the baseball diamond. I formed a deep abhorrence of the teenagers when I found shards of broken, amber colored beer bottles when I would explore near the old house foundation, along the edges of the baseball diamond, or on the beach that edged this part of my grandfather's purchase.

A long time seemed to pass, yet it was probably not more than three minutes. Boston was still gone. Then Lana and I both looked at each other as someone, somewhere, turned the music down with a careful slowness. We kneeled down to listen.

Another long interval seemed to pass.

A fear of the silence possessed us both, and we began to run.

Soon we reached the baseball diamond, and there was no one there; the sound had never come from there. We reached the narrow, corridor-like clearing that was the run from third base to home. We paused. The silence was terrifying again. Lana and I entered the last stretch of woods that encircled and fronted the backyard of the main house.

There we found my Aunt Elizabeth and Lana's mother, walking about nervously, calling to us. Everyone else was at the Paws'—hoping we would soon appear.

Breathlessly, I began to describe our trek when my aunt asked where Boston was.

Then we could all hear the piano.

From down the block, through the open screens of my Uncle William's and Aunt Maryland's came the sound of Boston's very articulate, very strong, playing. He had returned by the long way—having navigated back to Lana's grandmother's and then along the streets till he reached the head of our block. Or he had returned by a rough, faint path—out of our sight—that led to the back of his house. But I not did learn anything more that night of Boston's movements.

The police were on our block soon, and I was taken up to bed.

I found the following clipping in the *Pauktaug Press* a week later. I saved it in the leaves of a book, and I accidentally found it again a few years ago—the clipped column leaving a yellowed ghost around its edges on the white pages of the book. The areas beneath where it had been were still clean. I give the passage that describes the murder site and story. It contains, I think, the most sanguinary details ever given in *The Police Beat* section of the local paper:

After breaking into a home at 47 Sachem Drive, where kitchen knives and other cooking utensils as well as nearly $46 in cash were later reported missing by a resident, a group of seven teens assembled in a wooded area slightly to the east of Pauktaug Village. There the seven young men (five from Pauktaug Village and two from East Northport) carried out a loosely planned, alleged "demonic sacrifice" on August 5. After using large quantities of alcohol and marijuana around a campfire near a nineteenth-century farmhouse foundation, the seven members of the alleged cult drew straws to determine which of their number would be "slain." It is said that the notion of a *sacrifice-ritual was not regarded seriously until two members of the group went off to a private conference in an adjacent field. Both then allegedly used doses of the hallucinogenic drug LSD. Returning from their private talk, the two, one Robert Maranucci of Pauktaug and one Robert Pennypacker of East Northport, both 18, proceeded to make the group's till-then fantasized "ritual" a reality. After cutting the throat of one Thomas Adder of East Northport, Maranucci and Pennypacker proceeded to mutilate the body according to practices they had allegedly researched in an anthropology text describing mutilations as practiced in eighteenth-century Indian warfare in the northeastern states. Among the mutilations inflicted upon the body of Adder was the smashing of the skull with a large stone or boulder from the house foundation. An attempt seems to have been made to remove the victim's heart but appears to have been abandoned. Four of the members allegedly did not contribute to the murder or subsequent mutilation of the victim. They remained on hand as passive witnesses and did not interfere. All six of the remaining group fled the scene—while Maranucci and Pennypacker abandoned the process of burying the body near the front interior of the foundation—when police and nearby residents attended to reports of disturbances at 47 Sachem Drive. The six young men reportedly fled through the woods and exited on a residential street just east of Pauktaug Village. Pennypacker is reported to have left a suicide note implicating all six who were present and/or responsible for the actions of the night of August 5. Pennypacker took his life on the morning of August 6, at or around 5:30 AM. The remaining five young men were all taken into custody by noon of August 6, with the exception of Maranucci, who was apprehended at his place of employment in Huntington Station at or around 4:00 PM.*

After I returned from my walk with Sarah, I returned to the main house and practiced some of the required etudes for the competition until eleven o'clock. Then I met my aunt in the kitchen for tea. We talked about the competition until Uncle Harry came upstairs. Then we wondered aloud where Boston might be. Aunt Elizabeth said that if he did not call before noon the next day she was going to start to get angry. When we had last speculated about his whereabouts we imagined him to be as far as Ohio or Pennsylvania. As the next day was to be the second of August, the last of the two days that he gave as an arrival date, we thought that he must surely be that far in his transcontinental drive—if not as far as Harrisburg—if he was to make it on time. But if he did not call, there would be nothing for my aunt and uncle to do but to be angry. There was no one else to call to see if he had checked in with anyone else. He seemed to have evolved into a completely independent fellow—granting us a rare infiltration of his entirely soloistic habits if he indeed moved in with us. But as of that moment he was still truly independent and at large, driving across the United States with all of his possessions (save for his piano), and enjoying a last stint of answering to no other living being but his inscrutable, increasingly private self.

"Well, he knows that I expect him to give a reasonable account of his schedule and expected returns if he is going to live here with us. I just hope this black-out period is just a last gesture before he settles back here in New York!" warned my aunt.

After we finished tea for the evening and said goodnight, my aunt went to bed, and Uncle Harry went to look at the banister along the stairs to the third floor. He had yet to finish putting it back together after Boston's piano had been moved upstairs. After mulling over that task for a bit, he came back downstairs to the kitchen and went back to his little house for the night.

I went upstairs, then, myself. That is when I found Boston's letters sitting in a box on the shelves in the hall. I took them with me to my room. I did not think my aunt would mind, and there was a slight dust ring around where the box had been sitting. It was clear she had not looked at them for a few weeks—except to put a few new notes into the box.

I adjourned to my room with the box of letters. I was not sure where to start, so I resolved to put off my reading until I was more wakeful. Instead, as midnight neared, and just before I went to bed, I found the book in which I kept the old clipping from the *Pauktaug Press*. I read it through yet again, and I thought of the evening of the next day that followed that strange night of crossing the woods with Lana and Boston.

Aunt Maryland and Boston came over to the main house after Aunt Elizabeth, Uncle Harry and I had finished dinner. She and Aunt Elizabeth sat on the back porch as Uncle Harry and I played in the yard. Even though Aunt Elizabeth told Boston that I was in the backyard with Uncle Harry—and he eventually did wander out into the twilight in good spirits to run with me on the grass— he played first on my piano for about a half hour. At least three or four times, he played through a sonata or sonatina movement with shocking perfection, with striking digital accuracy.

My aunts began to speak in hushed tones of the detectives and of the police psychologist that had been brought over that morning. The police had thought it wise to have someone observe Boston during questioning—not only for his own sake and health —but so as to monitor the viability and veracity of his testimony. The doctor reported that she was shocked by Boston. He was in no manner physically suggestive of manhood in frame or manner. Nor did he present phrases or styles that would suggest an unnatural or unattractive attempt to affect premature maturity. But the substance of what he said, the grist behind the child's common syntax and observations was somehow, disturbingly sagely—and again, he never displayed any of the hackneyed or obnoxious qualities of the commonly precocious. She reported feeling a bit benignly disturbed by him—yet not feeling that *he* was unduly disturbed in any emotional way. Oftentimes a child may make unaffected remarks of the sort to which I allude here. But Boston seemed to do so with an increasing consistency and frequency, and during the morning's interviews, he not only accounted himself a clear, sober, reliable source of information, but an equal source of wise synthesis. For each of three or four questions posed to him that asked that one offer a sort of subjective, interpretive, if not purely speculative answer, Boston presented very finished, almost intellectually redacted observations.

I suspect, what with my busyness in the grass with Uncle Harry, and what with the distant sound of Boston's piano playing, that my aunts imagined I could not hear much of what they were saying. But I could hear them quite clearly as they swayed together on the glider of the porch.

The grave, stoic look of caution that had been the main thing I could gather of Aunt Maryland's state that day was still present. But then, when I could hear her speak, there was a confidence, a pride—not as for a child who was hers or in her care, but as pride, a confidence, for the child, Man. She spoke in a low confidence, with a cautious joy.

"They had just asked Boston to describe what of the actual murder he could see (which, my God, was everything about it), and the things that happened just after it—right up to the last horrible thing—when one of the detectives, who had hardly said anything before, perhaps for the sake of bringing some sort of distraction to the moment, brought up the issue of the radio. He frowned and half-heartedly said, 'Maybe the music made them do it.' And then there was silence that the other detective was probably supposed to glide back into, but Boston suddenly said, quite assuredly and with no preamble, qualification, or coda, 'No, the music didn't make them do that.'"

Thinking of my aunt's words of Boston's words, I put the clipping away into the box with Boston's letters, and left the new heaps of words, the box of letters, for later—for the next day, perhaps. Thus I ended my first full day back in Pauktaug, and the first full day of our waiting for Boston's return.

CHAPTER V

ROMANCE

On the morning of the second of August, I went downstairs to find my aunt already busy in the office and my uncle already laboring in the basement. We were going to have two viewings going on at once that evening—a second body had arrived while I was out walking with Sarah the evening before. Both of our two employees were down in the basement working with my uncle.

I practiced all that morning and then went downstairs again for lunch with my aunt and uncle. Keeping to my schedule, I intrepidly and proudly went back upstairs, agreeing with my aunt upon a five-thirty dinner time—a bit early because of the evening work that lay ahead in the business.

I practiced pretty well until about three-thirty, and then I felt a bit sleepy and low, but I pressed on—even when I had a glimpse of Aunt Elizabeth pull away in the car for a trip into the village. She was very agitated. Boston had not appeared, and there was no call from him.

Uncle Harry suddenly came into my room, however, and I had a little respite. He had left the rest of the day's work in the basement to our two employees, and he came to see to my piano. We spent a quiet hour together as he did a fair job of tuning. When he was done, he looked to me.

"I'm real proud of the work you're doing, Port. I have a lot of confidence in you—a lot. But just in case, you do know that this is all here for you should you ever need it?"

He nodded around to the walls to indicate the business.

"This is all for you now, just in case you ever need it. I know that this was never one of your interests—it wouldn't be mine either if I could do what you can do. And I know you're hardly thinking of such things now. Things are looking really good for you. That's what I want for you. But just in case, you do know that this is here for you?"

"Thanks, Uncle Harry. I'll remember."

Then we patted each other on the back and went to look at Boston's piano. My uncle put in the replacement bolts he had found for the third leg and left the shoddy pair on the desk in that room. I went back to my practicing and left my uncle as he started to tune Boston's piano.

"I think I have something in the basement that will take this scratch out, too," he mused to himself as I left.

Boston never appeared that day. I thought about him as I took Sarah for a long walk into town late that night. I passed Lana's house. There was a moving van in the Paws' driveway. For a moment, I wondered if they, too, were receiving a piano. But there were boxes stacked on their porch, and it was clear that it was a regular moving truck. It looked like a rather modest delivery.

Then I thought about Lana as I continued to walk—wondered where she might be in the world. Her mother and father still lived in that house, but I was not sure if my aunt or uncle spoke to them very much. I was not sure what Lana's situation was precisely, but I believed she was said to have been married and in Chicago.

And then I thought of the friend that she had living in her house for a year's time during high school—Denise.

The family of Lana's friend was going to move to Pauktaug in December of that year—which was to be in the middle of the final year of high school for Boston, Lana, and me (and for this Denise). Denise's father and Mr. Paw knew each other through business, and as this Denise and Lana had their own friendship, it was decided that the two might get along well enough as housemates until Denise's parents were settled from their move just after Christmas.

It should be observed that I continued to value Lana as an object of distant romantic fascination. As we no longer enjoyed the unburdened freedom of association that we had shared when we were children, and as no move was made or was in me to risk enjoining any sort of romantic connection as late teenagers, she became removed from my circle almost altogether—even though she lived very close. For good or for ill, I was not in the way of cultivating the mere friendships of girls, and as I was not ready to ascend into frenetic, jolly, operatic torment, I stood in rather quiet remove from that race at that time.

Lana had evolved into a richness of form and blonde hair, and she always smiled upon me at school and on the street, quite willing to be a friend. I was too interested to approach.

Of course, there was a certain part of me that hoped that Boston's practicing did not cover mine too often when Lana was at home. There was no hope for me then to compete—what with his house being just opposite Lana's and what with his immeasurably greater pianistic powers. But though I felt intense awkwardness in Lana's presence at this point in my life, there was no real complement in the form of jealousy or competitiveness in my connection with my cousin.

By this time in our lives, it was clear that both Boston and I were officially going to pursue the piano through college and beyond. Though we were both skilled enough to consider making the piano a career—in the sense of a professional playing career—

it was without question that Boston was the one who had the most hope in this line. His was a skill so refined, powerful, and consistent, that only a conspiracy of external circumstances would seem powerful enough to keep success from him. The failure could not come from him, for his technique and approach were near a level of infallibility—and he could call upon that infallibility with shocking consistency.

Aunt Maryland and Uncle William had allowed him to compete in a set number of competitions for young people in the northeast, and he had proven invincible in every one. Combining a general affability with such power, it was not difficult for Aunt Maryland and Uncle William to have Boston agree to hold himself back from committing completely to this competitive lifestyle until after finishing college. The joys of their quiet existence in Pauktaug and his cheerful yet still nearly unexplored intellect, compelled my aunt and uncle to fear that Boston may not allow himself to probe all the options that might interest him if he put all his time too soon into travel for the sole sake of the piano. And Boston was so confident of his pianistic powers—as were his pre-college teachers in New York City—that no one (without exception) thought it necessary to exploit his extreme youth while it was still combined with what appeared to be one of the most fearsome set of fingers in America, if not on Earth. This kind of confidence could create either an arrogant being or a fellow who felt free to explore with earnest and good-natured, humble interest, many tangents in the universe and the pleasures and profundities of common existence (his place of security and supremacy always harbored in the frozen future, ready to be thawed out at the moment the intensity of exclusive concentration shone upon it). Perhaps the latter state was a form of arrogance, as well. But it was a more attractive form—and perhaps a sort of arrogance was unavoidable if so much power were vested in a being also free from plagues of any and all sorts. Therefore, because the intensity of Boston's pianistic warfare was still unleashed, because he was genuinely convinced that I also had a place in the pianistic world, and because he was sincerely modest and affable (without seeming affected) as much as anyone with his imminent hopes could be, our friendship was not challenged by the extreme closeness of our goals. And since I confessed my knowledge of what he held at bay, we were free to discuss the challenging monsters of the piano literature without feeling ourselves in a race.

Yet as the year progressed and the autumn aged, I wasn't surprised (and I was a little relieved) to find Boston openly discussing with me the beauties of the slim, long-jet-black-haired girl who lived only yards away from his home. And after a time, Boston and I would time our exits from his backyard so that we would slowly overtake Denise on our walks to school. By gentlemanly pact it evolved by November that he alone would overtake Denise, and thus evolved a high school romance of an intense, distracting, but internally moiling poignancy. Boston even spoke of it to me with a fantastic sobriety and remove, with an astonishing interpretive maturity—that romances of this kind were painfully beautiful; that they were like painful, pretty, staggering, unrealizable dreams to be taken for their tragic tenuousness. He reveled in the transience of it. His walks, his movie trips, his time sitting in the leaves with her, were like the purities of seemingly non-sexual romantic dreams. He quite seriously felt a warmness in his chest when she came to mind. He reported all this with no admonishments toward me or entreaties that I, too, should seize the beautiful, tragic transience of rural American romance. He simply felt compelled to report how his mind broke down this inevitable new gravity he had discovered upon the Earth—a new force that could make objects fall in its direction. Nature and, hopefully, his own will would be able to leave this romance and love behind with the inexorable arrival of geographic change.

Boston's nights of speaking of his growing affections for

Denise were frequent that November. On the Friday and Saturday nights when they would go out, they had to return by eleven, and as it was too late for Boston to go to the piano, and as he was too enthralled to sleep, we would often go into the woods and then descend to the sand and the water for our talks. Ultimately, because of his generosity of spirit, he being first to venture serious talk of mermaids as we sat by the eyelash of the sea, I was able to venture more and more to him concerning my admiration of Lana. Again, I hardly ever spoke with the girl, then, from fear, so mainly all I could dwell on was how beautiful I thought she was. She was November feminized, I thought—her blonde hair looked like long strands of rich grained acorn and corn colors—and she kept a mild, rich tan to her skin from the hours she spent on the fields running and training for the track team.

On the last days of that year's November, Boston and I participated in a piano competition in New York City.

I had only been in a few competitions by that point in my life—and they were local and on Long Island—and I felt proud that I placed in one of them where I thought the other competitors were all pretty fine. Boston watched me in that one—it was held out east in a North Fork village during an autumn festival in October. The venue was beautiful, and it was held in a converted barn amidst the farm fields closed in on two sides by sea water. With my spirits high after playing and placing in the finals, Boston, my uncles, my aunts, and I went to dinner after the concert in the town out there, and Boston flattered me by taking out the application for an imminent competition that was to be held in New York City, which admitted any of high school age from the northeast region—provided that a live taped performance was submitted and approved. Boston had already sent in his material, and he insisted that I send in my second-prize performance recording to the competition, as well. To my surprise, by early November I learned that I would actually be in the fray with my increasingly renowned cousin. Boston had long since abandoned the small, local competitions for large regional affairs, but this would be my first step into that echelon. And I had never yet been to one of Boston's competitions as a spectator. I had seen the solo concerts he had been offered as a result of some of his winnings, but I had never seen the actual contest performances themselves. Our schedules were divided by school, and it was at this time when Boston's schedule began to intensify so because of these contests that he consented to pull away from entering too many of them. But this latest regional contest did not require any traveling save for three or four treks into New York, and so Aunt Maryland and Uncle William said it would be all right if he entered this competition to be held on the last four days of November.

When we learned that we were both in it, we took pleasure in discussing our pieces and the prospect of battle ahead of us. On the Sunday night of Thanksgiving break, Boston and I walked into the woods and milled about the baseball diamond in the moonlight, the paths between the bases still evident and hard even after years of disuse. We descended to the beach and sat on two large stones.

"I think I'm really ready for this one, Port," began Boston.

"I know," I answered, "I can hear you clearly, even through the closed windows."

"And there's no reason you won't be able to clear the field of all the other people, Port. I've heard most of them before, and you're better. I'm not just telling you these things to make you feel good. I mean it."

"Thanks, Boston. I don't know, really. We'll see." I think he really did mean what he said, and that is what made it seem so truly kind.

"Then, Port, maybe there'll be no one left in the finals at all except you and I, and we'll have our first real battle."

I only smiled, and then Boston started to speak of a fingering that was irking him in one of his pieces, and then we repaired home for the night.

That week, Boston and I played to each other at times in the lateness, until our respective guardians had to ask us to stop because of the neighbors. But I think we played to Denise and Lana, as well. Boston did not ask Denise to any of the stages of the competition. I had thought about what it would have been like to be brave enough to suddenly ask Lana if she would like to go with me on one of the nights that I was to play. But I hadn't the courage to say anything but an orchestrated hello to her during the early part of that week.

When the competition came, I played my preliminary offerings, and I thought I played very well. But I was not to be afforded another chance to perform in that competition, for I was knocked out right away. The other players did, however, shock me with their powers. What I felt I had begun to approximate in skill and strength, they seemed to display as an instinctive minimum. And then I watched Boston compete. What the other players could do—as the rounds headed to the finals—for their steel-fingered, impassioned best, was but an instinctive minimum to Boston.

Something happened in the final round—when there were five players left—that I recall with special distinctness. Boston came onto the stage looking his dashing best, bowed, took his place at the bench, and then he meandered for a time with a survey of things about him. He was the penultimate player of the night, and at first I thought he was lingering before he began so as to catch a bit of attention as a cavalier of confidence on the stage. But soon I thought differently. He looked for several long seconds to where the judges sat, and then to each main section of the auditorium as if to confirm something for himself. To anyone else, it may have looked like a nonchalant challenge. Yet not only did I know from having been in the same spot on that stage as a competitor myself that he could not see the areas where he was looking with any distinctness, but I knew somehow that he was not attempting to broadcast any definite message to any definite member in the giant room. He had taken on that abstracted expression I had seen in him a thousand times over since we were children—an expression generated by some link formed in a quiet or private moment with an inscrutable universality. He could oftentimes hold that visage of his deeps until well after one had approached him and called him to the surface to play as a child or to walk and talk as a young man.

I knew that all one could see from his spot were the lights that glowed from the outer edges of the balconies and boxes and from those that ran along the aisle floors in the orchestra After looking about the darkened room, he leaned hard to his right and put his weight on his right leg, resting both his arms on his thigh, assuming a posture in which he was stretching somewhat in the manner of an athlete. But then I could see that he was looking into the interior of the piano. What he could probably see there, at first, were the perfect lines of tuning pegs—all standing clean and shiny and altogether without dust in the new piano that had been leased for the contest. Beyond that were the sets of short lines of steel strings on his right and the longer steel strings in the middle, and in the shadowed areas near to where the lid met the piano's left side were the long, long, copper-colored strings. But most interestingly, he could look up into the inside of the lid and see the reflection of the various lights from out in the house, looking like dull yellow stars in the shiny finish—and the piano's insides shared the reflection and created a conflated image.

The tuning pins would have looked new and perfectly aligned, a finely groomed graveyard to Boston, with a slight trimming of red felt for a crimson lawn.

The strings wrapped around the pins like encouraged strands of ivy about stones, yet these strands strangle-held so tight that even the steel stones would have trouble taking a breath. The lower, the deeper, the farther to the left one went on the piano, the less strings there were, and eventually there was only one string and one pin for each note, and then one's left hand would hit a wood block below the last key on the left—that wood block like a definite, level, sea bottom. So there appeared to be less casualties in this graveyard from the deep depths, for there were less stones and vines for them.

This wood, copper, and steel cemetery revealed the ghosts in its graves. It was the evident burying place of stars. In the lid's interior reflection, the suns that seemed to glow from the lights in the distant, unreachable parts of the theater were tangled by the reflection of strings—these suns, effigies of thermal and gravitational splendor, these intimations of the grandest products of the universal laws—tangled by a tool of man, itself able to cast forth evidence of an art founded upon those same laws; tangled by an instrument which exploded and pulled and heated and lighted the Universe with waves of sound instead of fire.

Boston seemed to look upon all this before he started. Thus, the lid of the massive, nine-foot, instrument was not open so that it could project, but so that it could receive and embrace. There sat the giant piano, looking shiny and black like the old Universe itself—with Boston at the seat of this vague territory (enthroned there or subject to it)—and that old black personified bit of the Universe, its open lid looked like an aged sage's hand, cupped to his own ear so that he could take of the waves of the cosmos with rapt attention and hushed, furrowed brow. A piano's eyes are so squinted one cannot even see them. Where are its eyes, even? You will look in vain if you search. The piano is the cave fish of man's machines. There are some who think it is a giant mouth—bellowing forth and outward. But, no, that is one of the great deceptions in the history of man and Music, for the piano is as a giant ear—taking in, listening. Not only ivory gives an elephantine character to the piano, but also this giant flap of an outer ear! Attend a piano concert of real worth someday and be among those who sit in the overflow audience on the stage. Watch the lid closely. Watch it shudder at times though the rest of the instrument be perfectly still, anchored by three mighty brass casters. Watch it tremble as it listens—as it flicks away the flies and *listens.*

Boston sat upright and began to play. He played himself to victory, and it was difficult to watch the final competitor in his selections, for it was evident that Boston would win, and he did.

Boston won a sizeable monetary award and a solo engagement at the same venue in which the competition had been held. But that concert was not until February. However, a sudden invitation came by phone the next day to Boston's house from the Huntington Arts Council—for Boston and me both to play. They had just had a cancellation for a December 6 concert that was scheduled for the Pauktaug Theater. The Pauktaug Theater was a last-run, dollar-movie house that somehow survived right on our own Main Street. But on a Friday night every other month or so the Huntington Arts Council rented out the venue for a rather serious chamber music series. Boston and I never went to these concerts, just to be contrary, but we went to all of the regular movies at the theater. As the Council knew through the community that we were both serious players, and as Boston had just won a well-publicized competition, and as we were both from Pauktaug, they thought we might be an interesting and viable substitute for whatever chamber group had cancelled so close to the concert date.

I started to shy away from giving concerts in extremely local venues at that time in my life, as they seemed like attempts to elicit patronage and praise from people one already knew. Boston felt the same way, so I was surprised when he decided to delay giving an answer to the invitation. We went for one of our near-midnight walks on the close of the day that the invitation came, and we passed through the woods and to the beach.

"First of all," said Boston, "you should've had a prize in the competition."

"Ah, don't be silly—"

"No, I'm serious, and I want us both to do this concert so that you can play these latest things that you've worked on before you move on to other pieces. They're too good to let go of now."

"Boston—"

"Port, stop! So, I think you and I should play this concert. I want to play with you in this one because of another idea. Let's see if we can't get the girls to come to this one. I didn't want to have that on my mind at the competition."

I happily consented to let the brave Boston invite them.

Boston's involvement and enthusiasm—as far as a high school romance can be said to invoke true involvement and true enthusiasm—was far in advance of mine. But both of our fascinations were also based, I might fairly say, on a high degree of vanity. Lana and Denise were both powerful images to behold. They were as pictures from magazines given blood and three dimensions. Lana was a topography of curved features and blonde hair—and she brought the colors absorbed from the sun, the beach, into the shade of the trees.

Denise, her beauty was of a linear quality, though she was equally three dimensional. She had skin the color of a china doll's, and hair like the dark of the dark side of the moon cut into threads. When the night was totally black and there was no moon, it was difficult to see where her hair began and ended—the matte blackness of her hair was fused with the matte blackness of the night. When the night was that of a full moon, and Denise's hair shone with the lunar-blue and silver, then, too, there seemed to be no distinction between the ends of her hair and the ensilvered blackness. She could shake her head, and the Universe would shiver

Oftentimes I have seen girls with long tresses suddenly bend over and let their hair fall straight down so that it looks fuller for a short time after they spring their bodies back up. Once I saw Denise do this on Lana's porch when they were both leaving to go out one dark night in dark, short, party dresses. Denise halved her perfect form—bent it like a closing piano lid—and the void of her black hair engulfed her porcelain-white face and wolf-blue eyes, and it then seemed that there was no center to the universe. She had folded the last bit of light into the velvet of the cosmos. But she rose up, and her chiseled china face brought a point of reference again to the silken voids of space.

The night of the concert came. I arrived first—and then Boston a little later.

We both wore the dark suits that our families had bought us for the competition. My cousin did not seem anxious to take a turn at the unfamiliar piano. Instead, he pulled me aside from the bench and walked around to the front of the piano and peered down into its insides, and he beckoned me along. We rested our elbows on the thick outer rim of the instrument and both talked into its harp, more or less, in a happy, conspiratorial way. Boston seemed intent on confirming my excitement about playing formally in front of Lana and Denise for the first time.

"Well, I am excited about it. But I'm so preoccupied with the playing itself—just getting through this—that I confess I wasn't thinking about it much, Boston."

"You know your pieces, Port. Not thinking about it! Are you kidding me? Hey, on the way over, I saw both of them clearly in their living room, finishing getting ready in their party dresses. It was something. It was something," smiled my cousin into the strings of the piano.

My cousin dwelled on the silhouette of Denise in her dress by lamplight, and then he laughed at his preoccupation and tried his hand at the unknown instrument. As I walked offstage to find a chair, he asked me if I liked the piano. I did. Boston was pleased with it, as well.

Soon he had to withdraw to the wings with me, for what was to be the modest-sized audience was beginning to probe its way into the auditorium. Boston and I could see the faces of almost everyone who entered. Boston watched more than I did, since I was to go first—and since Boston seemed to meet these affairs without fear of any kind and could afford distraction.

As the hour for the concert's start approached, however, we could see no sign of either Lana or Denise. So, with a disappointed exchange of grimaces and then shrugs of shoulders, we both stopped looking around the edge of the open curtain that masked the wing of the stage. I jogged in place a bit backstage as a representative from the Huntington Arts Council made some introductory remarks for the evening. But soon the lights came up on the piano, and I had to forego any more hopes that the cold and damp of my nervous fingers would pass by any means except going ahead and playing the concert itself.

When I was done with my half of the program, I received a good deal of applause, and I was very pleased with my part of the recital. Not unexpectedly, I felt that the performance I gave that Saturday night was superior to what I had given at the recent competition

Boston smiled to me in his robust, inimitable, and sincere way, and shook my hand with real congratulatory vigor when I returned to the wing. After telling me of things that I had achieved that I had thought were too subtle for anyone but myself to detect (even if that other were as highly trained as Boston), I was able to relax in my own satisfaction—in the feeling that definite, salient points of summiting had been perceived by someone who knew the intimacies of the altitudes upon which I had just been engaged in a fierce, technical, climb. One might think that Boston was aware of such things because we spent so much time together and lived in such close proximity. But I had stopped speaking of particular struggles with pieces in favor of Boston's favored, generalized topics of speculation—so there was no way he could have known in most cases, especially when an entire piece came off with technical accuracy and power, just where the spots were where I might have felt I had achieved a new victory. One might think that pianists acquire after years of work a certain sensitivity to the non-verbal gestures of another pianist's dismay—even when that dismay is not projected through an evident compromise in the performer's sound, accuracy, or interpretation. This may be true. But Boston did not claim any heightened sensitivity to my state during this performance based upon his accrued experience of watching countless other pianists or me in particular. I asked him how he knew so precisely, then—as the Huntington Arts lady took to the stage to pitch some general advertisements and Boston's imminent appearance on the stage—where it was that the music had yielded to me and my slowly growing skill as it had never yielded before. He truly could not say.

"Then it is almost as if you were on the side of the music," I suggested.

My cousin only smiled and then looked away as he started to jog in place and shadow box while his introduction was being finished.

From behind the curtain I looked out to the audience and back to the lobby as the house lights went down again and as Boston went to the giant piano. In the light of the lobby I felt I could make out what appeared to be two attractive women in short dresses. But I could not see for sure. I backed away from the curtain as the representative from the Council passed by me, touched me on the shoulder, and then glided as quietly as possible from the backstage to a place she had reserved for herself somewhere in the orchestra seats. As she passed I looked to Boston again. I was ready to mildly scold the Arts Council woman in my mind for being in motion as Boston was about to start playing when I noticed that he was engaged in another inscrutable survey of his environment— just as I had noticed him doing during his performance in the finals of the competition of the week before.

As I watched Boston from the wings, I was not sure if he had the same kind of reflection to see in the inside of the piano's lid as he had at the competition. I had forgotten to look there myself during my half of the concert. But he did continue what seemed to be a new habit for him—this looking about the performance space and studying the piano with intensity before beginning to play.

Because Boston was seated with the common nineteenth-century orientation of the piano, his view—if he merely looked forward—was of the dark void of the opposite wing of the stage from where I was standing. One could see the full length of the piano, of course—and the complex, ominous reflections on the inside of its lid if the lighting was right. But it was the piano keyboard itself that was so well lighted that night. There was a great deal of light pouring down from the ceiling above the stage. And there were several impromptu lighting sources that came from the back corner and the back wall—so that Boston's back, the keyboard area, and the general forward section of the piano were clearly illuminated. And because the piano itself was lighted so clearly on its outer shells this night, he had a view—even I could see it from where I was standing—a view of his own hands clearly reflected in the keyboard lid.

The look of his hands! That the piano reflected nothing else in that area but its own keys and the pair of agent human hands that controlled them in the fray of battle seemed significant. Thus he seemed to be controlling, playing, what was himself. Thus it seemed to me that if his image might come from within the piano, might not the wave of sound that was emanating from the instrument also be of him—not just sound that he was causing, but he somehow the sound itself? His fingers, by reflection with the keys, were already in the very wood of the piano. What else was in there, as well? He sat before a sort of player piano and only pretended to play as a fallible performer.

There were no errors of chance occurring in his performance. Some predetermined holes punched in the rolls of his mind were letting loose a performance fully formed and insusceptible to the vicissitudes of human weakness, instrumental flaws, or other external conditions. But it was not the talent or the medium of this rendering that fascinated me the most. It was not that my cousin was as some new kind of pianistic or intellectual or artistic genius before the world. It was that here my cousin, connected at that moment in the act of performance, was in union with laws—and it was as if he had found one of the old laws in its purest form.

Imagine that no man, woman, or child had ever before been able to show the pull of gravity with clarity; that they were the first to sit before a vast audience, representative of the sea of mankind, and show that a marble dropped from the hand would always fall to the ground—without fail, every time, every single time without exception, always. Boston sat dropping this new marble in this new demonstration of an old, old but till now only suspected law. Music, Sound, that old, old suspected law, built of the same inscrutable sinews of physics and ancientness that guide all the falling marbles of the old, old, suspected universe, could be shown to be commanded without fail like an absolute law. And Boston Gourd had found the marble-drop demonstration of this always felt, always known, always suspected, but never infallibly demonstrated gravity that was Music. Here was no struggle as found in the biographies of the great composers and the great performers— no struggle toward a grand yet imperfect realization of an only suspected absolute. Here, with their old marbles, Boston was showing—like a little boy sitting at the edge of the stage—that a marble dropped from his hand would fall to the ground. He had a giant bowl of marbles before him that evening, and he dropped them patiently, quietly, again and again into a little unseen bowl on the floor of the house at the foot of the stage.

I had felt different types of fears in my life. But here was a new kind of fear for me—something new to feel as I stood watching Boston play to the audience in the rented movie theater that night. This was nothing of one pianist's dread of another. This was a fear of pure proximity. Here I was close to something new and powerful to an unknown degree.

The music continued to roar forth unstopped by the common compromises of realization. The ivories, though false, thrust forth like resurrected, goring elephants. The ebony sent forth new root systems with a daring propinquity. The spruce in the sound board seemed to have the brush as of new, palpable, evergreen needles near one's brow.

I decided to creep back as quietly as I could to the top of the balcony.

When I reached that height, I leaned against the back wall, and let my fear abate into speculation. I watched Boston now from as far away as possible in that venue. Yet the infallibility of his march was still evident. His discovery of a pure demonstration of a natural law—or combination of natural laws—of Nature was unabated and proceeding. The house was full and sat in stillness and perfect silence—watching the marbles drop from the hand of the pioneering boy as if for the first time.

I had foolishly hoped to see if a little bit of physical distance would distance me from this terrible nearness I felt. It did not. Then I pondered what form the dread took in me. Was it fear, really? No, I thought. The balance of power had long been established in Boston's favor, and this new, perhaps supernatural augmentation did nothing to raise any old jealousy I may have felt when I was a child. In fact, there were many—increasing numbers, really, who thought we were almost equal. I had in me I had been told—by others and by my own conscience and observation—the potential to match, perhaps, the heights that had been achieved in the long, good history of the piano and its players. Boston's power was something beyond that—beyond where I had set my sights.

His level was reaching beyond a matching of the legendary past. Boston would not even have been thinking of such things, not with what I could hear coming out of him then. His was a new affair. He was consorting with something. He was consorting by some directness with a power that had never been consorted with so directly ever before—though it had always been present.

I watched with unbroken attention as Boston careened through his program. Each work was met with a laudation more glorious than its seemingly unbeatable predecessor. When Boston was nearing the end of his last work—also a piece I had heard him play at the competition the week before—I noticed yet another thing that seemed to me to be startling. I felt I had heard him play this performance before! By that I do not mean that I merely acknowledged in my mind that I had heard Boston play this work at the competition and at his house before this particular concert, but I had heard this particular rendering before, as well. I did not feel that I was hearing another performance of what was perhaps a series of similarly styled articulations. I was hearing, I felt—and this was uncanny, given, as well, the differences of the dimensions of the venue space, piano, and countless other considerations; not to mention the challenge to human intellect and physicality to achieve such an effect or reality—felt that I was hearing the exact same performance.

Boston was somehow summoning, it seemed, a consistency that was beyond my ability to explain. It exceeded, even, what one might expect from carrying a recording from one place to another and playing it back in different locations. In this latter case, though the recording was immutable, the ambient space could have its effect and change the perception. But Boston was somehow superceding such variables. I could not understand what I was hearing.

My cousin finished his last work, and the response was cacophonous. Boston had not only achieved a repeat of the performance he had given at the competition, but he was also able to evoke nearly the same response from the audience. Whether the roar was in acknowledgment of the trans-musical, trans-aural, phenomena I felt I was perceiving, or whether Boston simply controlled this response as he controlled his playing, I could not say. I did not feel that I was observing something supernatural—but something as yet unseen in the world.

As Boston walked on and off the stage to receive an incessant wave of acclaim, my eyes fell upon the only thing that could somewhat divert me from what I had just seen and heard from the stage.

Lana and Denise were part of the balcony's full crowd. When the applause subsided—when Boston's revelation of gravity was concealed again for a spell—the lights came up, and I watched them both slowly ascend to where I was standing near the projection booth. Both were in party dresses, as Boston had said they were. Denise was in black, but Lana was in a deep maroon. Lana tilted her head slightly when she saw me and smiled and waved. I was embarrassed by my good fortune, for all this seemed a gesture of tacit consent to erase the gap of over a decade that had elapsed since I had ever really spoken to my neighbor in any significant way. Yet it was also, in a way, an instant invitation of intimacy from a sort of beautiful stranger, for I could not say how much of our childhood connection Lana preserved—still it relied on that memory so that the leap could be made without total absurdity. When the pair reached me, Lana jumped up and down ever so slightly, put her hands around the back of my neck and kissed me on the cheek.

I have since read in books that many large predators (as in, say, some of the big cats) will instinctively stalk, chase, and catch prey. But they will oftentimes not know of the final step unless instructed by their mothers. I must have been lacking some figure of instruction, at least, for in my years since that smile and kiss from Lana Paw, I have seen other young men given the beautiful glance and gesture that Lana gave to me that night, and they seemed to know that the hunt was over. She remained standing next to me, her left arm around my side, and I awkwardly returned the gesture—yet it was difficult for me to think of anything to do or say to carry the situation along. The texture of her dress was like the firm velvet that is on the edge of boxes in concert halls. It seemed to be there to bring a hush to sudden movements of arms, hands, or elbow.

Despite my awkwardness, I felt some bizarre pride in my affectation that seeming ignorance of another person's interest in me was attractive. Why I held to that policy when I desired nothing more than Lana's company and admiration is unknown to me. I seemed bent on affecting a sort of historical, rural American callowness in romance. We unlocked, and Lana, Denise, and I very slowly walked down to the lobby. I was between them.

"We only saw the end of your playing, Port. I'm so sorry!" Lana said.

And then she whispered in my ear, "I couldn't get her to finish getting ready on time." The whisper was as fine to me as the kiss.

"Yeah, Port, you were both really, really good. I was impressed. It was just like a summer day back on your street!" smiled Denise, in reference to the open-windowed practicing that Boston and I did on warm days.

In the darkness of the turn of the landing of the stairs, Denise's black hair—augmented by her black velvet dress—rendered her visible form into only a beautiful, chiseled, porcelain face and cold blue eyes. Her dress had long, tight, sleeves—so there were moments when her white hands and legs were also evident. Lana's dress had long, tight, sleeves, as well, and just as I was noticing this—and perhaps Lana saw this—we reached the lobby floor, and Lana crossed over to Denise, put her arm around her friend's waist and pulled her close, so that both were standing before me, tightly pressed side to side. Lana did a second's worth of aping the shake and the shimmying of a model or showgirl showing off a dress—

raising her free arm into the air and flicking her hand and fingers out. Denise answered the gesture.

"How do like our dresses? I made them," asserted Lana, and she raised her eyebrows up and down with mock arrogance.

"Wow, I—" I started to say, but Lana could not hear me because of the crowd that was passing by.

"The hems aren't quite even—on either of them," she continued, and she fingered at the ends of her dress with her tanned fingers. The two girls parted, and there was a moment of silence.

Lana's display of her dresses and self seemed to me not so much an act of cuteness or foolishness, as it was a statement of the terms that had to be suddenly expressed if we were to be reconnected as young adults. It seemed a clever, subtle, intellectual statement made with an ostensibly silly gesture of her body. To have spoken as much would have been a presumption upon our future. But it was well-spoken in this silent stretching of form that otherwise seemed but a passing celebration of youth, beauty, and lightheartedness.

I noticed, then, as well, that though Denise was present in most respects, she seemed a bit conscious of time. I thought perhaps she might be wondering if she could move on to see Boston.

"How do you move your fingers so fast? I could never, ever, do that," continued Lana.

"You could. You really can. Like running around the track. You just repeat certain things over and over until you can do it. You could—"

"No!" Lana laughed, and she rolled her eyes.

When I took a step back from her involuntarily, an elderly couple stepped in to congratulate me. Lana made a pointing gesture over to another part of the theater—as if to say, I thought, that I could find her there when I was done. I felt safe in my passivity, for I knew that Aunt Maryland was going to have a small reception. Lana's mother and father were going to be there.

I then had to spend a full half-hour talking with the friends of my uncles and aunts. But when the theater was empty, I looked for Lana. I went back to the stage and saw Boston and Denise talking in a distant, private corner. Soon, Denise left.

"So, what happened with Denise, Boston?"

"Well, Port," he said, "we didn't win in this one. I don't know why I was thinking there was so much invested in this. Maybe I held her hand a few times, I think. Anyway—and I know this is silly—but she said something like—and this she said when I acted surprised that they weren't coming to the reception back home—and this made me think that *she,* then, invested too much in the whole thing—said that she had been attracted at first by the whole idea of the piano and all. She was interested in me as a friend, but the piano carried her a little past that. But it stopped when I stopped playing. I can't believe I'm repeating this foolishness. Anyway, they're both off to some party somewhere. They didn't even ask if we wanted to go."

I was proud of myself that I did not tell Boston that I thought that Lana might really be interested in me. It was doubly futile to reveal as much since I knew at that point that she was probably not going to put herself in my way any more than she had that night—and I knew that I was not yet at the point of life when I could apply agency myself to such things.

Because he laughed at himself on our walk home, I was able to take comfort and amusement in the transient vulnerability that my cousin seemed eager to share. He sounded plain and uncomplicated for a spell, and he would clench his fists and grit his teeth—and then laugh in self-mockery at the whims of the blood—as he recalled and described the receding sight of Denise and her velvet dress.

In the midst of one of our most vigorous mutual laughs, a laugh coughed and gasped as we crossed onto the street that was directly perpendicular to our own, I volunteered that Denise surely got her material about *liking someone for the wrong reason* from some column in a teen magazine. Why she felt she had to have such an earnest, grave, yet comically hackneyed statement to make that night! This made me laugh. It seemed very much like what I might have expected, for she was always posing it seemed, and probably imagining what few phrases in the world might go with her few poses. I laughed at this, and I turned to Boston.

Or perhaps Denise was more perceptive than I knew.

My cousin did not fall silent in a threatening way. He genuinely did not seem angry at me, but he suddenly stopped his contributions to the levity, though he tried to maintain a mild, friendly, approachable smile. He was considering something. But he was not utterly removed—as I had seen him as a child when playing in the yard alone or as I had seen him as a young man when playing the piano. He was not quite considering of his deeps, I thought. He did not seem to have to go quite that far away.

But as we approached Aunt Maryland's and Uncle William's house, my cousin did not awake from his mild contemplation—the kind of remove that could be the prelude for either an extended rumination or a sudden ricochet back into the unmindful whirl of passing exchange. As we came onto our street, I looked to Lana's house, and her car was not in the driveway. When we came before Boston's house, he seemed to be near breaking free of his rumination—but all at once he turned on his heel in his own front walkway, paused, looked about the street, and then put an odd question to me.

"Port, could you do me a little favor?"

"Sure, Boston, what is it?" I answered with amused curiosity.

"Could I use your piano for a little while?"

"Oh, gosh, I don't know why you'd even think you'd have to ask me," I said quickly as I resumed my walk toward Boston's porch. "So what happened to your piano? Did the upper strings—"

"Port, I mean right now. There's nothing wrong with my piano.

But—" And then he nodded to the front window, where one could see some of the dozens of people who were inside, somehow all squeezed into the four large rooms on the first floor of Boston's house.

"Something wrong, Boston?"

"No, not at all. Not if I can just play—just check something, really—on a piano for a little bit," he smiled in a meek way, rather like someone who knows that it is worth hiding a passing pain that he knows he can cure himself momentarily, rather than speak of it to those who really cannot help at all—save, perhaps, in some small pragmatic way, like offering a glass of water or a room to rest or work in (or, in my case, mysteriously, a piano).

I just laughed and said sure. I told him that I had wanted to change before the reception anyway. As we walked up to the business, we both observed that it seemed funny to have the street so filled with cars but to have no funeral or viewing going on.

The main house was totally dark, and we had to stumble through the backyard and up to the porch so as to go in the kitchen door, which was almost always unlocked.

Boston paced in the room adjacent to the kitchen as I got a quick drink of water. Then I left for my room and simply said, "It's all yours, Boston."

He went down to the piano in the business section of the house.

"Thanks, Portsmouth," answered my cousin, tensely, as he went down the stairs.

I really did not think much of Boston's request, for I was just then waxing rather elated by the end of a successful concert. The happiness of my own victorious battle with some hard works was just then dawning on me, and my later observations of my cousin and the mildly jarring near acquisition and quick loss of Lana left my mind as I thought of the concert itself. It was also not unusual (especially for a pianist like myself) to wish to check certain things after a recital. It was odd, however, that Boston should wish to do so. But that did not occur to me that night—not even with my dawning realization of Boston's true technical achievements and intimacy with Music, itself.

I was rather hungry by that point, as well, and such a simple, primal expectation as the food at the reception, I must confess, leaves me with the embarrassing confession that I was thinking of little else as I finished changing my clothes.

It was when I was sitting on my bed, tying my shoes, however, that I could faintly hear Boston begin to play—because all the doors were open. He started with one of the most hair-raising passages from his recital material of that night, and it was then that I paused to wonder what it could possibly be that someone like a Boston Gourd would need to check in such a rendering as he had given that evening.

And then it came to me that I was hearing the same performance yet again, and I paused in my small labors to wonder at this once more. I opted to keep this observation to myself. If I had tried to describe it to Boston, I only would have intended it as praise of a skill that was astonishing to me—but I did not yet quite know how to articulate what it was that I felt I was hearing. I felt then that it would sound like I was only intimating that he was playing things in the same manner—as if he lacked imagination and was feeding his listeners' and his own boredom—if I did not think for awhile how best to describe what I was suspecting in his playing. It was not static. The degree of sameness I was perceiving was a freedom from the chance happenings that bring credited variety to commonly lauded performances. There may have been some differences in the actual volume or speed or attack, if I am truly honest, but there was a remarkable, benign sameness to what he was achieving. But I could not yet describe it. I also felt that any praise would sound like a meek attempt to distract him from the real melancholia that was striking him, I felt, because of Denise.

Though I knew it was but a high school romance in the smallest sense of external realization, it still interested me, almost amused me, to see my indefatigably forward-moving cousin made to pause for even an instant by such a maudlin little story. Finally, I felt that trying to describe what I then heard in his playing seemed like a sort of attempt to put myself on a plane of equal observational skill with my cousin—as if I were trying to counter his comments to me during the concert's intermission with some of my own.

I did my best to clear my mind as I looked out my window and down the street to the lighted house of the party, and then I looked to Lana's house and grimaced. Suddenly, the sound of the piano stopped. I thought I might hear it start up again, but when I went down to the kitchen, Boston was there waiting for me at the table.

He looked very present and untroubled again.

But I still asked him, "Everything all right, Boston?"

What amazed me was the amount of unaffected sincerity in his answer, for he was in earnest and truly forgetful, when he said, "Yeah, what's wrong, Port?"

Now I had to respond, but I did not mind inventing an answer.

"Oh, nothing. Just sorry to keep you sitting here so long," I said, and I forgot our time in the main house very quickly as we walked over to Boston's yard.

"You know, Port, you played really well tonight—really well. You know, you're going to be a famous concert pianist someday. I know it."

Boston had a way of giving his high praise that made one feel a great affection for him—for it did not sound like affected affability suppressing condescension and untouchable power. He seemed to mean it. We went to the party, and I did not leave until it was very late. Aunt Elizabeth had already gone home and to bed when I got up to leave, and Uncle Harry was in his kitchen reading as I passed by and walked up the driveway.

Before I went all the way into the backyard, I looked back to

Lana's house. Her car was still not back, and I sighed over her in connection with that concert for the last time. Though we lived on the same street and went to the same school, I do not think I saw her more than five times outside of school before graduation—four times, perhaps, in busy, passing, moments in her driveway or in the village when she did not see me. And there came another time when we were all assembled and it was not appropriate for me to sound her out, even if I had mustered more courage by that point—which I had not anyway.

So I sighed that last sigh and caught view of my own breath for the first time that nearing winter. I looked down into a puddle that had collected from a recent rain, and asked my reflection, rather like I had asked Boston earlier, "Everything all right?"

Yes, all was well, I felt, as I stared down at my reflection and saw only an image of the always nearly smiling, ever reset-able self.

CHAPTER VI

FIRST LETTER

W hen I returned with Sarah from my walk at the end of my second full day back in Pauktaug, I practiced in my room until about eleven, and then I went down for tea with my aunt and uncle. They were tired from the double viewing of the evening, and so my Uncle Harry took Sarah out one last time for the day, and then he said he would just take her back to his house for the night. Sarah oftentimes liked to stay at his house for variety. My aunt went to bed, yet I retired to my room not quite ready for sleep.

I decided to start looking into Boston's letters. Most of them were of astonishing length, and I could only imagine, when I began, that Boston decided to disburden himself of so much in this set of letters because he felt that he owed an intimacy to his aunt now that he was going to be in her daily routines again—or because he was trapped in a foreign environment with a great deal of time to spare. Perhaps it was something of both. I could not say for sure.

I spread the first letter out on top of the closed lid of my piano, leaned against the curve in the instrument, and began to read.

Dear Aunt Elizabeth,

Thank you very much for your letter.

I am here in Maryland now. The trip here was uneventful. But your persistence with me is what drives me to write at last. Your persistence has been that I send word to my old home from time to time (and for me to know that I have not been forgotten). But before I send just plain word let me start with sending my thanks. Never during all the years—I think eleven now—that you have tried, from time to time, to contact me have you changed your tone of basic affection and simple inquiry. The only reason—this is true no matter how poor an excuse it seems—that I could never bring myself to answer you or my old world of Pauktaug was that I feared once I communicated with that world again I would never be able to stand being away from it. Even for all your truly staggering, placid, kind notes, surely you must be asking your old nephew, "But couldn't you have sent something, anything, some few lines, without breaking your code of distance?" Perhaps. But you are kind enough to suggest that I might reopen my channel with you, and Mr. Gull, and Portsmouth—as if I had never let it go. You have even suggested that the offer extends to my actual return to Pauktaug and the old street. Would I shock you—and not seem like I was just creating some story, some false bit of excitement to appease an aunt—if I told you that I am thinking of accepting this offer? In light of such generosity, can you excuse the rudeness that asks for time to think such a thing over?

I have three main options that I must consider. One option is vague. It is a sort of contingency plan that allows me to imagine myself either returning to California or to some other place that might come up as a result of this competition.

There are the two other options, as well. Both see me back in Pauktaug! One is more practical and the other is a dream of mine—even though I suppose the latter could be realized. The first Pauktaug option has me returning to the old street and accepting of your offer of a room in the old main house! That would be like a dream, too, but since I know you mean it, I don't merely have to think it an unrealizable dream. If things do not go precisely as I hope here in Maryland, there is a new, massive international competition in New York that is being held there this fall. I am entertaining the idea of preparing for that back home in Pauktaug and maybe even attending graduate school in the company of Port. Would he let me tag along with him? Can he forgive a fellow who was not being reclusive but merely in need of a sort of distance? I needed silence to work all those years, as well. Not merely in a practical sense in terms of practice. I needed to be away from so many suggestive smells and sights and sounds—so many things that always set me to thinking good things, contented thoughts of the past. Life there was always so beautiful and full that it never provided the bleakness I needed, in a way, to justify the pursuit of the piano to the extent I have. I needed to create a void to fill. I needed to be so by myself that the piano might seem my only constant companion when there was no one else. Despite what you might think, I could have forgotten the piano had I remained in Pauktaug. Well, I like to think that I could. It would be nice to forget it at times. Perhaps *that* is my most dreamlike dream—for when did I ever pause from the keyboard when I did not have to even before I left New York?

Anyway, going back to school and entering that new Manhattoes Competition is the idea if things do not go as I would like them to in this contest. What is it if things go well for me? To lose here on certain terms so that I can return home and no longer have to play the piano. That is the second main option. Then I will be satisfied. If I can explain it, my hope is to play here at the highest level and prove that I will, most likely—certainly—lose.

What is it if things go poorly for me? To win this competition. Then I might have to return home to Pauktaug—and this is the third main option—and forever have it an only occasionally seen home-base as I continue with another two- or three-year phase as an itinerant competition winner. That is the third option—and the dream in that is a bad dream for me.

But of course I will not play as if to try to lose. But I am reasonably sure that I will. I expect and hope to. I have not lost my faith in Man so much as to think this impossible. If I win the first prize—or any prize, for that matter—then Music wins. I lose.

You might ask how I have come to this unusual conclusion. Many of the foolishly illusioned—as opposed to those who have come by their illusions with sound and sober reasoning—might ask, with their shallow, ostensibly revelatory idealism, "But are not the piano and the player, the pianist and the music that he plays, one?" They are not. They are two things. Of course, I speak of a highly qualified situation. I speak only of pianists on a level of unimpeachable standards—pianists of the highest form on the international competition circuit (virtually free of technical flaws or any errors in realization). And they are so accomplished that to question or critique their interpretive abilities is simply to give an idle critical mind something to do—a reason for imagining it has a purpose. I speak, as well, only of the highest form of music—of pieces that can safely be said to be representative of not only music, but of Music, so to speak—as if it were a being that has a purest, infallible form, that can wear a given number of forms that Man has given to it and still somehow be of that pure, infallible form.

Thus, if the infallible player plays, engages, some part of the seemingly infallible Music, and loses, or is not recognized, is the loss always chance? Is it always just ill luck? Can such questions even be asked when the flawless player plays flawlessly before a throng of attentive listeners? They are there to say that chance was not against him. The audience is there to give recognition. Thus, if the evident partner (the pianist) on the stage has not failed, could it not be the other half that has fallen short at last? Could it not be that the Music itself has failed? Should it not be that there are winners of competitions who walk away victorious, given a first prize of intellect and soul, and the Music knocked out at the screening level?

If these two beings, Man and Music meet and there is some imperceptible disappointment, not attributable in any discernable way to the performer, is it, then, the pianist that is at fault? Could it not be Music that is losing?

Yet no one asks such a thing. No listener, no performer walks away from a concert and asks, "Is it music that is fallible?" Yet why not? Music, this sly, prevaricating yet always praised third part of any human musical endeavor is somehow embraced, celebrated, yet ignored every time it appears. How else to explain for Man's dismay when Man does not fail—he the other two parties, player and listener—yet the concert does?

I am not one to decry the medium of the piano competition. In fact, it is not even an issue in what I try to express. It is, rather, a perfect microcosm of the world of music. Its seven or eight, or nine, or ten, judges are just a small representation of the world. And that representation is idealized, for they are all experts in their fields—pianists of the infallible line that I write of above. They are no more and no less political than any other microcosm or macrocosm anywhere else in the Universe. I will have none of the complaints against competitions come from me. In fact they are a perfect opportunity to prove what I must prove.

Yet the evidence for questions against Music are so easily come by. Can I be the first pianist with enough skill and enough time logged in battle to have noticed that there is a third party on the field?

When I left Pauktaug, Aunt Elizabeth, I was free for the first time. I don't speak of the hackneyed college freedoms. I was free to demonstrate without hindrance of any kind from Aunt Maryland or Uncle William my absolute command over the piano. I hope it does not seem vain if I imagine that you followed my career—perhaps with the help of Port—through all of the major international competitions that have taken place since I was about twenty or twenty-one. As you know, I think—maybe I did not tell you—I am only just finishing my undergraduate degree. That is how busy I have been. That is how spread out my life has been because of these cycles of competitions.

I have been in nearly every edition of every major competition in the last eleven years. I have four recordings (do you have them?), and I have enjoyed an international career. But after the hundred or more dates I would get as part of the representation prize from one competition—after I had played them—the interest would simply burn off, and I would be compelled to enter another. There was some overlap of dates from one competition into another, sometimes, but, generally, my observations were correct—that not until I would win another contest would the cycle of sure dates be offered to me again.

Because of the overlap, I was charged in the press with a sort of lust for redundancy. But I do not think that critics could see that after a time I was hunting for bookings and not for prizes. Granted, I perhaps entered more contests at some points than I should have. Sometimes the overlaps were so severe—causing me to have to cancel and explain my situation so many times—that I lost a lot of ground with a concert series or hall in many a place. But there was always another competition to win that would have its own peculiar avenues of bookings, and I would be safe.

I lived this way. I have lived this way for over ten years— now almost twelve years—of my life, Aunt Elizabeth. Yet it worked. I had honed my skills to such an extent that, save for a few competitions early on, I never—never ever—failed to place.

Then, two years ago I was in a pair of competitions. I played in these to perfection, yet I did not place. My reaction was reasonable. I shrugged it off. But the level of my playing (matched with the general approbation I received) did cause me to be puzzled. Then last year I was in no less than three large competitions. I did not place in any of them! I did not get past the preliminaries in any of them! This concerned me. No, this made me reel within.

Why the reeling? It wasn't the idea of losing. It really was not. I have always known that there are some inconsistencies in the Universe beyond one's control. But my playing was no longer subject to any kind of vicissitudes. It was something totally under my control. And I could command the same level of performance to come out from within no matter what. Therefore, I had lost five times in a row, yet without any diminishment of my powers—and no discernible political campaign against me. I could not understand it. And each time my placement was lower and lower in the overall rankings of the preliminaries. It was as if something had been discovered—not consciously by those who were judging me, but through me in a way, I thought. Some discovery of Man, through these small, idealized, representations of Man (juries, audiences) was unfolding.

I noticed, then, as well, I thought—though there was no absolute evidence for this in straight concerts as there is in competitions—that my ranking was falling. I do not mean that concert dates fell through—of those that remained from the last of my long good streak as a competitor—but that there was a waning of response. There was an almost palpable sense, to me, that the audience was seeing some new, disturbing, element through me. They would applaud, even give frequent ovations, but there was, indeed, an alteration in the tension of their responses. But I could not perceive, could not imagine, what it could be.

In anticipation of a competition that was scheduled for December—and with the last of my dates from previous victories nearly expended—I withdrew from what few external routines I had, and I lumbered into the practice room for three uninterrupted months. Not able to perceive what my new, unfolding flaws might be as a performer—and unable to hear any decline in the level of my playing in recordings from the recent competitions when compared with recordings from my decade-long streak of invincibility—I resorted to the only option I had left to me: self-doubt.

Yet it was unique self-doubt, for even I could not cite the source of its foundation. I had no belief in my self-doubt, one might say, but it was the only stance I could take. Thus, I took to the practice room, the woodshed, for three solid months—not only in preparation for the December competition in San Francisco, but with a pressing desire to locate the leak in my hull. I took to the practice room sea looking for this leak, notwithstanding the fact that there was no water on board the ship.

Into the woodshed I went (the practice rooms at school and at my own piano in my apartment) with an intensity I have never applied. I would often enter at eight or nine in the morning and not leave until one or two in the morning of the next day.

You asked me in your letter if there are any women in my life. There was one of great importance to me up until last November, but now that situation is such that I am sure it will not interfere with any plans I may have of returning to Pauktaug. This girl, this woman I should say, was solicitous of me even through the first month or two of my intense retreat into the woodshed. She seemed to see a sort of fun in this new start I had taken, and when she was done with her day of work—she had just finished law school and was already doing well in a large firm nearby—she would make a ritual of coming by the school practice rooms or my apartment and bring me out at eight-thirty or nine for dinner.

Oftentimes, she would bring things with her—bring a whole dinner—and we would climb to the top of the school's stairs and go out on the roof of the music building and eat our dinner there. I had known this girl for five—almost six years—and as we survived her vigorous years of study and internships during law school, and my itinerant existence and few empty evenings, I started to suspect that we had achieved a level of permanency. When it began, I felt that she was so attractive that I should not invest too much attach-ment—in the deepest, most hidden, most personal sense—until after a very long time went by. Yet it evolved despite my early fears. But perhaps because of that early hesitancy on my part to strongly attach to her I may have never really started to attach strongly to her at any time. I had thought I had. We had even started to spend so much time at each other's apart-ments that she just suddenly proposed to my great surprise that we should move in together. Despite our liberal use of each other's places—such that to say we were not living together was a only nominal statement—I could not cross that line.

By early November of last year, she started to question what I was looking for in the practice room. Soon her suspi-cion was that I was heightening my practice regime to such an intensity so as to passively escape her. I truly did not have that intention. But then I thought of it—and though it really had not been my plan—being free from even the distraction of a stunning, intelligent, Venus seemed appealing.

My practice—my research in the woodshed during those three months—seemed to be asking a fundamental question of the Universe and the world. I realized suddenly that she would have been perhaps undisturbed—for she was a secure and confident gal in many ways—if it had been that Music had merely taken an even higher role in its competition with her for my time and affections. She was actually prepared for that well-celebrated and rather hackneyed contest. And I think she was simply enamored of having a boyfriend in my field. She did not want to give up her vocational world so as to be around other people in the arts, but she did not want to give up her connection to them through me.

But I finally told her, in early November of last year, what it was that I was asking the world in the practice room each day and night. Had she understood my answer from the start, an inner turmoil of how to hold on to a beautiful woman who understood what I was proposing would have ensued. But she made it all easy for me.

I told her that what I had learned and would continue to confirm up until the competition, which was then just under a month away, was what it was like to endure the crisis of losing self-doubt. To truly lose self-doubt is a blow that few men are willing to face. I had practiced and worked by then for two uncompromising months, actually working and re-working and honing the already world-class technique and skill that had been mine upon entering this phase of practice.

What had driven me on? The belief that there was still some hidden flaw in my playing. The belief that the self cannot know all of an aspect of the self. The belief that one can never be one's own severest critic. But this drive waned and was gone after two months, for I had looked in every corner of my self and in every corner of the aural picture that emerged from my steely fingers. I found that I could not support self-doubt. I could not. I found—what with the intensity of my review—that if I was not still looking upon perfect playing in myself, then now upon perfection per-fected because of my intense review. It was perfection refined, filtered free of an inability to soberly know of its own per-fection. And my realization left me with no resentment or anger for the scores of judges who had begun to vote against me and for the thousands who seemed to merely applaud and stand and roar at my recital dates as if such noises and stances of approbation were a manifest cloak to mask a fear of recognition. They had all begun to see something through me, Aunt Elizabeth. They had seen the infallibility that I had been too well trained as a human being to acknowledge. But my three months in the woodshed revealed to me, as well, what they were seeing. And I had a new faith in Man and where he is going. And the only self-doubt I was left with was whether I could hold up and see to the end the task that my peculiar skills left me to accomplish.

When my blonde Venus floated out of orbit for all time, I took to the woodshed for one final month. With a terrified joy I practiced for streaks of time that often lasted for nineteen hours a day. A few teachers and fellow students stopped in to inquire after me and to enjoin me to rest, but more often than not they left with heightened brows that were only meant to question their own intrusions, for they found me in a bliss of energy and animation. I reported nothing to them save that I was well, and they left with the confirmation of my words and a true red, ruddy, glow that fired my entire face.

With a terrified joy I practiced, chipped and carved at the wood in the woodshed until it would seem that heaps of sawdust must have been all about me, pouring forth under the cracks of the practice room door and causing a flood in the hall—filling the building itself ultimately and spilling out into the street, not resting, this wave of sawdust, until it reached the sea and was sunk, dissipated and dispersed by the strength and cold of the true deeps where it was truly swallowed. I sawed, cut, chipped, and sanded at Music and Man until both were down to stumps and cores.

Then one glorious night, after having performed the experiment over and over, day by day throughout that catalytic, purgative, thrilling November, I produced the same result yet again. I had sanded until it would seem there could be nothing left of Man, yet there was always more. And his wood would never crack and give way. But Music! Music, though it did not give way or crack, it vanished in the ether of its own prevaricating, uncommitted, nebulous silence. It yielded to something in me. Music meant nothing to me! And this was no great disillusionment of the self! It was, rather, a great discovery of Music's waning reign! It, not I, was fallible. Music had a lifespan, not Man.

Now I knew what judges and audiences, a thousand honest, grand souls had seen, but they without the notion of what to do next. But how could they? The very man who was showing them the way did not know he was shining a light on a frontier. I had by some sextant of the fingers and ears and mind and heart of Man captained the way to a shore unpeopled altogether. Not even Indians hid upon this shore and looked to the old notes that trumpeted and faded as we came to rest in the harbor of this new continent. Nothing save Man—nothing that he could bring with him save himself— could live on this shore. During the approach into the bay of this new find, I had still been the careful captain, and had not looked up to see what New World I had sailed to for my pilgrims. But in the woodshed I looked up and pondered the forested shore for the first time—pondered what my passengers had seen before I had looked up from the charts and down from the sails, pondered what gave a terror in the report of their eyes.

Thus I studied for three months this shoreline that my audience and judges had seen with clarity while I had tended to my duties of navigation—and brought them closer and closer, until one could hear the crash of surf on the untrod beaches. Thus I had discovered my ship not only had no breach of the hull, it also had no mysterious, unwelcomed water on board.

It was where I had piloted the ship that had caused the change—it was where the greatest effort with Music, where the greatest skill to meet with its challenges had taken me, had taken Man. Music cannot follow Man always. Man is greater than his discoveries. Surely Man will want to land on this new shore—where he can carry nothing of the old with him, where not even laws of the Universe can follow. Presumptuous Music! I scrape you off for a barnacle. Man is enough. Music! It is you that are fallible. You are the law that is subject to laws. Not I. I see your fallibility now. If others could see this through me, before I could see it in myself, then imagine the demonstration that will follow when I carry self-awareness into concert with me. Music! Your smug supremacy is at an end. I will not walk away from your impotency, but bring it to its life-importuning knees by rendering its greatest manifestations with such perfection that its fallibility is appallingly evident. I will complete the vision of my sagely audiences and sagely judges, finish and clear their view of the coddled monster that has ruled so long by its presumptuous precedents! I will free the discoverers that are too meek to proclaim what they have seen—had seen even before I had seen it. I will play music so well, so perfectly, that I will show that Music is vanquished!

I emerged from the practice room in early December of last year and traveled to San Francisco. In a raging, private, silent elation I drove up the coast, for I was in a new relation to the Universe. No longer was Music safe, but I was safe from Music. Music receded in light of my new occupation. I was in vanguard. I could not say what I did or what I would do precisely. But I was ahead of all and everything. I may not offer an alternative, but I would recite the obviation of the very Laws! Music born of Laws! You cannot follow me. You cannot follow Man.

For thousands of years Man had written forms unto proud Music up to the end of those forms, to its double bars. And what when they reached the double bars? Back to the start once more! Reinterpret. Explore your same, trodden, packed-down tract again! Yield us a few tears and laughs you smug Music from the labors upon you. But beyond the double bar! Who has gone there yet? There is something better after the concert!

I drove to San Francisco, ready to play as no one has been ready to play. It is sometimes common for a great competition to award no first prize when it feels that no competitors merit a first prize based upon comparisons with past competitors. What if no first prize could be awarded because the very matter upon which the contentions were being fought was shown to be beneath such a battle?

Show Music fallible! Music weak! Music old and down upon its paltry, now humbled, brittle, feeble, elderly mortal knees. Play so well that its arrogant, glassy head would roll and shatter before the throng, and all would leave in silence—progress beyond it, free of compulsory worship, free of Nature's laws. Build, then, new Laws, as if they floated in the liberties of the unreached, weightless voids of unlighted space, or the cold, manumitting pressures of the yet unsounded darkness of still unprobed, still un-life-sounded, unevolved, undiscovered trenches of the deepest sea.

People often ask me if I am still nervous before my concerts. A strange question, this. Nothing can happen to me in a concert; no personal harm can come about; no embarrassment. And I confirmed that in my final woodshed bout with humbleness. Thus I am tempted to waive any answer to this question as the house lights dim and the stage door opens and the piano appears to me. The lights come up on the piano and there it sits, a captive on casters. Some of my competitors will chime in so as to break the awkwardness of my silence—this as I begin to walk off of the wings toward the stage.

"I don't know about him, but sometimes I look out at what he is looking out to now and feel like I am on my way to an execution."

But have you heard how a musician—especially one in jazz —will refer to his instrument as an axe? Well, fellow pianists, if I were to answer your question in the wings, I would tell you that I hold the real axe in hand. I walk out to the stage and the last of the house lights fall, and I am not walking toward my sentence but to render one. I hold the axe, and there is a hush in the crowd. I raise my hands before the black victim and see my nearly black-masked face appear in the reflection of the wood's finish. I steady my hands as the executioner. I would ask in answer to the question of nerves:

"Isn't it the Music that is terrified?"

Music! Where should the fear lie now?

I steady my black-masked face and raise my hands, the true axe, to bear against the prisoner. But the lights of the stage come up fully and show that my face is white. My hands fall with a sudden, virtuosic, seething, earned malice. Yet there is a silence in the hall, from the stage and from the crowd. Then the silence of the platform is met with a roar from the crowd. Thus the execution shall be met by the throng, as in the days of yore when the voices of lavish kings were given their last soundings—only by the falls of their imperious, presuming, prevaricating skulls.

CHAPTER VII

VAMP

After I finished Boston's first letter from May, I thought about it for only a little while, for I was very tired from a full day on the bench. The only real thinking I did about the letter after I put it down and turned out the light was that Boston might be simply having a sort of joke at my poor Aunt Elizabeth's expense—giving the letter a weighty tone that she was never accustomed to reading or communicating in herself. I did not think Boston would choose my aunt a confidant for earnest speculation. So I drifted off to sleep after putting Boston's letter back in its envelope—hardly being awake enough to think seriously on its contents. And I laughed mildly at the thought of my Aunt Elizabeth ever really reading it (she probably had skimmed it after a point).

I had never seen Aunt Elizabeth (or Uncle Harry, for that matter), read anything save a newspaper, magazine, or trade paper for as long as I could remember. I never mentioned the letters to my aunt. Thus, Boston's letters to my aunt became letters to me, in a way.

I fell quickly into a deep, full sleep—the sound of the crickets the last acknowledged grist of the end of my second full day back in Pauktaug.

When I awoke to my third full day, I went down to the kitchen. I had breakfast with my aunt and uncle, and before I left to go back upstairs for a day at the piano, my aunt asked me to run down into the office and see what message was on the business line's answering machine. She had heard the office phone ring, she thought, when she came in from being out with Sarah. I went down, and that is when I found the message from Boston.

More than anything else, the message shocked me because of the sound of Boston's voice. In addition to the evident maturity in the actual tone quality, the spirit behind the voice seemed somehow younger, in a way, than the voice I remembered. It was as if I heard an unknown man speaking in a tone of voice from Boston's very early years. I tried to explain this to my aunt and uncle. But they were obviously more interested in the actual content of the message.

It was clear to me that Boston had consciously made the decision to call the office phone at an early hour so that he could reach the machine. His message was this—

That he had not spent even a fraction of the money he had saved for his cross-country trip; that he was going to spend some last weeks of solitude hiking and staying at a campsite in northern Pennsylvania; that he would be back in time for the start of school and in time to start his preparation cycle for the October competition; that he would call to check in a few more times as he enjoyed "the last few days of his freedom before he had to check in each morning and evening with an Auntie again." That was his message.

Uncle Harry just shrugged at this and remarked that he thought it meant that we would soon have a message from Boston that he was not coming back to New York at all. Aunt Elizabeth expressed her worry about his staying in campsites and the dangers of hiking alone. Then she expressed her fears about his fingers and hiking on rocks. I ventured my irritation at his indirectness, and then we all went our separate ways for the day.

My third full day in Pauktaug unfolded as would a whole string of days that late summer. With Boston only a vague and unlikely imminence at that point, I sometimes forgot about him altogether.

I would have let him slip my mind completely had it not been that he was true to his word about calling Aunt Elizabeth every few days. He was, indeed, staying at a full service campsite somewhere in the mid-section of northern Pennsylvania, and he said that we could count on his arrival for the start of the autumn school term. But I no longer counted on it, and began to find him, frankly, annoying. His box of letters also remained on my desk in my room. I forgot about them completely and never looked at them.

The heat of summer returned, and there were nights when I lay abed sleepless despite my fatigue from practicing for the Manhattoes Competition. At last, however, the imminence of autumn truly settled in sometime in the middle of about the third week of August, on the eve of my last two full days before the start of the fall semester. It, that first breeze, came when I went down to the kitchen for dinner with Aunt Elizabeth and Uncle Harry.

We had just started to eat when the phone rang. My aunt was still moving about with some last things to bring to the table; I was tired of all my city friends and feigned to be utterly unmoved by the ringing of telephones. My uncle rose and answered, but it was for me.

"Portland? Oh, my! Sorry. Really sorry. What I am thinking? Portsmouth! Professor Silver. This is Neil Silver!"

"Hey, Professor Silver. It's all right."

"Listen, Portsmouth! I'm playing tomorrow night with the Philharmonic in town, and I have a small block of tickets. I can offer you a few if you'd like. It would be good for you to see this—to hear these pieces. Good things are going to come of this concert. For once I feel the accompaniment has been well-rehearsed, and the repartee, the sense of real give and take—the sense of real music-making—is going to be quite extraordinary."

I hated when Professor Silver made such a call. He was so near the apex of the business that one could rule out such calls as a desperate act to fill the hall for one of his concerts. But one could also rule out the gesture as a magnanimous one toward a student—for he was not offering the tickets. He was selling them. This action, combined with a unique, oblique, delivery of self-praise—which was tinged with his sadness when the listener remained silent and refrained from confirming his self-praise—made what might seem like an altogether insufferable, even obnoxious, approach, sound somewhat pitiable and even tolerable.

He continued for a bit about the concert that was for the following evening, and even made a play at humor. "I wouldn't tell you about this unless it would be really good for you, because, the concert is, after all, on the last evening of summer break, on a sort of school night!"

I had already resolved to yield to him.

"Okay. I'll take a ticket," I said.

"Just one?" he asked, with laughing but earnest disbelief. I was surprised that he had the nerve to imply that I was either too cheap to buy more than one ticket or that I was too down and out socially to find someone with whom to go.

"All right. I'll take two for tomorrow."

"Great, great. This will be a good experience for you—really will. This is great, great literature that we are dealing with."

My aunt was already well into dinner herself now and paying no mind to my conversation, but Uncle Harry waved to me and frowned, as if to emphatically reassure me of my right to pull away—that Professor Silver had already worn out his welcome and his advertising time.

The sale was clinched, and it pained me when Professor Silver would then commence with what he thought was a requisite amount of chattiness—affecting, then, to speak to me as if I were a sort of colleague or professional friend. It could be very trying.

"So, Portsmouth. You know, I thought of something the other day. Should you and your cousin make it to the finals this October (of course you will!), I'll have to pass on voting for both of you—

since you both study with me. There'll be other judges for the other rounds. But I'll be on the finals' round jury for the solo half-recital and concertos. If you and your cousin get to that stage (which you will!), then I have to pass on voting for either of you."

Only then, as he was finishing this last streak of talk, did it become clear to me that Neil Silver was sure that Boston was going to be his student. I asked him if he had talked to my cousin.

"I talked to Boston just the other day. Told him he's in the Manhattoes for sure. Yeah. He said he'll be in town for the start of the semester. Yeah. I thought you knew that. He's admitted and registered for the master's program—and, oh, he has the lesson hour just after the one we agreed on. So, I guess you'll be coming in together more or less. Yeah, he played for us at one of our regional auditions—just at the time he was giving his senior recital for his bachelor's. Can you imagine someone like that playing a senior recital? And, gosh, I hope he doesn't take as much time to finish his master's! Anyway, I didn't see the audition videotape, but I told them just to admit him to me if all the paperwork was fine for him. So, great, I'll have a sort of family in my studio family! Cousins! I think I have had some Asian girls who were sisters—or maybe they were cousins too."

Uncle Harry had gone into the front room on the second floor and then called out to me, as if he really needed my help with something.

"Oh, my uncle is calling me, Mr. Silver. But I'll be there tomorrow. I'll pick up the tickets. I'll be there."

"Great, great. Let me let you go. And, Portsmouth—see, I've got my Ports right now—don't be a stranger! Come back to the green room and see us after the concerto!"

"Okay, I will, professor. Thanks."

"No, please. I should thank you, Portland," he closed, while getting my name mixed up once more, and I returned to my dinner—with gratitude to my uncle.

Before much time had passed, my uncle dismissed Neil Silver as he always did, much to my pleasure.

"Well, Port, I'm free tomorrow night, but I don't want to go all the way into the city to listen to that fool!"

I smiled, and then I looked to my aunt. She smiled back, and it was a full smile that had more meaning behind it than the phrase she offered to go with it:

"You know, Port, I only really like the concerts when you're in them. I don't want to go either!"

She said this, but her smile did not pass away. I could not imagine the smile's source, as for nearly a week we had taken no business on account of a summer vacation—and as no one from Pauktaug had passed on who had expressly wished to be handled by our home. We had seen virtually no one for a week, and had not spoken to anyone, really, of any significance. Instead, a blissful routine of practice and evening walks and tea had ensued. Thus, I was intrigued by her smile—not knowing what could be fueling it—and I waited to see how long it would take before it assumed a spoken form. I said nothing—so eating just a bit more and looking about the room with her smile, she began to speak slowly after a time.

"While you were practicing this afternoon, I went into town, and on my way back I saw Mrs. Paw—the one on this block. She had me in and we had some tea. Port?"

I looked up and answered yes and looked down rather indifferently, as I was beginning to be disappointed with the story.

"I know someone who might like to go to the concert with you!"

Now my Aunt Elizabeth's smile was enormous. I felt she might laugh a bit at what she thought was the enormity of her idea.

"Ah, no, no. No way! No way, Aunt Elizabeth! I'm not going to the concert with Mrs. Paw!"

My aunt just laughed. Then I jumped in again before she could speak.

"I don't want to go this concert either. Give both of the tickets to Mr. and Mrs. Paw. They can both go."

"No, Port. I know someone else who might like to go with you," smiled my aunt.

"Who?" I asked, yet I could not imagine that a slim hope I was developing could possibly be true.

"Lana," she answered, and she rose and turned away with her empty glass and went to the counter. I made my next question aggressive so as to make my aunt and uncle laugh.

"So? What? Now you'd rather have me running around with married women than practicing too much? Is that it?"

"Port, she's divorced. I never thought I'd be steering you toward a divorcée, but Lana divorced her husband, and now she is taking a job in the city. She's over in her old house—living there again, for now. I don't mean that you have to marry her. But maybe she'd like it if a friend called her."

"When did she move back there? How could I have not noticed anything happening over there?"

"She's only been there a little while. But I didn't know until today that anyone had moved back in."

I remembered the moving van that I had thought at first might be bringing a piano to the Paws.

"Would Lana be expecting this call? Would Mrs. Paw be expecting this call? Aunt Elizabeth, how good is the intelligence you're giving me?"

"Well, what do you mean exactly, Port?" my aunt asked, with a bit of her endearing vagueness.

"I mean, what are my odds? How much softening up have you done with motherly cabals and artillery? Is it safe to send in the infantry? What are my odds?"

It was difficult to make my aunt comprehend analogies like that.

And it was more difficult to push the buttons for the call than it was for me to start pressing down the piano keys for some concerts. In fact, I stopped and redialed twice so as to confirm I was truly hitting the right numbers. I had been right each time, and I finally allowed the connection to go through and the ringing to start. I made this call in my room.

"Hi. May I speak to Lana, please?"

"Who is calling?" asked Mrs. Paw.

"This is Portsmouth Gourd, Mrs. Paw."

I suspect that Mrs. Paw not only expected the call, but that she would have known my voice anyway. I often saw her at the end of the driveway during the early part of that month—and there, as well, whenever I would go for my walks when I visited home from the city or from the west when I was an undergraduate. I did appreciate it, however, that she did not betray, at least over the phone, the quiet but pregnant silliness my aunt seemed to harbor for this contact.

Mrs. Paw must have put her hand over the phone, for the next thing I could hear was Lana herself—but only after a long minute had passed. I thought it would be nice if she would jump right in and say hello to me by name—since I am sure her mother told her who it was—but the conversation started only with Lana's "Hello?"

"Hello, Lana, this is Port Gourd from down the block!" I began, determined not to let the mock-question of her hello throw me off a resolve to make an intrepidly amicable start. I was relieved to hear a highly-stylized and femininely welcoming reply.

"Hey, Port! Hey, you! I'm so sorry. I'm not usually such a ditz! I didn't even think to ask my mom who it was. Gosh! Hey! It's good to hear from you! What is going on with you?"

"Oh, pretty much the same thing that I was doing when we were in high school!" I laughed. "Getting ready for school right now and practicing."

"That is so cool! You and Boston, doing what you always wanted to do! I have one of his CDs, in fact."

"Oh! Which one is it?" I asked.

"I knew you were going to ask me that. I don't know which one it is. Sorry! Gosh! Which one is it? I wish I could—"

"What pieces are on it? Do you remember?"

"Gosh, no! I knew you were going to ask me that, too."

I was starting to feel foolish for pursuing this tangent for even this long, but for some reason I asked next, "What is on the album cover, Lana?"

"Oh, you, I don't even remember that. I think it was red. Wait a minute! Here are my CDs—still in the box from my move. Wait a second—"

"I'm sorry, I didn't really mean to—"

"Here it is! *Boston Gourd, piano.*"

"Oh, that one! I've wondered if Boston didn't think that cover was funny?"

"Why is that?" asked Lana.

"Well, the cover is so plain, just those three words written on it—and that title makes it sound like Boston himself is the piano. I mean, it doesn't say, *Boston Gourd, pianist.*"

She laughed, but I could tell she really had not tracked my last observation with enough interest to have it register in her mind.

"But it's so cool that you guys still do what you have always wanted to do. I'm, like, at this point now where I feel I have to find something like now or else I'm never going to find it."

"Well, I hear that you're going to look in New York for a job."

"Yeah, but, it's not something—well, I shouldn't really say that. I'm hoping to be head-hunted into a good advertising job, based on what I already had in Chicago. I'm hoping it works out. It's still just strange to be back in New York—not even just New York, but Pauktaug, even—and getting a lot of stuff, new stuff, started for me. Yeah. That's what's going on."

Then there was the start of a difficult silence, and then she offered another sighed "Yeah," so as to cover the gap. This made it seem to me that she felt responsible for the lull, and more embarrassed by it than eager to be free of the call.

I proceeded: "So, Lana, do you have some pity in you for an old high school friend and elementary school playmate? Some pity for a poor, reclusive, workhorse?"

"Pity! Listen, you—" she began with a laugh, but I forged through her laugh—like holding the sustaining pedal, the damper pedal, down, and playing new chords that gently mix and clash with the old. It was a beautiful haze (her voice) under which I wanted to hear my own chords. I only hoped she could hear my question.

"Hey, would you like to go to a concert with me in the city tomorrow? I have to go in to hear my own teacher play. He is wildly successful and has all the confidence in the world, but somehow he just isn't happy unless I'm there to approve of what he is doing!"

I stopped my own laugh to hear that hers was gone, too, and then there was a beautiful, clear, "Well, sure! Yeah, let's do it! I'll be home—here, Pauktaug home—by three or four and then I'd like to go over to the gym for an hour. If we leave by six, can we make it?"

"I think so. We might. We'll have to drive then. I had thought we might take the train. But we'd pretty much have to race right there. I was going to ask you if you might like to get dinner before, but—"

"Hey, we can grab something after! I haven't been to any kind of a concert or anything for a long time. Sounds fun. Thank heaven for New York, huh?"

"Yes, right," I said as earnestly as I could—at the same time putting out of my mind the prospect of not being able to eat dinner until almost ten-thirty or eleven the next day. I still felt such an overwhelming sense of anticipation at the prospect of this date, that I had not yet realized that Lana had already seized control over the pacing of the entire proposed evening.

"So, what should I do, then? When should I get you? We'd probably—no, we'd have to leave by at least six to make it, and just make it at that."

"Listen, why don't I just take all of my stuff with me, and you can just grab me at the gym. No, how about this! I'll try to finish up, and I'll just come by and grab you in my car when I'm ready! All right? Oh, and call me tomorrow between, say, three-ish and four-ish, before I go over to the gym."

I assented to this last takeover of control, and her request to call again. All I had were the tickets in my name.

I went back to the piano and practiced with more concentration than I expected I could muster. In fact, I closed the window and let the air conditioning take over as I played away with rapt attention. I had thought the romantic fable would take me for an evening, and maybe in some part of me it had. But there seemed to be something else at play because I was freed from a long, perhaps always-monitored and latent preoccupation with the status of the fable—that mythology that governed me even before the time I had seen Lana on the balcony and in the lobby of the Pauktaug Theater so long ago. Now somehow, no matter what the course of the fable, of long-held youthful expectations and suspicions of certain heroic and romantic inevitabilities, I was free from a tangential waste of energy—no matter how beautiful I had thought that waste to be. The tangent seemed somehow self-fulfilling now, and I practiced with a precision never known to me before. A sense of perpetual delay, of beautiful remonstrance against ever really getting started in life, had passed away from me, and I practiced as with a new set of hands. My memory was free and its freed spaces received a flood, and notes became engraved in me, and I practiced with my mind as I had never practiced before. Rote work suddenly lay dead in the corner, and I looked with intermittent fascination at the course of the moonlight moving across the closed top of my piano, marking the speedy passing of the hours.

My aunt's knock at the door startled me. It drew me from a deep revelry of labor that was altogether new to me.

"Port! You don't have to jump like that. I made enough sound coming up. It looks silly when people react like that. Don't let yourself get used to it. Anyway, Port, it's eleven. Do you want to come down for tea?"

Soon, I was downstairs, and I did not include a review of my unusual practice session when I sat down to talk with my aunt and uncle.

"Are you going to call Lana tomorrow? I think she might even be there in the mornings now," asked my aunt.

"I already called her. She said she'll go to the concert."

My aunt suddenly launched into a hesitant stream of qualifications about the prospect, but she was more pleased than anything else. Interestingly, after we parted for the night and I went back to my room for bed, my thoughts only just glanced across the prospect of seeing Lana. In the weeks of my full return to Pauktaug, I had mainly been preoccupied by the labors of preparing for the competition. What alleviation I had felt from the pressures of my self-imposed schedules and anxieties had only come briefly and intermittently—from what little advances I had measured every few days or so. On some evenings I could count a new piece or a lengthy passage memorized; on others I marked the grasping of some new technical peak; on others I noticed self-connecting elements in a work for the first time.

Advances had only come as I had always known them to come—slowly and with a harrowing sense that they would vanish without a zealous effort to maintain them that was equal to or greater than the effort I had made to attain them. But during that August night of practice I had discovered some extremely latent skill within myself that had, perhaps, lain dormant within me from the start of my life. I could not imagine, at least, that such a skill— such a sudden sense of facile ease and confident retention—had suddenly formed within me. Something had allowed it to come forth. It was if I had suddenly entered an adolescence of the pianistic mind and there were wise whiskers jutting forth from the ghostly chins of my fingers. It was inexplicable, but a delight.

Again, I kept it to myself, for my aunt and uncle were already too much my admirers. They would have thought this latest report just another passing observation of a day's practice during a streak of confidence. But I was so sure of this change that I remained silent. Yet I wished to sleep on it and see if it survived a night of total surrender to an indifferent mind left to cobweb by unconsciousness.

When I awoke, it was still there, this new skill. How to describe it? It was as if all the skills that are necessary for the formation of a pianist had been streamlined and empowered. Was it that my acceptance into a world-rated competition and a promised date with a school beauty of the past had freed me from a waiting? Perhaps. Perhaps I merely made a considerable jump in the particular pieces I then had in hand. I cannot say for sure. But I think it was more than that.

On that penultimate day of the summer break, I practiced with shocking productivity and efficiency. The work was no longer plagued by the labor of figuring the work out. Only the work remained. If I did the work, the result came. And I worked, and I was shocked.

If in the weeks since my return I had accomplished, say, a quarter of the primary work that needed to be done for the competition's preparation, then in that single day I reached a three-fourth's readiness. Perhaps I only discovered in a single day, in a single instance, that I had already achieved a three-fourth's readiness since my return to Pauktaug. But, again, I tend to think otherwise. Something was different.

It was as if I had been taken to the moon and I could breathe, or taken to the deeps of the ocean and I could breathe, and was free in those places to indulge my weightlessness and explore the un-self-conscious dark. And without there being any supernatural intimations to what I speak of, it was as if there was something else already there in that dark—or some part of myself that had always been there, and I was only just then being reunited. This reunion was not total however. But I felt I was at the start of something.

When I closed up the piano at four-thirty on the afternoon of that day of my date with Lana, I felt confident that work would yield a rich field in direct relation to my efforts. Never to need pray for rain again! Never to fear locusts! Never to fear any vicissitude or randomness! I worked in stone now and not in clay. I worked in absolute likelihood and not in chance. I felt as if I might finally have a chance at the pianistic prospects I had always imagined for myself. And yet my ego did not soar. I was quiet inside.

As I showered and dressed for my date with Lana, I realized I was not sure if what I had observed in myself was a peak or a continuing upward slope.

I called Lana's house, as she had requested, and only got an answering machine. I left a message and then finished dressing.

Soon it was a quarter to six, and as I waited—hoped—for Lana's car to turn on to our street, I began to realize again how long it would be before dinner. Soon, as well, I thought of how tense I would be, marking the landmarks of the car drive into the city with such a narrow window of time before the concert's start. Lateness was something I could tolerate, if need be, in anyone—save myself. And I suspected that Lana was conspiring to make me late. She had until six before she was truly late herself. But I already had my fears. I looked about my room for something to distract me from my vigil, and it was then that my eyes fell upon my aunt's box of Boston's letters.

CHAPTER VIII

SECOND LETTER

Dear Aunt Elizabeth:

I hope all is well. Since I scribbled that last, long, letter to you two days ago, the two rounds of the preliminaries here in Maryland have come and gone. I have been advanced to the semi-finals. Unlike San Francisco last December and the competition in New York this autumn, there is no chamber music round in this competition. But that suits me. The only thing that has bothered me here so far is the lodging. If I did not have the prospect (if I decide to come for sure) of being with you and Port in the old house for the competition this fall, I would swear, no matter what the cost, to stay in a hotel for any competition in the future. The host family I am with is fine. They let me be, and the house is enormous here. But one can never quite rest altogether under such circumstances. Tonight, as in my first night, I'm not tired enough to sleep here in my room. I'm just tired enough to wish to wander about at my leisure. But I hate having to give account of myself to my hosts. So I remain here in my room and affect to sleep. I hope you won't mind if I wile away another evening hour or two in writing you another letter.

Nothing has happened here so far that did not happen in San Francisco last December. Before anything else is said, you might ask, "Did everything go as I had hoped it would in December?" It seemed as if it were going to; then it did not. Did you read about what happened in San Francisco? It was a rather unusual competition. I'll do my best to describe it for you—just in case you did not follow it.

On my first morning in the San Francisco affair, I gathered in the hall with a dozen others who had drawn numbers as I had—making us among the first to play on the first days of preliminaries. After a time, Aunt Elizabeth, there is among the older competitors a whole list of faces that becomes familiar to one who competes enough. Among the dozen there that first morning, I knew at least four others. Through the course of the competition I met at least ten pianists whom I see rather regularly in this competition-circuit way of life.

But of more interest to you, perhaps—for it was all that interested me—was strategy. What was my strategy at this point? Of course, in the competitions that preceded this one, I had failed to advance beyond increasingly early rounds in the contests—until it was that I was being knocked out even at the preliminary stage.

I was in a unique position. If I risked underplaying so as to cover Music's weakness, I, the player, might be knocked out— and Music would win. If I risked playing as I had before my recent months in the solitary woodshed, I risked exposing Music too early, and I might be knocked out as usual by the terrors and pathetic fears of Music loving judges and auditors in the hall—and Music would win.

This brings me to the question I feel one might ask on reading what I have written thus far. Why the competition as a means? Because of the venue, because of the view! If I could get far enough with my new purpose not yet fully revealed, then where else could I gather as many witnesses in my fight for Man as in the finale of a competition? Though I had a name as a sort of professional competitor, I had not—and have not—the power to have a venue in one of the greatest halls of the world, with all the most influential critics and pianists of the day present (with even, perhaps, a television presence at hand to carry over the wires and air the exposing of an equivocating monster). But competitions, they offer nearly as much to the pianist who can scratch his way to the finals—when they are competitions of note and prestige. But how to scratch one's way to the end when the other pianists and one's self are the least of one's foes?

If I could play to the end, play all the way to the finals, and play such as no one could think to knock me out or think another pianist my better—but also to think that to award me any prize as a pianist was unthinkable! That was my woodshed-wrought purpose! I must play to be unbeatable but under no circumstances win! That was my dream for my fellow man, my hearers. To come to the apex of victory and then have my fellow man see (and confess that he had seen for some time) what I had forced myself to see in myself of late—that the only prize that can be awarded is to Man himself on the defeat of Music! To come to the end of the competition and have the judges and audience stand to their feet in silence and cry to the only remaining competitor (in a noble, rasped, hush), "This is no contest! Not among Man! But for Man! Music loses!"

But why not walk away? Why not beat Music by never letting it speak through me? Because of late too many have heard it for the meek, weak, tyrant that it is. And they heard it through me! And now that I, too, hear it through myself, can I trust that there is anyone of my skill to do this battle of exposition for the sakes of the growing witnesses who have not the physical means to uncover the monster? Perhaps I am the first to hear the great flaw and be able to play at the same time so as to expose the great flaw. Who can say? But I cannot surrender the responsibility. If I stop playing, stop competing, perhaps this strange window that I look through in myself—that so many had looked through before I had known it was even open—might close with my silence. I will not close the window. I will jam my free soul in the jamb of this thus far protected, feted, despotic ghost!

I am not the first who could have played with such skill to expose the faulty, burdensome angel. But my predecessors were in league with the angel, and formed a compact by which both faulty angel and faulty man might continue for the adulation of infant Man. But I will not harbor this organ grinder's monkey on the back of Man—not when more and more have seen him, and through me! I will not adjust my playing, attach blinds to the window of my own realization! I will stare through it, too!

But my strategy. What was it to be? I decided that there were no longer any acceptable risks. I could not risk underplaying. And I could not of course play again as I had in the competitions just before my retreat—that is, play and expose Music yet not realize what I was exposing. Thus, there was only one option. To have faith in Man!

But it was Man that knocked me out—even in the first preliminaries of the last contests—Man that had heard this new truth and wished not to have any more of it! This you might say. But it was because there must have been something awful, something pathetic to them—to those many who could see—in my not knowing what I exposed. There is, ultimately, something repugnant in obtuse, mentally deficient, virtue to the thinking Man. This you must give me. This you must confess is an awful but irrefragable truth. They put me aside with good reason. No one wants a great advance of Man, an enemy exposed, by a child's thoughtlessness—an animal's, meek, mindless posturing that is as some heretofore undiscovered display that humbles one of the oldest of savage beasts.

One wants the revolution to come by self-aware agency! How they had seen what they had seen before I spent my time in the woodshed I cannot say for sure. How I had learned to see it in myself was somewhat clearer to me, but was ultimately a mystery. But if they could see it in me before—could see that Music was meek under my hands—surely they might see, as well, some invisible sign of confidence that I had now taught myself to deliver the coup de grace—to this beast that lay helpless but before my reform still breathing under my able but unclosing claws. They would be for me, surely, if they knew I would be willing to fight for them—to kill for them, to kill for Man.

Oftentimes, people will speak of the giant responsibility that comes with winning a competition. Or they will speak— speak tired, but still energetically righteous talks—on the responsibility one has to music or to art or to the piano or to the public or even to one's self. I have no responsibilities. But I do wish to do this thing—this thing, this idea. Ultimately, I do not feel possessed or mad. I do not feel I have to do this thing. I want to do this thing. I'd like to give this advance to Man.

I took my place in the wings when the pianist before me had finished. He played very well, and the audience warmly received him—gave him, even, a minor ovation (the first of the competition). He strutted off the stage and was called back. He was called back twice, in fact, and Music took the bows with him and then labored to the wings—its old, fat, wheezing self, still adulated and confirmed by a hundred fools in the early morning quiet of the preliminaries. As I waited for a cue from a woman working in the wings in concert with the judges at tables inserted into the front of the house seating, the pianist who had just finished—Brian Matthewson of New Zealand— passed me. He was flushed with self-satisfaction, and he expected to pass me without incident, thinking, I am sure, that my only thoughts were of my imminent bout with three compulsory etudes. But I stopped him, shook his hand, and patted him on the back—in a sort of sincere paternal way, I now recall—for he was but a poor innocent.

Soon, the animated little woman with a headset nodded to me with an earnestness that was hopelessly outdated and filled with a false sense of the importance of the ritual. I nodded my thanks to her, however, and received some sincere supportive touches on my back from two other pianists just as I was about to enter my stride. One was a Korean girl. I've never spoken to her. She didn't seem to know any English. And the other was a pretty girl from Germany. Their encouragement was endearingly sincere, and I looked back to these flowers who thought they still grew and shone on a minor battlefield. But they were safe on the ground they could see. Nothing of note would trample them where they thought they struggled to bring kindness and beauty during their own race to be among the noticed objects on the superficial field.

Attendance and ticket sales for the early sessions of pre-liminaries, even at the largest, most notable, competitions in the world, often attract only a moderate-sized business. Applause was scant as I made my way to the piano, for the hall was not even half full. But it had made a considerable noise for Mr. Matthewson—almost as big a noise as such a crowd, enthralled by the old, common, rumble of Music, could offer. They had pegged a choice for the public's favor even this early in the competition. But such things were not unusual. Nor was it a surprise to me that they selected Mr. Matthewson. In two of the competitions that fell directly before my retirement to the woodshed, and in several when I had still been carrying victories from one contest to another across the globe, Mr. Matthewson had been my nearest competitor (nearest when I was still winning, that is). And he had been the winner in the competition that directly preceded my three months of prac-tice and pianistic self-examination. He has a technical skill just below or just equal to mine. I find him here in Maryland, as well. I did not take too much notice of him before my increasing inability to place or keep safe from early elimina-tion began to emerge. But then—when I had time to linger, not being a part of the competitions I had been eliminated from—I often watched him and Helmut Krepps (a pianist from Germany who lives in Great Britain) win support of the crowd as they vied for first place in the finals. Again, Matthewson won the contest that directly preceded my little retirement. Krepps won the competition before that. And Krepps is also here in Maryland.

Both these fellows are celebrated for their piano playing— and for their temperaments. Neither of them betray the slightest bit of tact when commenting upon the competitions themselves, their rivals, or even the judges. They either strive to fulfill the image of the mad, angry, tortured artist—or they are all too susceptible to those tendencies because of the pressures of the business. I have met my fair share of affable, balanced, generally and genuinely kind people in this business—so I tend to think that Matthewson and Krepps tend to err on the side of affectation. If one catches them off guard, at times, they are, well, oftentimes less guarded—especially after coming off stage from a successful and well-received performance.

The applause I received as I took my place at the piano for the first time in a competition—or even in any kind of performance—since my months in the woodshed, seemed a combination of indifference at the prospect of hearing another pianist after the furor of Matthewson had passed and of pity for any that should have to follow him. I nodded with ritual politeness to this vague clapping. These meek clappers were not the crowd I was in league with. It was the other faction in the audience, along with the keenest part of the jury. I was going to play then to all those who had meekly applauded me before my retirement—to all those who clapped lightly not out of pity or indifference or boredom, but out of sentient fear, from a shocked view of the dead and further dying Music that shuddered upon the platform and shivered in their ears and in the hall. I was going to play to those others. They were there, I knew. They had to be, for they had been everywhere—in my last five contests and in my recital followings at that same time.

I settled into the bench and let the unimportant applause die away. Affecting to need a moment to compose myself, I looked at the massive new instrument that sat before me. The lighting was so intense for this preliminary, that I was taken with innumerable images that could be seen reflected in the instrument. Not only could I see warped, bent, images of some on the panel of judges, and some of the audience just behind them, but also an odd, stretched, image of myself reflected in the interior of the piano's lid. And mixed with that image were reflections of the piano's steel and copper strings, its bits of wood and felt, and stretches of its mighty, iron, frame. But of more interest to me was the flawless, perfect, reflection of my own hands on the label-exposed underside of the open keyboard lid. My hands reached into all of this, or seemed to reach out, with the very same dimensions that I saw for them just before me in life. And in between, one imagines, in between all the mottled reflections and in between the webbing in the image of my perfectly reflected fingers was the piano's blackness.

Just before the playing starts I think Music is all in there. It hides in there before it sees how much surfacing it will need do at the hands of the player. Is the player beneath waking it? Is the player in league with it? Or is this new player the dreaded one? Is this newest of players the one who will dispel Music for all time from its pitiful despotism over only slightly more pitiful hordes of earthly followers and subjects? I reached to the opposite ends of the keyboard and grabbed the ends of the piano's sides and pretended to take one last, personalized stretch before beginning to play. Instead, I shook the piano ever so slightly, and the comprehensive reflection shuddered before me.

I righted myself, took one last breath, and began to play my three compulsory etudes. There was to be a mandatory silence between the pieces in this first part of the preliminary. Applause was to be held until the completion of the third study. This was insisted upon by the program and an announcement of the judges at the start of the morning's activities. But the result of my performance upon the audience and the jury was not yet of interest to me. What was then emerging was all too fascinating.

I imagine that every pianist dreams of carrying the sense of total command that he feels graces his private practicing from time to time into the fray of battle and onto the concert platform. But it has always been a bit of a challenge for me to identify with the everyman when it comes to pianists, as you know. I do not say this from immodesty, but from sheer point of fact and observation. I have always felt—ever since I was in my late teens—that I could achieve a near unquestionably consistent level in my own private playing once certain tasks were accomplished. And I have had more than a fair share of moments in carrying that same sense of control into battle. But even I—and even in times when I have won competitions with hardly any question as to my front ranking by anyone— have felt a bit of frustration in my attempts to bring the perfect command of the practice room into the changeable environment of public performance.

Imagine, then, Aunt Elizabeth, when I discovered, as I began to play my first etude in the San Francisco competition, a command confirmed in public that was so total, so comprehensive, that the colossal confirmations of my late term in the woodshed was bested by a confidence and control that was hitherto undreamed of by even myself. Each attack upon every single note was graded and shaded as it had been in my mind in the long struggle within to create an idealized realization of the works I was playing. But I was not then hitting only a fair share of those idealizations—so that an approximated intent could be gathered by the judges and audience. No, I was hitting the idealized realization down to every last component. I was not sculpting a beautiful vague figure in sound. I was rendering every last cell of it in its most idealized form.

If I had discovered, say, in my unconscious labors in the woodshed, that note 3034 in the right hand was best, was ideally, was unquestionably suited to an attack of the hand that registered at, say, six pounds of impact at nine miles an hour—and I could render that note with those specifications on command in the woodshed—then that is also how it emerged upon the platform! And yet! And yet allowances for the idealization were also made for the instrument and the ambient space—but the absolute value of note 3034 in the right hand still landed with the result of six pounds of force at nine miles per hour.

I was past vicissitudes. Though I had been to such a level before, never had I felt that its command was absolutely mine and mine for all time. But there was something much more gripping to me than even this. I was playing this way for the first time before others—playing at the height of what mankind had thus far esteemed as technical perfection and command, and with the fullest extent of interpretive rendering extended to the pieces I was playing. Yet I knew that I was exposing with my infallibility of rendering something that was fallible and weak, incapable of infinite renewal. Though performing with the sound that had marked the highest passions and physical achievements of all men that had trod before, I played with the full knowledge that I could no longer mark such passions or achievements with that sound. With the height of seeming passion and seeming physical impossibilities, I plied the waters of a complete indifference. I was impassioned with indifference. I felt a thrill at how little I felt. Now I, too—like my pre-woodshed witnesses—would look mildly about the room when this performance would end and wonder why it was that Man still kept feigning gratitude to such a tyrant. With magnificent indifference the Music raged through the pistons of my fingers. It raged outward in its old, old manner of show, raced from the guts of the black piano, barreled to the back of the hall, and ricocheted a return to the stage. Surely I thought I heard it beg me for some compliance with my old unawareness as I continued to throttle up and down the keyboard. The faintest report of my last attacks would return to me as I commenced with my next—and those reports would indeed seem to beg. It begged of me for surely there were fewer and fewer left in the halls to beg from—surely fewer even than when I had left the platform just before my long journey into the woodshed. And it begged of me, for when there had been fewer and fewer to beg from in my last performances, there was always foolish, unknowing, me to appeal to, and I could be counted on for some flush of face, some old twist in the gut, some old dampness of impassioned brow, some old memory triggered by its strains, some old writhing in my inobservant, deaf and blind and thoughtless heart. But now it pleaded to me in vain. The notes bounced off the last row in the balcony, made some second desperate second appeals during its return flight, and then begged me in a weeping, meek, pitiful sob to feel for it, to think something of it, to have some use for it still. I felt nothing for it, and I was enthralled.

Surely, as well, it was meeting with its greatest indifference yet from those in the hall. How else to explain the absolute rigid silence as I finished the first etude? How else to explain, then, the silence when I paused before beginning the second piece? There was not a sound. And I am in earnest. There was not a creak of a chair. There was not a single cough. I even looked into the hall to confirm that it was still peopled. Yet there was the same crowd, the same panel of judges—all staring back at me with some look of new, dumb, terrified silence.

Never had Man been in such legion against a common foe! Never had Man united in such legion against what had so long been thought a balm, an ally, a never ending resource to bind him to his own soul and to his fellow man's when all else seemed debatable. Never had Man so instantly united against such an infamous, false, yet invisible thing before. All the fears of Man were this one fear, this one foe. All secret fears of invisible things seemed revealed—and revealed upon one, discernible, distinct invisible thing. How else to explain the silence? Surely they all saw it then!

The silence seemed even greater as I played and then finished the second etude. I even took an inordinate pause so as to revel in this sign of seemingly imminent victory. Were it not for some almost imperceptible, ambient, sounds in the hall—the ceiling fans above, or even the hum of the lighting—I suspect I could have heard the pulse of my own nervous system deep within the entrails of my ears. But the silence was such that I could, indeed, hear the ticking of my own watch—as one can on rare, rare, days when all is perfectly still in a room.

I commenced my third etude, and all was perfection in its rendering. It was comparable in all measurable ways to the finest of performances, to the finest performance, from the days when Music as faulty entity was still yet unsuspected. And yet it was beyond that. It was emerging from the instrument rendered as if each gesture was free of the demands of passing time—each note, each depression of a pedal, each and every gesture of attack and mental recall and preparation put forth only as the finest, most idealized example of the millions discovered by experimentation in the woodshed. And an art rendered in real time was seemingly rendered with the reliability and safety of a plastic artist's temporal liberty. Music, gasping in its eternal remove where it needs still to breathe the air of mortal time, shook and shook and pleaded to me as I barreled with inexorable power to the close of my final etude. I had not wished to show so much so soon to the public. But what choice did I have? I could not pretend ignorance of my role, and I could not throw the fight. I had to fight with full force and know it—and play unlike any musician ever to play before me in the history of this old, ringing, tintinnabulating, world.

I came to the end of the etude, and I listened as the last, pounded, stabbing chord made its desperate rounds of the enormous room. When I heard the last of its decay, and the piano stopped shaking with life, I kept my head down and my eyes closed. For perhaps a magnificent, pure, half of a second, all fell to perfect stillness and clean, unquestionable, victory. Music was out of me for all time. It was dead for me, and I basked in that frozen silence as the decay yielded to comprehensive quiet, and suddenly the tick of my watch into the next second became evident. And Man was free to march ahead into a new void of frontier. I reveled in this last, complete, comprehensive indifference. I reveled in the completion of my first true, sentient, performance before what I knew must be my ever growing sentient audience. I rose from the bench.

Then came the wave.

First it was the sound of the seats springing to their vertical position—hundreds of them, like the sound of concert grand lids when they are opened quickly and recklessly. Then the sound of the human roar, empowered by its self-righteous urge to declare its tireless allegiances. It roared a fidelity, a faithfulness. I had to turn to see if this were true, and I stood in terror-ridden shock as what I thought would be my ending loneliness festered into an absolute isolation, and my beautiful silence died.

I stood against this only with my hard-won, impassioned indifference. And I glanced behind me when I was forced by the onlookers and the lady in the wings to witness this defeat again and again and again, glanced behind me when the sounds of hands and roars yielded to stomping feet in some slavish corners and looked to see that contemptible, massive shackle, carved of wood and steel and copper and felt and brass and bone and mystery by that most indefinite priest of the pantheon—glanced behind me and saw the piano shudder from the din and chuckle with life.

CHAPTER IX

CONCERT

When I finished reading Boston's second letter from Maryland to Aunt Elizabeth, I had time to think only a few things without distraction. Mainly, the second letter made me continue to suspect that Boston was toying with my aunt—almost as a child might suddenly hold up something he had found in the woods only so as to see the reaction of his skittish auntie. If there was more of the same in his third letter, then I thought I might begin to credit his peculiar narrative as a sort of experiment. Yet even when the sudden excitement of Lana's car horn brought me to the window, I put the peculiar letter back into its shroud of an envelope with a splinter of malaise that there was something of a yet-to-be understood earnestness in his idea.

I resolved to ask my aunt later whether she had really read Boston's letters with any care. All I had time for at the moment was a hasty call of goodbye to my aunt and uncle who were down in the office. Then I ran out the back, around the porch, and down to Lana's enormous, shiny, gold, SUV.

When I slid into the passenger seat, Lana greeted me over the mildly blaring rock music on the radio.

"Hey, you!" she called.

She leaned over to hug me, and then she kissed me on the cheek as we broke our embrace. I started to say something, but she could not hear me. Then she saw my eyes flick involuntarily toward the stereo knobs as I began to repeat myself.

"I was just saying, you made it!"

"Of course I made it! Oh, gosh, it's so good to see you. I'm so glad you called. I haven't been to anything in the city in so long—anything for fun, I mean. This is going to be great. And it is so good to see you! Don't get me wrong—I love my mom and dad. They've been great as I've been going on interviews and all that, but sometimes! But, gosh, don't get me wrong. It's really nice to be back—and the old street exactly as it was. It really seems exactly the same. You guys have the house looking so much the same that I thought you might come out of there looking like you did twenty or twenty-five years ago!"

I was looking at Lana as she said all this. She most certainly did not look like she had looked twenty or twenty-five years before. Nor did she look, even, as she had nearly twelve years back—when I had last seen her, in our final year of high school. She still had the same presentation of mind and voice, it seemed to me, but her form was hardened and firmed into a tanned, delicately muscled, intensity that was still feminine in shape—but defined a sort of excess of perfection, a redundancy, that many attractive women invoke by means of intense daily exercise. If it were covered, her form could still have been that of very young woman's, but by discreet means of exposure—sleeveless blouses or tops; skirts with slits revealed when sitting—she demonstrated quite well this consummate, labored, redundancy.

Her long, straight, brassy blonde hair was still ever so slightly damp from a recent shower and rushed blow drying—and the tips held together subtly in select places like sandy-colored fountain pen nibs that drew watery lines along the shoulders of her form-fitting black velvet dress.

I looked to her fingertips as she drove, and I recall wondering how long her immaculately manicured nails and fingertips would last if she started to practice the piano at all. I asked her about her piano playing.

"Oh, gosh. I wish I'd kept it up. I haven't played since eighth grade."

It was not until we were in the concert hall that I could really study the rest of her and what it seemed to tell me of her last dozen years of history. We had had a rather swift trip into the city, and because I offered to pay for a garage, we were parked and on our way into the hall itself with an astonishing quarter hour to spare. The way in to the city had been occupied by a brief compulsory summary of her college years, her work experiences, her very brief marriage and divorce.

When she asked how it was that I was still free, I countered by intimating that I had been in a couple of relationships that were equally difficult. These relationships I alluded to were merely a series of dates that hardly lasted more than a couple of weeks in any case. I offered this not so as to sound boastfully jaded, but so as not to sound still too eagerly hopeful and unscathed—so as not to let her sound like a casualty and I a survivor. Somehow a full report of my bright outlook seemed like it would sound aggressive.

But romantically hopeful and unscathed I was, indeed. I had been drawn, too, by the calls of life. I had not been totally excluded from the conduct of such things in my third decade. But I had been so consistently industrious that I had been preserved (with but a few torrid ups and downs thrown in as challenges) rather in the same optimistic romantic state that I had always occupied.

The rest of the ride was consumed by a running, laughing, commentary on the hazards of the road trip into New York City.

But, again, it was not until we were in the hall that I could really study Lana. She had on that black velvet dress and black shoes that were enormously flattering to her legs—which were themselves as evenly tanned as the rest of her body. Stockings would have been like an affrontive orchestration to an already flawless work of piano scoring. The colors and tones were already present in the work.

When we took our seats, she seemed to check herself, not with the vanity that any young person might apply, nor with any intimations of common, superficial vanity, but with a self-survey that seemed to confirm that something was still holding as reinforced. She had the look of some long distance runners that know they are no longer on any of the miles that can provide enjoyment or exhilaration. She was holding and checking herself by sheer will, with a promise to herself that a relief was surely to come at some point—for no one runs indefinitely, and she was indeed on some sort of measured course. No one runs on a totally unmeasured course. There is always some sort of precedent of time and distance. She had, with her marriage, perhaps, hit what marathoners call "the wall." But she was driving herself on, still—with the same stride that had taken her to and past the wall—inexorably to some line just a couple of tenths past a figurative twenty-six mile mark. Despite the brevity of our reunion, and because of my naively low expectations for spiritual compatibility, and because of the shocking allure of Lana's supremely tended form, it was with disappointment and sureness that I could already sense that Lana never looked to me with that imperceptible but definite glance that would have intimated she had hope that I might be holding, if not representing altogether, at least part of that inscrutable finish line. Thus, with only that most tenuous of reunion catalysts, mutual pasts and mutual childhoods not mutually esteemed, I settled into my seat with the blaringly attractive Lana Paw—her blonde hair as golden as a trumpet's bell under stage lights.

Lana took her seat and crossed her legs, and then I looked about the auditorium for the first time. Though I had been bullied into buying the tickets for this concert, Neil Silver had bullied me, at least, into buying a pair of tickets from a block of seats in an excellent section of the orchestra—and the price printed on the tickets was much more than I had to pay. Though I doubt that Mr. Silver was personally responsible for the reduced price, I was still grateful, mainly because it had given me such an attractive impetus for contacting Lana again and having somewhere to take her.

I was still basking in the sense of infinite pianistic advancement I felt I had made that day and the day before. And despite my suspicions of Lana's ultimate romantic indifference, I felt reinforced from all sides by either beautiful object or encouraging portent—next to me the perfect combination of stunning, modern divorcée; and childhood romantic object, figure of the fable. And all about was an old and revered structure that validated the world I had practiced myself into and hoped to remain within with more practice.

Bending, stuffing, folding, and rolling themselves in seats—like eggs being rolled back into places in their cartons—were thousands of people gathered for an altogether sanctioned and esteemed activity. These thousands were not of one mind. But more or less, when they took their seats in such a hall, they were overawed by a suspicion that they all should be of one expectation and one conduct. There might be tussles and irritations, family rages, before a concert. But generally—as I had observed was also the case in literally hundreds of instances back home during wakes, viewings, and funerals—very few brought their indignations to bear into the auditorium. They might be festering beneath the placidity, but I have almost never seen anyone fail to leave a hall or slumber room for the out-of-doors before bringing their personal narrative to the fore. There might be displays of subtle aggression and self-expression—I have seen snorers and seat-shifters and whisperers in both venues—yet almost no one ever truly challenges the assumption that the subject of the main venue is to be deferred to in all cases. In both instances, a hiss that enjoins silence is all that it requires for one human being to remind another that there is one main will to which all should submit. Few other places can boast of such a minimal requirement to maintain the peace. And few other places can boast that such a minimal requirement is generally so revered and effectual. I was always pleased to think that I was part of a business with such a powerful, implicit, code—part of two such businesses, really.

Soon the lights went down and the preparatory sounds of the orchestra yielded to silence, then applause and the appearance of the concert master, then applause and the appearance of the conductor.

Lana leaned over, touched my leg briefly, and whispered warmly with her breath.

"Thanks, Port. This is fun."

I whispered back that I was glad. She seemed to want to continue to talk to me, and the start of the concert appeared to frustrate her. But she settled back and began to read her program, especially as the opening work was a new one for full orchestra—of the sort that would be tolerated and executed brilliantly by orchestra and conductor, then recorded, feted in a few magazines and journals, and then never played again. Lana seemed able to abide the violence of the new piece when someone nearby whispered that the work's composer was in the row right in front of us. She whispered this to me, and then she seemed to take pleasure in looking for the one who seemed bent on showing the least reaction to the work. This struck me as clever, and I joined her in the search, and it gave me an opportunity of looking at her when she herself was looking far down the row.

I eventually gave up this diversion and started to listen to this new piece. I was at best ambivalent about it. But what focus it did bring to me sent me down a path in my mind quite apart from my admirations of Lana. Through a long trail of thoughts and associations, I thought of Neil Silver's imminent performance, then of Boston, and then my cousin's unusual letters.

To begin with, my thoughts were rather self-centered. I knew that we were then in the portion of the concert when the pianist appearing in the concerto that was to be played before the intermission was probably offstage gauging the nearness of his starting time—if not by the warnings of a concert official or stage hand, then by the status of the work that was nearing its end on stage. I have heard that sound for myself on a few occasions, and it can be a terrifying sound—for the concert has started and is alive for nearly all but one's self at that point, and enduring the first breath of exposure to the light and air of the vast world of the hall is a forbidding, solitary, experience.

I have never known anyone to walk away at this point. I have never seen it, though I suspect it must have happened many times in the history of this old concert-giving world. The call to give life to that piece one has been charged with resuscitating is strong. Or perhaps the fear of the accusations that would attend abandoning one's charge is the real fear. One is rarely forgiven leaving a scene of distress—especially if he has been appointed to perform the restorative work. Thus, one often walks out in terror and gives forth all he can so that the music can live again for a time.

I knew that Neil Silver was off in the wings hearing the muffled sound of the work he had probably heard perhaps once before in a dress rehearsal. But considering his age and experience, and the fact that he was just short of being regarded as one of the, say, five, most highly regarded pianists on the Earth, I wondered how much fear really attended his last moments in the wings.

I did not really know Neil Silver well. I had logged many hours under his direct guidance, and we presumably shared discussions that embraced highly volatile, deeply personal, emotional facets of our lives. But I still could hardly answer to what he really thought about anything, not even music. His reverence for interpreters of the past and present was so deep, or so affectedly deep, that I never heard anything from him that I had not already read for myself.

Generally, piano lessons for me only confirmed failings that I already suspected of myself in my playing. I have always walked away from my lessons with a sense of disappointment that I have never felt any measurable intellectual gain from being in the company of a celebrated performer-teacher. But this is, of course, only my personal experience.

So, again, it is impossible for me to say just how Neil Silver felt as the first work of the concert's first half was ending. But then I thought of one of whom I was sure, even though I had not seen him play for nearly twelve years—Boston. My cousin's pre-concert demeanor in the years that I had known him in person, and now through his letters—made me suspect that he did not approach the concert or carry it out with personal fear as a consideration. What the muffled roar of the music preceding his own playing and the applause preceding his appearance on the stage meant to him I could not yet precisely say.

As I thought intensely on this, and as I thought of the thousands of times that Neil Silver and Boston Gourd had stood on buried wings and then heard the muffled applause suddenly uncovered—as the conductor would leave for the side of the stage after the end of the first work—a terror went through me as I thought of myself seeing what they could see and hearing what they could hear. Seeing the door open to let the conductor leave the stage let the remembered sound of the unmuffled roar back into my mind. And I sat privately embarrassed, humbled, and filled with dread for the autumn competition. But before Neil Silver appeared I had a sudden flash of admiration for Boston, and I began to think about his letters for the first time away from reading them. I started suddenly to suspect I understood his theme— and I did not feel the writing had been but an extended narrative developed solely so as to tease my aunt. But when I started to formulate a summary for Boston's new cause in my mind, the applause died away, and I became aware of Lana once more.

"I guess you have to know a lot about music to like—to appreciate—a piece like that last one," she whispered and smiled.

I grinned and looked back to her.

"I think you would have to know a lot. A real lot!" I said.

We both laughed.

I continued: "I guess that composer wasn't too happy with his piece or the orchestra wasn't. He wasn't asked to stand at the end, and we still don't know who he is or if he's here!"

"Maybe he's shy," Lana laughed, and she lightly tapped me on the shoulder with her rolled program. "Oh, that's the piano they're rolling on now! Have you ever played in here, Port?" Her question was truly innocent.

"Oh, gosh, no! But they are going to have the final rounds of the competition in here this fall. I probably won't make it that far, though."

"Oh, you! I'm tired of your old act. You used to play like the way people play in here when we were still in high school. I used to think that there would never be a way that you'd be able, then, to be interested in anything else!"

I was stunned and flattered by the latter part of this. And Lana confused me, for she gave no ultimate signals of interest in the present, but seemed to like alluding to lost, irretrievable, and now unviable signals of the past.

"Are you kidding me, Lana? I used to—" I started to say, but then the conductor and Neil Silver appeared.

"Oh, is that—Oh, I'm sorry, Port. Go ahead."

"No, go ahead, please," I insisted.

"Is that your teacher? I've seen pictures of him. I actually know about him, I think!"

I confirmed that the pianist was indeed my teacher, but before anything else could be said, the concert continued with an aggressive, fast start that hardly allowed the last clap of applause to die away.

Lana unrolled her program and looked at the piece's title. She pointed violently to it and underlined it with her polished nail. She nudged my leg and then whispered warmly to me again.

"I know this piece! I love this piece! I've heard this before!"

"Good. I'm really glad, Lana," I whispered back.

I was old enough and just experienced enough to put Lana out of my mind as the music unfolded, and in the solitude of my considerations during the performance, I returned to my developing conclusion as to what Boston's theme might really be. But I did not come to that speculation without feeling a direct response to the concert itself—which seemed ultimately to work its way in tandem toward the end of my latently forming ideas as to the meanings and purpose of Boston's letters (or, at least, those that I had read so far).

Though I had felt of late a sudden surge of advancement—and the suspicion that I was closer than ever before to thinking like one of the world's great, infallible pianists—I had not shaken another feeling that had been growing in me for several years, a feeling that there was something predictable, fatiguing, a bit sadly old about all the music I was playing and hearing—all this notwithstanding my late advancements in skill. Thus, I knew in my heart I was not affecting a new indifference so as to rationalize my own professional failings. I had every reason to love the piano more at this time. Yet, somehow, with my increasing skill came something of a dread each morning at the prospect of having to go to the piano. At first I thought this was merely a battle with a realization of inescapable routine. But the dread did not diminish at the end of a day's long work. It lingered with me, and tempered all the joys of my advancements. It seemed, in fact, to heighten in direct relation to my advancements and confidence as a player. I would like to characterize it merely as the boredom that sets in during the labors attendant to any long preparations, but there was something inscrutably different about what I felt. However, I could not yet begin to imagine what it was. At first I felt a sort of guilt that I was allowing a merely blue feeling, a dark common pall, to fall over me in late youth. Yet at the same time I could not surrender my suspicion that this feeling was some sort of benign discovery. Yet if it were some sort of discovery, I had only a theory of what my theory might be—and no idea what application the theory might possess if I could discover its nature. I imagined that I may have happened upon some sort of notion that I could never fully prove—for if I decried something in music, surely everyone would cite bitterness and regret as the catalysts for any such statements from a still-developing and vulnerable concert pianist.

Neil Silver thundered through his warhorse, and he gained on the end with a steely strength. He was slated for a massive victory with this performance, and I felt overcome with an enormous surge of resentment and anger as he closed on the double bar of the final movement. Yet this anger was not directed at Mr. Silver, precisely. It would be, ultimately—that night, at least. But as the piece rolled to its inexorable, crowd-thrilling, conclusion, I felt on the verge of remembering something, or knowing something, as if for the first time. If I could just know the object of my resentment, I might be able to see Mr. Silver later and be the congratulatory admirer and general lover of music and general lover of general success that anyone might hope to be.

As the final bars rose up and up and all the members of the orchestra and the pianist shoveled and threw their power forth with concentrated force, I felt nearer and nearer to my remembrance or discovery. It had something to do with predictability, with inevitability, with stasis, with sameness. The pianist and the orchestra rushed forward and ahead, yet they pushed as if into an obscene familiarity that I could not yet identify.

Lana reached over to my leg and squeezed my thigh as the final bar of music sounded. Then she rose as did all—not even allowing the echo to die; therefore viced between the seats and the stage, in a way, by this echo—and they gave Neil Silver seven minutes of continuous admiration. The roar broke my thinking, and I sat in my seat, as if sitting up in bed in the morning trying to force the mind to conclude an unfinished dream. Thus, it appeared for a moment that I sat angered and frustrated and infantile in my sitting. I could yield only to the suspicion that such was all I really felt as my nearness to my memory or discovery faded away in the powerful roar.

I stood and smiled to Lana as she wiped away tears from her face, and I pretended to fumble with something unseen in my seat—so as to justify my slowness to rise.

"I'd forgotten about things like this, Port!" she said above the din, without the levity that had attended her previous whispers.

"Well, it's always here for you, Lana," I responded, and then I quickly gestured to the stage—for I suddenly felt it may have sounded like I had coyly, obliquely, indicated myself with what I had said.

Then thoughts of intense frustration attended me as I struggled to remember or discover why I felt such resentments—and they turned into a common jealousy of Neil Silver as my nearness to realization became more and more distant as the wailing continued.

When the ovation was finally over and the intermission commenced, Lana asked me, "Since you're his student, are you supposed to go back and congratulate him?"

"There are a lot of people here. I don't think I'd be missed or expected. But want to go back for fun?"

"Okay," beamed Lana, and she stood and smoothed the subtle creases from the velvet of her top. "I'm not going to say anything, but it would be fun to walk around a bit. And I've never been backstage at a place like this before."

Lana and I made our way toward the left side of the house and out a door that led to the backstage. An usher was slowly admitting people to the green room, and we waited on a line many individuals and couples deep. My almost remembered thoughts or my almost accomplished discovery continued to fade.

As I waited in the line, I began to imagine what it might be like to pursue the quietest of employments in some remote place, where there were no concerts. I imagined that Lana merely looked diverted and excited for my sake, and that she secretly longed to leave behind such a ritual where it could never be seen, and that I would have a beautiful partner from my ancient past to escape with to an ostensibly routine life of a sequestered middle-class existence—far away from the truly patterned, truly stasis-bound, truly tyrannical routine of the existence promised by the path that surrounded me. Oftentimes, a romance is feared as a seductive alternative to one's chosen path. Standing in that line, seeing Lana's approval of the world of my choice, made me fear that she might be a seductive reinforcement of it—just when, inexplicably, I seemed terrified, even angered, at the prospect of having to remain in the piano's sphere. Yet the almost-known reasons for my fears continued to slip away from me, and by the time we were near to Neil Silver himself, waiting to extend our hands, I could only look to Lana with forgetfulness once more and feel that her still-running race of vanity and physical self-preservation in no way considered me as part of her course or as a possible finish line. But she was pleasant, present, and attentive, despite this suspicion of mine.

All I had, then, was a fatigued feeling of jealousy for Mr. Silver.

We neared him in the line. Then the line halted for five minutes as live television cameras consumed Silver for a planned commentary for the night's national broadcast of the concert. Silver recited a well-rehearsed repartee with a man from New York's public television station, and then Silver ended this interview as the humble founder and spokesman for the imminent first running of the Manhattoes Piano Competition. After this was done, he tended to his line of admirers once more. Lana and I soon reached him.

"Hello, Mr. Silver. This is my friend from way back in elementary school—even before that—Lana Paw. We really enjoyed the concert! I'm jealous. That's about all I can say!"

I was pleased at my thought to use confession as a form of praise. And it sounded and was sincere. I was free, then, to notice that Mr. Silver looked slightly possessed—not as if he looked maniacal or extremely out of sorts. He seemed, rather, plagued as if the height of his ego had been appeased with the height of achieving its deepest intent—yet there was something in his face that betrayed a sense of not being responsible for what had happened. He looked like a man, I thought, surprised and secretly disappointed to have achieved all that he had ever imagined for himself—but this not a man intelligent enough to be fully aware of his disappointment. Thus there was a smug emptiness to him that I found repulsive. And then I could tell that he could not remember my name.

"Well, thank you very much for coming. It's a great work, this. It's a great work. It's probably one of the most valuable works of this kind of repertoire. You know—but this is just my opinion— it's probably one of the most valuable gifts given to Western civilization. No matter how many times I play it, it is always above me—it can never be played well enough."

His eyes flitted like an animal's around the room—like a large, advanced, predator that continues to hunt even after it has been sated. Just then a bit of prey attacked him, and he responded— another couple moved in when I was silent after his last affectedly self-deprecating line. I withdrew with pleasure, for my jealousy had subsided into pure irritation. Neil Silver—though perhaps somewhat excusably distracted and flushed with the first excitements of the post-concert reception—had seemed surprised, even puzzled, at my appearance at the concert. I could not understand his behavior, really, considering it had been he who had called me about coming to the performance. I suppose I did understand it, actually, for I had always thought him—and most others I met in classical music—rather trying, cloying, and, well, goofy.

Feeling foolish for having approached someone who had pressured *me* into coming to his concert—and being so peculiarly received by him—I sent my thoughts away from such things with plain anger and suddenly recalled how hungry I was.

Lana did not mind the idea of leaving the hall before the second half started.

We had our dinner in a restaurant with sawdust on the floor and dark little booths with candles on the tables, and she told me stories of her years waiting tables and tending bar in undergraduate school. Then we had a sincere laugh together, and she put her hand atop mine for a long minute when she realized that I thought she had suddenly begun to speak of a disillusionment with a certain composer.

"One gets tired of bar talk pretty quickly," she had said.

She saw my puzzlement. And it endeared me to her that I had lost the sequence of her narrative and made this foolish mistake because I was so intent on her that I could not always hear everything that she said. It was this demonstrable perceptiveness and her general openness to the humor of language and the sad beauty of reunion that made her even more appealing and hard to think of as fragile. Yet hers was a fragility of larger things. Hers was the fragility, not of a crystalline feminine wisp, but of a flexible, feminine power perhaps exhausted before its time. Thus she did not seem fragile so much as ponderously precarious.

I did not see this until we drove home. Lana said she could not bear the thought of driving back to Pauktaug, and I obliged. Therefore Lana did most of the talking as we drove home into the gradually consuming quiet of the north shore of Long Island.

She told long stories filled with an affectionate, strong wit—not stories that would seem to drive on a melancholy, brittle, teary halt—and yet twice she started to cry.

When we returned to our street and pulled into Lana's driveway, I carried the memory of the noise of the city into the silence of the village—as my ears still rang from the drive, for we had opted to roll down the windows and listen to the night air as Lana talked and we curved along the winding road that ribbons its way east near Pauktaug.

With the crickets sounding, I faced Lana one last time after first intimating that I should return to the main house. She lingered a bit so that I felt I could linger a bit, too. Lana asked me a little bit about the business of my aunt and uncle, and then she asked me if I still took walks in the woods behind the main house.

"I mean, did they ever build back there? There aren't, like, houses back there now or something?"

"No, Lana, it's the same woods that we knew."

"They're spooky, then, still," she smiled.

I was flattered that Lana asked nothing about Boston—and nothing more about my aunt and uncle. Then she stood staring at me for a long instant, and I felt a bit embarrassed and unsure of what to do. I probably could have kissed her then, but I did not. But Lana leaned forward, put her hands—perhaps a bit awkwardly—on the sides of my head, such that my ears were covered and the sounds of the crickets were muffled, and she gave me a kiss on the cheek and said thank you. Then she kissed me one last time in the same place and withdrew.

As I walked away, I affectedly turned about and walked backward for a moment or two so that I could smile and appear in my old callow fable again. But she did not expose my affectation by lingering to watch this gesture for very long. She turned only once on her trip up to her porch and waved good-night.

When I reached my own back porch and quietly entered the house, I thought of Boston's letters again. My aunt was asleep, and I went straight up to my room.

As I sorted through the letters and found the third he had

written from Maryland, I sat by my window and looked out to Lana's house and her second story blinds, then aglow with yellow light. Lana maintained herself in my mind, my mind that wished to cloister itself upon the many letters still unread (that seemed to bear some strange sympathy with the speculations I was only just then beginning to form and explore), she a new sort of wedge, a passionate preoccupation to alleviate my lonely, imminent journey.

But Lana remained a predominance as I hesitated to start with my reading. She represented to me an alluring precision of my desire—just familiar and historied and sad enough to be someone whom even my aunt wished me to pursue, but also worldly and seductive and divorced and advanced and tight and sinewed (like a daily-tuned concert grand). I did not look backward, then, as I looked out of my window and down the block to her lighted window. But into some tugging mix of always I stared as I leaned against the top of my closed piano, and, in the absolute silence and stillness—save for the crickets—of the late August night, I began to read Boston's third letter.

CHAPTER X

THIRD LETTER

Dear Aunt Elizabeth:

I hope all is well at home. Now I am altogether certain that I wish to return to Pauktaug this summer. I'll be entering that Manhattoes Competition this fall. But I hope that it will be my last competition. I hope there I can finally lose on my terms. I did not lose on my terms in December in San Francisco, and it seems likely that I will not lose on my terms here in Maryland.

There is to be a luncheon this afternoon, where the competitors and the judges are supposed to lightly and indifferently mix. Perhaps I'll have a feel for the way things will go after that is over. Yet I am certain, almost down to the very ivory of my bones, that I will not lose this competition on my terms. I will either lose on their terms or win on their terms. These options are no longer acceptable to me.

But I had such hopes. I felt that no matter what happened in San Francisco in December, I would not let its result seem final and representative. But now that the same thing seems to be happening here as in California, I am beginning to have my fears. I will give it one more try in New York this fall and then hope to be done with this business no matter what happens.

But what happened in December? I'll tell you as best I can before this morning goes by and it is time for that luncheon.

I try to recall what I wrote to you last—more than a week ago. It doesn't really matter precisely where I left off, but I believe I told you so far of my time before San Francisco and of my bout at its preliminaries. I think I ended there. Thus, if you have followed my course this far and have even a shred of sympathy for my dilemma, you will understand the shock and distress with which I left the stage after that first preliminary.

I had brought my own knowledge of Music's numbered days to the platform with me. I had thought to augment—with my own new knowledge of Music's fallibility—what the audiences and judges had increasingly seen through me before I retired for three months to the woodshed and learned to see it for myself. But though I had no real notion of what the judges thought after that first preliminary—or for some time into the competition, for that matter—I left the stage with a fear that Music had gained some sort of peculiar hold again upon the audiences. But this was only a freak occurrence, I reasoned. Surely the roar of the crowd was in reaction to some latent old habit of my former, unknowing style of playing. I had served Music inadvertently somehow and had given it one last bit of cover.

But I reconsidered this upon hearing a broadcast of highlights from the preliminaries that night over the radio. I taped that and studied it more than once. It was clear, then, I knew, that any thinking person, that any human mind that had belief in human destiny could hear what this performance proved: that Man is still but in his infancy; that Man has all ahead of him; that the environment of Man's birth has yet to define the limits of his ultimate life. If Music, and thereby the laws of sound and pitch, could be proven to be exhausted, spent, seen to their limits of service and their will to confine the aspirations of Man, then what other Laws might be questioned next? Might not light yield? Might not time? Might not gravity?

Indeed, I floated above this performance, as if in command of all—though I hovered above a planet-sized mass of history, natural law, and tyranny. I was able to float above it and to control my flight in defiance of Natural Laws. I flew ahead; I stopped; I turned though I had nothing to push against and nothing to cite as my source of thrust—save my own infinitely young soul and will. What infinite reaches of silent space, of the galaxies, of the heretofore chiming Universe might we reach even here without ever leaving! This very world might have the differences of worlds seemingly unreachable—where perhaps the Natural Laws are different (where perhaps by happenstance light, sound, time, gravity, have no reign)—if we allow ourselves to realize here, in and on our own world, even one of these differences.

I attack Music, Sound! It falls before me as I prove myself its master. That masterful level defined by my complete command of the physical aptitudes required to render Music unto perfection, by my complete command of recollecting its representations, its heretofore ostensibly moving, ostensibly sublime, ostensibly heart- and mind-bound flames, by my proving Music's complete obviation for the human soul. Others saw this before me—otherwise I would not have been moved to retreat and discover that I was demonstrating this new state through myself—so, thus, I do not serve some maddened purpose for only myself, but for all Man! Music soothes the savage beast! The presumption of this natural law, this Music! To soothe savagery! It is we that should shed and slay this ancient savage, Music. Savage in its tyranny; savage in its stasis; savage, beastly in its clutching and control of meek, unimaginative hearts via a stranglehold through the ears. Savage beast! How can it answer to my civilized indignation?

We can reach these other parts of the Universe, my aunt,

my fellow traveler. I am sure of it. You know, Aunt Elizabeth, that the illusion of legato, of connection from note to note, can be incredibly augmented if one depresses the rightmost pedal on the piano. What happens within the instrument when this is done? The pedal is connected to a vertical rod which raises the dampers that rest atop the strings—letting, then, the strings ring freely without the muting effect that otherwise attends the release of the finger from any given key. Man needs only stamp and kick and flail like a benignly questioning, benignly wild child of the unappointed guardian Universe until he finds the pedals that raise the dampers of his iron strings. This figurative application of a Law of the piano—that its strings will ring unabated for a time when the dampers are raised (and cause other sympathetic notes to vibrate across that iron harp even when they are not struck by a hammer)—also points to Music's and to Nature's weakness. If I kick and depress my secret pedal and show my control over even just one note, just one law, in the Universe—and, then, that note shakes and quivers from the hammer I sent to pound upon it—then what other notes, what other Laws, will shake, as well? Infinite laws will shake in sympathetic vibration. There need not be a pedal depressed by every man of every appropriate discipline to question it, Nature's Law. I depress the pedal and strike one note and send all notes into a quiver. Though that sympathetic shaking may be hard to hear, it happens nevertheless. The very lights in the hall, the very gravity that keeps the patrons in their seats, the very time by which they measure their wait in that old velvet-lined tomb of hall; all shake and quiver when the honest man plays.

But what happened at the latter half of the preliminaries? We drew lots again for the order, but this time I was to play very late in the day. I did not watch—from the hall or from the wings—the performers that preceded me. Instead, I listened for the mild applause that reached me faintly in the distant green room. Matthewson and Krepps, respectively, had notably drawn places in the order right next to each other—and directly preceding my performance time. I was able to mark the ending of Matthewson's performance by distinct roars from the hall. Soon, a representative of the competition came to warn me that my performance time was imminent. She led me to the wings. There I watched as Krepps finished his last piece and met with his roar.

Krepps—having earned, then, the title of second of the two men to watch in the competition—strode off the stage, darkly grinning towards me and enraged with pride in his performance. The applause and the roar continued unabated as he stalked the wings. Time and time again Krepps was sent back to meet the acclaim. Each time he returned he challenged me with an aggressive smile. I only smiled back with a sincere affability—concealing only pity for this prisoner of Music's maximum security cell. Do not such men—or the mass of mankind—realize that there is something of the most pained fool that walks out to meet the ceaseless ovations that from time to time fill the world's concert halls?

Do they not realize that the applause continues in between the performer's marches on and off the stage? Is the applause to bring the performer back? No, it is for the intervals when he is not there! Then, the obsequious masses fete the invisible monster with their baby gestures of musical performances themselves—claps of the hands like pathetic, chubby infants; shouts of bravo like terse, hoarse, singers. Even foolish whistlings attend to praise of the monster Law from time to time. And the ostensibly praised pianists go back and bow to the foolish masses who know not what they clap for—they all merely rattle the bars of the cells of their life sentences.

Helmut Krepps's second preliminary round ovation finally died away, and I looked back to see him settling in one of the wing's chairs to watch my performance. Not far behind him, I could also see Brian Matthewson leaning against the wall, also preparing to watch me play as he dried his brow and took drinks from a water bottle. It was rare to see such decided rivalries so soon in a competition, I felt—and even more rare to meet with such a thunderous and many-peopled reaction from the usually scant audiences of preliminaries. But there was an unusual sense of crowd and event surrounding even the earliest phases of this round. Perhaps it was because of the intense radio and cable television coverage that was being accorded to the contest.

With the intent of playing, as I had played the day before, at a standard beyond that of artful, beyond that of the commonly human, I marched to the gleaming black piano on the stage. I met more than the applause of common reception I had first heard a day earlier as I made my obligatory bow and took my seat on the bench. There was a wave of slightly more excited applause. It was a hopeful applause—somehow made in remembrance of the preceding day and in anticipation of things to come.

I played the first of the two works I was to perform in this round. As was the case for the first day of the preliminaries, the audience was strictly instructed to hold any applause until the conclusion of the final work. I played as I had played the day before—to the heights of technical, interpretative, and ostensibly emotional levels, yet I was altogether free. And when I finished, I felt my hard-earned indifference, could almost see its emptiness before me. I discovered, as the silence grew after the last chord, that I smiled at my freedom, and I noted that I was even free of sweat. Then it came again.

The roar was monstrous. If it was not exactly equal to the previous day's ovation, then it was greater. I had greater difficulty hiding my shock this time. Before falling asleep the previous night—with the sound of my own recording from the radio still reeling in the machine and reeling in my mind—I had still hoped, in a sense almost hopelessly, that the following day would prove the true starting point. The first day was, perhaps, but a last temptation of old Music working its way through an obtuse crowd. Thus I had mustered the courage to return to the stage for the second bout of the preliminaries.

But now there was no deceiving myself. Though I was undeceived about the fallacy of Music, the crowds were in its hold again. They saw nothing in me, nothing through me but Music in all its power. I was utterly invisible to them as I took a shocked bow and nearly stumbled to the wings. I looked to Krepps and Matthewson then. They were both—especially the singularly aggressive Krepps—eyeing me with disdainful, fearful faces, and mildly clapping with their enslaved hands. But these expressions were as nothing to those that I had for them. Though the daylight thinking of my mind knew that these fellows were unreachable due to contentions that were not even among my concerns, I reached out from the twilight of my pure realization, from the ecotone of my new frontier to these two most pianistically able people in the wings. With my eyes I pleaded with them—even pleaded despite their own vain desires to achieve their personal, enslaved and ostensible victories. I looked to Krepps and Matthewson, as if to say—This was not supposed to happen. This isn't supposed to be this way. And though these fools would never understand me, I'll credit them with this—they did look back with a peculiar splinter of recognition in their faces. They looked back, their anger stupefied by incredulity, for on my face was something that could only be read as a sort of apology—sympathy for their thwarted, obtuse, desperate concerns. I do not suspect that they were even Music lovers—but they were intensely trapped by it, as I had been. But neither possessed the insight to know that it would be noble to play to escape. And though their pianistic powers were akin to mine in many measurable ways, they were as dissimilar as could be in the immeasurable ways, the intangible ways. Their playing might be said to reveal something—but these were only of the old, tired, already well-known, cyclic revelations and discoveries. Let us pretend to be surprised, says the world when it hears the Music through them.

I do not remember how many times I was recalled to the stage. I do not even now recall the end of my time in the hall that day or my journey back to the hotel. But I recall awaking from sleep to see if my performance was featured on the highlights show on the radio that evening. It was. Again, I taped it, and I listened over and over to the recording of my second public battle with Music—in which I met it on its highest terms yet walked away a free and indifferent man. But the roars, the roars. What to make of them? Why, now that I could see through myself the tyranny of Music could the public no longer see it through me?

Finally, I shut off the tape, and went walking down the precipitous slopes of town for a very long time until I reached the Bay. With a desperate reconsideration of what the ovation, of what the roar from the audience had meant, I stared out upon the water. Perhaps, I thought, the roar had been for me and not for Music. Perhaps they applauded now my own recognition of what they had begun to see in me before my retirement to the woodshed. Perhaps they leaped from their seats like unshackled slaves, or like men and women feeling a sudden lightening of the Earth's hitherto inexorably constant pull of gravity.

Or perhaps the mass was but a mass fool. But they led me before, if even by accident and chance, to this realization and inescapable truth. I knew that there had to be some who heard what I could hear in myself now. They had to be out there—sitting, even, in considerable numbers on the judges' panel. They, at least, might follow me in the larger cause—and allow me to begin to win the greater battle against Music by allowing me to lose on my terms this smaller battle of the competition.

With less promise of reinforcement than I had hoped for from the public, I climbed the steep slope back to the hotel with increased resolve to impale Music upon the spike of my own indifference, until with the bloody trail of its silenced incorporeal body I could lead Man to his silent, illimitable, open spaces of flux and dawn.

Before returning to my solitary room, I took a detour to the street where the halls for the competition were. There I pondered with wry outward fatigue a new poster that had been put up late in the evening at the box office.

It boasted of "The Three Men to Watch: Krepps, Matthewson, Gourd."

The dates of our remaining competition times were given and the hours for the box office were written below—even though it was already clearly marked everywhere else. Thus, tickets were marketed for a manufactured rivalry. As far as the other two pianists knew—or anyone else—it was, indeed, a three-way rivalry. But there were actually two separate contentions involved. There was indeed a common two-way rivalry between Krepps and Matthewson. And then, too, there was another contest. There was the intention of this Gourd fellow, I thought the poster should say. He wished to mark the rivalry of meek but better-destined billions, living and dead and yet unborn, against the seemingly intractable but secretly vulnerable Laws of Sound.

Piano competitions—competitions and contests in general—invoke and invite those who wish to serve themselves to do so. As contests generally feel they serve the higher cause of the discipline to which they cater, their attraction of those who wish to serve exclusively the self through such forums is rarely a source of disturbance. Music is served, ultimately. Yet they do not suspect what eternal, massive, grandiose selfishness they really serve with their conglomerations of petty, seemingly self-serving but really driven slaves.

If the man or woman who had made up the poster I

looked upon, in the mist of that Pacific midnight, had really wished to announce the most fantastic yet veracious elements of the imminent bouts of the ongoing contest, he or she should have written:

"Charity Concerts Ahead. Pianist to Slay Music and Free the Mind and Heart of Man."

This alternative poster would have gone on to announce that admission was free, and that the hall would be closing for all time after the date of the final performances of the competition. I walked back to my hotel in a light rain. I alone held a ticket in my mind to the unannounced programs that were yet to come.

CHAPTER XI

FOURTH LETTER

My Dear Aunt Elizabeth:

I am on the plane now—on my way back home to California for the last time. Next time I leave California (in July, when my lease is up), it will be to return to my other home of New York. I've been thinking how nice it will be to avail myself of the room you promise me. When Port and I weren't playing with the pianos in the slumber rooms of the old house, it was our next favorite thing to go up to the large, empty rooms on the third floor. Never did I suspect all those years ago that I might have the prospect of living and working in a room up there someday. It will be nice—despite what you may think— to be able to look out from there and down on my old home. Has that house changed much? Do you know the present owners well or at all? If you do, please do not tell them that I ever lived there. I would not want anyone to ever feel funny about the changes they may have made. Advancement, evolution, is the greatest right of all, I think.

But, Aunt Elizabeth, it is hard for me to think of another competition at the moment—even though I know I must go through with just one more. I still have my hopes, my peculiar hopes for my fellow man. I can hardly begin to describe the happenings of last night; they are so odd—so horrible for some.

I will begin by telling you that I did not win the competition, nor did I lose it on my exact terms (the latter, as you may recall, was my deepest hope). Though I am sure you know what strange happenings plagued the end of the San Francisco Competition in December, yesterday's competition in Maryland wasn't quite such a national or international news story for those outside of the business. But I'm sure it will make its rounds of the non-piano-playing and listening world quite soon. Yet, perhaps, what has happened will make the news because of its extra-musical bizarreness. Perhaps after I am off this plane and can see or hear the news again, I'll have an idea of whether you would know or not. For now, I carry on with this letter. I am coming to rely on our quiet, one-way confidences.

Though there are considerable differences in what plagued the ends of both of these last competitions, I dwell on the disastrous, common, misfortune of both. You know something of the judge's strange death in December that altogether halted and dissolved the competition in San Francisco, disbanding the entire enterprise for the year with no result? Surely you have read of what happened in magazines or newspapers? There were features about it on several television entertainment and news programs. Or surely you have heard of it through Port. But if it has escaped your notice despite all those possibilities, then my home in Pauktaug would seem an even more wonderful retreat—if free from the reach and repetition of over-beaten media preoccupations.

But what happened in December? I'll tell you, Aunt Elizabeth. I played with pure power and self-awareness through all the remaining rounds. Why I met with such an increasing perversity of reaction from the public, I could not fathom.

Before my retreat to the woodshed, I had met with increasing, almost profound, distancing from the public that had given me an audience. Then, as you know, I found in myself what they had fearfully begun to hear and see through me. But with a sort of epic contrariness they reverted again to a fearful blindness, a terrifying deafness, when I emerged to confirm what they had discovered. Perhaps Man did not want such a powerful confirmation as I had developed in those three months of retreat. Perhaps what I had shown before my brief retirement was, alone, nearly too much for them. Thus with a shocking, colossal denial, this public applauded, stood, roared for the warden, the aristocracy of Nature that I so deftly exposed for a spent, expended, false ascendancy. They refused to see their master die, thus they cheered my skill, my exceeding Music's requirements of performance as if it were a tribute to Music. This is how much they fear Music—fear losing a master when they have been led so long. Rather than dare credit the challenger, Man, who has exceeded the false law at its game with its rules, they credit tirelessly the originator of the game and the game itself.

Thus I placed hope in those who face Music by profession. For had not the judges an equal, a greater responsibility, for driving me unto my period of self-discovery? There was a period, you will recall, before my three-month hiatus, in which I could not even escape the preliminary rounds of competitions. Those judges saw something, I know.

And as proof to myself that I was not entirely mad, satisfying and gratifying rumors of dissension among the jurors of the San Francisco competition began to circulate among the competitors and the media—especially concerning the celebrated leads that seemed to hold firm for Krepps, Matthewson, and myself. Yet this gratification was soon qualified within me when I learned that the main substance of the rumors contended that the jury schism had as its main theme the debated issue as to whether or not I would ultimately win the competition—take first prize with no contest. I listened with impassioned silence to reports from the cable channels and radio stations that had risked giving almost all their airtime to complete coverage of the competition's events, behind-the-scenes information, and gossipy sub-terfuge. Someone had thought the subject worth an all-out media risk for an experiment—little did the man or woman who made such a proposal know of the impending spectacles that would make that risk pay off so handsomely.

I also monitored the talk of other participants. Of course, I hardly knew how much truth there was in anything I heard. Yet there was a striking consistency in it all. The rumor was this—

Through the chamber round the media and public were matched with the rumored sympathies of the judges—that there was heated battle not for the top three spots, but for the topmost spot by three strikingly powerful and seemingly equally equipped combatants. Then came a phase when the word seemed to be that I was losing ground among the judges, this during and after the semi-final solo round. Of course, this marked a rise, though slight, in my renewed hopes—at least coming from the judges in a literal sense regarding the result of the competition—for a loss on my terms. Then came the concerto and my hopes rose even higher, for the public seemed to study the rumored reactions of the judges. I felt a glimmer of disillusion in their roars for my concerto performance, and I had hopes for them. But I was only fooling myself. Yet I held onto my hopes for the declining approval of the jury and the imagined declining love of the public for Music, which I knew had but monar-chial hold upon them.

Then, two nights before the closing ceremonies—all the concerto performances completed—I returned to my hotel room to rest. Out of habit, I turned on the cable station that was giving its ludicrous-all to the competition. As I was changing my clothes, I turned with interest to the television when I heard the latest speculation. The lead that I had held was not, after all, so precarious as had been rumored before. Now the rumor was that the jury was nearly divided, but with one juror undecided as to where he stood.

Who was this juror? Again, I suspect that even you, Aunt Elizabeth—despite the fact that you protested way back to never follow the careers of any but Port and me—must know the name of Carl Loewe. Surely you know the name now from all that has been written and splattered on television and radio since December? Carl Loewe, born in Brazil in 1912, the pianist's pianist, the composer's pianist? The encyclopedic pianist? The pianist who has embraced all the hackneyed categorizations of which many are grateful even to posses only one: poet of the piano, intellectual pianist, romantic, classicist, wild, spiritual, controlled, pyrotechnic? His discography enormous? His sagely image one of the most coveted presences throughout the world of the piano and music? Surely you know this name. If not, these things I give are the things he represents. As a teenager I admired him very much.

Late that same evening I found myself suddenly a bit hungry and driven, as well, to take my usual night walk. I left my room and went to the elevator. I started to descend to the lobby, but the elevator stopped on the floor just below mine. To my great surprise, Carl Loewe himself shuffled in without looking at me and pressed the button for the lobby. I had met him once before many years ago, but I decided I was not going to initiate anything. He grunted a few of the elderly, geriatric, Old World affected snorts of a venerable artist, and I think he was going to follow these noises with some sort of address to me, when the elevator stopped yet again after descending only a single floor. A large group got on.

This was not just a group of insignificant bystanders, but a group made up of mainly competitors from the competition.

There were two men, two girls, and two other girls not from the competition. I had never seen the latter two before.

I should say, Aunt Elizabeth, that I had sunk nearly every last spare dollar I had into that hotel stay in San Francisco. I could not bear the notion of staying with a host family on that trip, so it was that I found myself a room very near the competition venue—but at a rather extreme rate in a rather old and established hotel. Thus, only a few other competitors were lodged there. Several of the judges were registered there, however.

Helmut Krepps was one of the people to get on the elevator during the second stop of my descent. I think that Krepps was the fellow who had a room two floors below me. I had not run into him in the hotel before—nor would such an encounter have yielded any sort of exchange. His absorption in his quest for personal victory was so extreme that his performances, his chattel servitudes to Music, did not end with his departures from the platform. He was an angry slave—one of the angriest I had ever met, yet too much a coward to attempt (or to even suspect the possibility) of escape. He was filled with an unattractive, unproductive hatred, yet he still lived only so as to please his master. How he did not know, after a time, that his labors served only to augment the powers of an invisible, tyrannical, aged grandee, I cannot say. He reserved his hates for those slaves who seemed to be nearly equal to him—those who stood the best chance of attaining the coveted positions of house slave to the ghostly master.

Krepps seemed to hold an especially ripe hatred for me. I am sure he had no idea I was preaching a secret hope of escape for all. He seemed only to have a consummate disdain for the fact that I was his equal, his better, as a pianist, a rival with no regard for the petty prize he coveted but to which I was closer to capturing. I would have given him the prize had it been in my power.

The group seemed to have come from Krepp's room, and I imagine that they had just been watching the same cable channel I had, for with an unnatural boisterousness, Krepps and another male pianist (both a little drunk) both yelled (and then laughed at the coincidence of their perfect ensemble), "Hey, made up your mind yet?" to Loewe.

Carl Loewe looked up in surprise, and he seemed more alert than I had suspected him to be before we made this stop. The two female pianists were rather meek and quiet, but they were also drunk, so when Loewe grunted "Huh?" to the question from behind his glassy, watery, elderly eyes, both of the girls laughed like poor students trying to stifle themselves in a classroom. The other two girls were just women who Krepps and his companion (the latter knocked out from the semi-finals) had picked up at a club or bar, I imagine. The two female pianists seemed to have only disdain for these other women—for these other girls seemed to represent attractiveness earned without labor. And they gained access to what may have been a little social clique without suffering any of the original club's mutual trials and danger.

The elevator continued its descent in an awkward silence, and no one repeated the question for Carl Loewe. I had stood in the back corner behind Loewe when they entered, so that everyone could fit. At the risk of sounding immodest, Aunt Elizabeth, one of the sultry bar gals sounded me out with her eyes suddenly. I'll confess, taken with those eyes, and with all else that they plugged into, I looked back for a relieved, parenthetical moment in my lonely day, and I smiled to her. Just when we were both about to speak to one another, Krepps looked to the girl and along her eyeline of focus and over Loewe's shoulder and saw me in the corner.

"Bastard," he muttered, when he saw me for the first time, rather loudly because of his drunkenness.

I just gave a mild little smile and a neutral, sibilant, puff-laugh through my nose.

The elevator landed at the lobby then, and as everyone filed out, Loewe looked back to study me. He paused just far enough from the elevator's exit to allow me to get off. It was then that he held my gaze with a knowing, sagely, stare. I stared back with the deepest of hopes, and he seemed to stare back as if he knew, for his look seemed as one of true sympathy for one who has keenly labored in the most unspeakably lonely endeavor.

For a moment I thought he knew. For an instant I was sure he looked at me and smiled a confirmation that he had heard through me, seen through me, when I was on stage, some evident hope of manumission for Man. His old man's eyes seemed bright with the possibilities of a future he had only just lived long enough to see—but he glowed with the brightness of having seen it born even if he could not survive to see it live fully. I cannot tell you the hope this long look gave me.

And then he broke my hope. With a commonness of gesture, the shallowness of which I could not mistake, he reached out his arm and patted me on the shoulder with a true sympathy-negating touch of assurance.

My immediately resurgent thoughts of isolation and melancholy were deferred, however, when Krepps wheeled about in the lobby, just in front of the hotel entrance (his arm around the sultry girl) and pointed to me. He squinted his eyes and shook his head slightly to express real incredulity, fatigue, and exasperation when he called out, "Gourd, you bastard!"

A timidity seized hold of Loewe, and he waddled off not far behind the drunken party and into the street and went his own way. I lingered in the lobby for a moment, a bit self-conscious about passing the front desk just after everyone there had watched me as the subject of the last address, but I was too hungry merely to go straight back up to my room.

After a moment, however, I strode out the front of the

hotel and headed downtown to any restaurant I could find that might be open late. I found a place, and I ate quickly by the window as an intolerably loud, miked jazz pianist pounded away with his trio in the adjacent bar. The only thing of note I can remember from this quick, lonely, dinner was a brief glimpse out the window—just as I was being shown to my table—of the other pianist who was among the "three men to watch."

Brian Matthewson went jogging by, holding a rather respectable pace though he was near the crest of a long ascent. He hardly seemed to be sweating. I start to sweat even if I play a single scale while sitting at the piano. Yet I did not think on him for long, for I knew him to be only a shade more amiable toward me than Krepps. Matthewson was more cautious than Krepps, yet he could be just as vocal in his formal and private complaints when he felt so inclined. He buried his contentious angers in more civil, less-likely-to-be vociferous affairs, however—like this midnight run—when he had no definite remarks to fire off.

During my noisy dinner I weighed one last time the possible meanings of the nebulous look Loewe had given me before Krepps had called out and made Loewe reveal more, and I was forced to conclude that it did not augur well for my cause. I resolved that things were not going my way with the hope for the self-reliant conversion of my fellow Man through inspiration. I was certainly not going to lose the competition on my terms—and I might even win. How could I assure a loss if my fellow man could not acknowledge the truth? There were ways to force a loss, I thought. I could withdraw. But who, then, would know Music mad and not I mad? I could think of no other ways to force my living brothers to see the death in Music. I could not withdraw. I could only proceed—but proceed in fear that I might only be feted as Music's keenest lieutenant after all this arduously wrought investigation and belief in self. I decided to think this round of Man in this splinter of Time asleep, perhaps. Onward to another interval of time—where surely a chance for me (and thus for Man) might emerge again. But that this present sleep could, would, wound me so! These vicious sleepwalkers to carry me to victory in their slavish night-mares. How to inflict something upon them so that they would know that the dream was death they saw in their sleep-walking? I could not let these sleeping dogs lie! Yet how I had kicked at them as I kicked the pedals in my perform-ances. But never did they stir from their sleeping ovations. Usually the soldier, the reformer, is abetted by the sleep of his enemies. But the lazy dreams of submission were as a most bellicose assault upon me. The most raging roar of Music's slaves is followed by their ever-constant soporific lullaby. They had heard nothing—but slept on and on. My most ferocious renderings of perfection could not wake them. The Music overpowers its prisoners into an excite-ment of sleep, a frenzied sleep. I am powerless. But I would not give up.

After my simple dinner I took an aimless walk about the town—found my way down to the bay and then back—and was about to return to my room when I noticed two police cars and an ambulance racing through the otherwise quiet night in the direction of the venues for the competition. I reached the main hall and found the cars and the ambulance parked just by the stage door. I went in myself and met with no opposition. Soon I heard voices coming from far off, but I saw no one until I worked my way around to the front of the hall and entered the orchestra section of the seating.

There, on the distant stage, were two police officers and two paramedics. The two ambulance workers were already putting their coats back on and backing away from the scene. One of the police officers was busy shouting things into the radio that was attached and wired to his uniform. Another stood by and stared with disbelief at the piano that stood where it had stood during the last concerto performance—right at the front and center of the stage's lip. On the piano were some books, and on the music rack was an open score—as if someone had just been practicing on the instrument.

And hammered between the weighty lid and the immovable rim of the piano—right at the meeting point of the giant brass locking pin and its female brass complement along the piano body's inner edge—was Loewe's crushed skull, his head turned on its side. And, of course, there was Loewe's lifeless body, as well—depending down from this dullest of guillotine blades, still attached, but hanging as limp and withered as a single sheet of music manuscript paper that had been rotted from damp and neglect and stillness.

CHAPTER XII

FIFTH LETTER

Dear Aunt Elizabeth:

It is nice to be home here in Los Angeles one more time—
glad to be here knowing that I won't have to stay here much
longer. I hated doing it, but I saved just enough money by
skipping my usual indulgence of a hotel room in Maryland
to help get me through the end of May, through June and
July here, and through my move at the end of July. And I
have just enough savings to complement that. I'm going to
call tomorrow and make a reservation for the shipment of my
piano. I'll have it trucked over a day or two before my antic-
ipated arrival in the beginning of August or the end of July.

I feel compelled to keep scribbling to you, Aunt Elizabeth, mainly because I feel that I owe you a great deal of
catching-up since you have been kind enough to invite me to
return into my old world on a daily basis. I am trying to
school myself into answering to other human beings again
with these descriptions of my late musings and travels. I do
not mean that you will find me wild and uncouth in basic
manner. I deal with many about petty things with perfect
pleasantness every day. No, I mean that I have no one—no

one at all right now—to whom I feel compelled to explain my mind. I like to think people who live under the same roof should feel that obligation. At the risk of sounding too forward, I really mean to say that I do not recall what it is like to talk with you. I do not recall what you are like, really. Though I hope to fall in well with Port as we did when we were still only boys, I really long at this point for a mature female confidence. If you've been worried about having to lay down ground rules in the house for yet a second young man and his women friends, I can say now that I am out of that arena for a time. All my relationships with women, since Aunt Maryland passed on, have led inexorably to romances, brief and torrid, or torrid and dragging, and I long for some gender-polarized conversation that does not lead to such inevitabilities. Perhaps I venture too much. Forgive me, I am still agitated from the plane trip yesterday—and the colossal surprise of the last day of the competition two days ago.

But let me return to San Francisco once more. What happened in Maryland will seem all the more odd if I review what happened upstate in December just a little more.

After I went into the auditorium and saw Carl Loewe trapped in his polished black death vice, I wandered down through the orchestra seating to the edge of the stage in shock. There was a policeman there talking on his radio. He stopped his conversation when he saw me and asked me who I was and how I had gotten into the hall. I told him that I was a competitor and that I had followed the cars there and had walked right in through the side stage door. The officer yelled to his companion to make sure that all the doors were locked and to see that I was shown out of the building.

The next day (the day before the closing ceremonies were supposed to be held), I slept late and then watched the competition cable station to hear the news. (I found news on all the local stations that day, as well, however.) Loewe had gone to the hall to practice. He and another judge were supposed to have shared a recital venue for an informal concert the night before the competition's last day, and he had just started to use (for his own private rehearsal) the instrument in the main hall that was still in position from the last performance of the concerto round.

What brought about the gruesome accident? Somewhere into his rehearsal, it is believed that Loewe decided to raise the piano's lid to its fully open position. He rose from the bench, and being somewhat feeble in strength, it is imagined he had something of a struggle raising the lid, and it is believed he never placed the stick in the little hole or fixture that keeps it securely in place. With the stick in such a precarious position, it is then believed that Loewe struck the stick (after stumbling forward a bit, or after reaching into the piano to inspect its interior), causing the stick to slide down and fall—and allowing the lid to come plummeting down with all of its massive weight. Loewe must have tried to pull himself back with a quick reaction, but the fall still caught his head. It is believed to have killed him instantly, for there was no evident sign of struggle or effort to free himself. The blow to the head was said to have been enormous. His skull was cracked severely, and there was terrible bleeding. In addition to all this, the large brass pin that helps hold the lid in place when the instrument is closed was said to have pierced or severely indented his skull above the right ear.

The brutal, swift, death meted out for Loewe by gravity and chance and elderly human weakness left little mark on the piano, it was later noted. Save for a relatively minor scuff on the inside of the lid, from the stick being pushed and scraped against it during the fall, the piano bore no permanent mark of its part in this tragedy. There was a large amount of blood that trickled down the outer right side of the instrument, but it was removed rather easily, and hardly any bleeding made its way into the heart of the piano.

All this was noted because next to Loewe's lifetime passion for music and the literature of the piano, was a passion for instruments themselves. He had been an instrument collector before he had fallen on a streak of hard times because of the protacted illness of his wife. He sold nearly all he had for her care. It was concluded, that even in death, Loewe would have been pleased to have left any fine instrument he had played upon in no worse shape than that in which he had found it.

Now, Aunt Elizabeth, I am not versed well enough in the history of piano competitions to say whether what happened next had any precedent. But surely it was a nearly unique occurrence. While the media delved into an examination of the death of Loewe, two main issues surfaced. The first had to do with pianos and their makers themselves. Though I— and I am sure any other pianist who has spent time around grand pianos—have thought of the remote danger posed by the slight possibility of a piano's lid falling over in some bizarre way upon the head or hands, I never thought that the piano makers were in any way liable for this slight risk posed by the inherent shape of the traditional grand piano. But, to my amazement, a cry went up calling for the piano companies to answer for what was being called a flaw in historical design. Discussion of such concerns began to fill the television stations as much as talk directly related to the death of Carl Loewe.

The second issue was that of the state of Carl Loewe's widow. As quickly assembled biographies appeared on the local and regional cable television stations, more and more attention was given to the fact that the terminally ill wife of the long celebrated twentieth-century master of the piano was left with hardly a single resource with which to suffer the last months of her life.

What was announced at the closing ceremonies came as a surprise to everyone, even myself. One of the jurors read a statement after nearly a half-hour's worth of thanks were offered and minor speeches were read by others. After an interminable biographical essay, the new presiding member of the jury offered this resolution to the competition in San Francisco:

"Thus, we cannot guess what Carl Loewe's last decision of adjudication would have been. We will not presume to make that decision for him. As we all know, it is not uncommon for the great competitions of the world to refrain from granting specific prizes when it is felt that no performers have come forth to properly claim them with their performances. But we have seen many prize-winning performances here, and though we have reason to suspect that the remaining jurors could delegate the awards in a fair and satisfactory manner, we are going to acknowledge for a time that we cannot go on without Carl Loewe. For, indeed, in most respects we cannot go on without this, this highest-ranking artist of the twentieth-century. Competitions are for the fostering of young talent. Carl Loewe, despite the many factors that are constantly cited in criticism of the modern piano competition, still believed that we could make them work. Let it not be said, then, that this competition forgot to observe the memory of established talent (and its families) when an unusual and tragic circumstance has put forth a new and critical challenge to the music making community. Therefore, our sponsors and our treasurers are going to waive the awarding of prizes this year in favor of bestowing security on the widow of Carl Loewe. Let it be said that the spirit of the piano will carry her peacefully through her final illness, even in the absence of one of its greatest artists, her husband, Carl Loewe."

At the reception afterward, I noted that the tenor of this announcement and decision was so incontrovertible in its public correctness that it paralyzed those who would have complained under any other circumstances. I watched in amusement as Brian Matthewson made some quick nervous rounds of the tables—then was caught several times as he tried to leave unnoticed. Helmut Krepps went from table to table and, ever so just perceptibly, muttered obscenities under his highly-accented breath.

Yet I should be sparing in my observations of others at that point. I left the reception as soon as I could, and the next morning saw me driving back to Los Angeles—all that time unsure how much my distraction must be showing. The directors of the competition had decided merely to take the money that had been intended to support one aspect of moribund life and direct it to another, though smaller, thing that is slated for death. I had entered the competition with such hopes. Now there was no loss on my terms, their terms, or any terms, just nothing—and I was not sure how I felt about it.

CHAPTER XIII

SIXTH LETTER

My dear Aunt Elizabeth:

I'll send a note tomorrow or in a few days giving the details, but I've made arrangements to have my piano shipped east in the last days of July. I am going to get rid of nearly everything I have here, pile the rest into my car and drive it into the ground in a cross-country trip home. I look forward to it. I've planned my finances pretty well. I should have enough for the trip and for any unexpected little detours that may happen along the way.

Surely you have heard by now what happened in Maryland three or fours day ago? I don't consider my San Francisco story over, really, until I tell what has just happened this month in Maryland.

What happened in Maryland? Almost precisely what happened in San Francisco—with a horrible coincidence at the end to make the similarities uncanny, almost touched with supernatural likeness. But there were differences.

I need not summarize the early rounds, Aunt Elizabeth. I have given up hope for the time being that the common crowd, the common concertgoer will ever show again the accord and mighty vision it did before I possessed accord and vision within myself. Thus I will not tell you how through all aspects of all the rounds I did nothing but infallibly show the truth about fallible Music. But the public did nothing but cover the eyes of its soul and conscience and then stood and roared. There was never even a moment when the public seemed to abate its unwanted support of me in Maryland.

But there came, through the channel of traditional gossip, word that the jury was unsettled about my fate in the semi-final round. This competition had only five judges, and they functioned on a strict system that there had to be unanimity among them as to which players would be voted past the semi-finals. (The finals would be judged by majority.) But there was word that two judges were quite up in arms about what they would decide in the case of one pianist—and I heard it rumored that the one pianist in question was myself.

You must have heard what happened. But I will continue. And I will forego expressions of my amazement at the odds that must stand against such tragic events occurring in such close succession.

Though I was rumored to be finished as of the semi-finals, I went over to the practice facilities on the night preceding the announcement of the finalists. The practice rooms were part of a university music school that was adjacent to the forums for the competition, and the building was busy despite the late hour of the day. I think it was nearly nine-thirty when I began to practice my concerto—practicing just in case the rumors and Man should fail me.

At a little past ten, I went out into the hall for water, and I could not help noticing a group of pianists and students huddled about a locked doorway that led to the university's main hall. I asked what the great interest was, and they hissed at me to be quiet. Soon it was evident that all were listening to a rather heated argument between a pair of contending judges. I smiled at the devotion of this crowd to their eaves-dropping, for it was very hard to make out anything but vague shouting, even if one pressed their ears to the miniscule space between the door and its jamb.

I left the spying group to their labors after only a few minutes and took a turn about the practice room halls. Nearly all the rooms were filled. But at this point in the contest some of the rooms reserved for competing pianists were empty—due to the attrition of combat. A few of the reserved rooms boasted faces that were new to me as of this competition. The competition circuit and the world of the piano are always ready with new legions to take the places of those who fall away—fall away either finally too old by the rules of the competitions or finally too sick at heart to continue. I, myself, Aunt Elizabeth, have only just about two more years in which I can register for most competitions. But as I have observed before, I am going to apply all my force of will and hope so that this competition in New York might be the last.

Yet some of the faces in the practice rooms were familiar. Both Krepps and Matthewson pounded away at their concertos as I passed by their rooms. Krepps was too intent on his work to notice me as I lingered outside of his window. He had his eyes closed as he repeated a slow passage with some intermittent, high-register, filigree. Moving along from room to room, I eventually came across Matthewson, as well. Taking a pause and looking out toward the window just as I passed, our eyes met, and I smiled. But he just wiped his brow and turned with mild indifference back to a relentless drill for his left hand.

Perhaps because of the memory of the San Francisco competition in December, the competition box office and the press hesitated to resuscitate any pronounced rivalries between particular competitors. However, there was still a sense, even from the start in Maryland, that the race of Krepps, Matthewson, and Gourd would be close. There were

two Asian girls who were also extremely powerful and celebrated throughout the course of the contest—so there was a
latent sense of five main figures to watch in this instance.
The lightening of an atmosphere that would foster great personal antagonisms and contentions led to an ostensibly more
affable environment in this Maryland competition.

Both of the Asian girls I just mentioned were among the
group of eavesdroppers, and a sense of amiable hilarity
attended their participation in the light-hearted spying that
was going on outside the main hall's locked entrance.

I returned to my work, but at midnight I left my room
again—rather groggy after having let myself put my head
down and fall asleep on the closed keyboard, perhaps for as
much as a half-hour. Yet upon entering the hall and rubbing
the sleep from my eyes, I felt for a time—and I really mean
this—that I might still be in some sort of dream. Here was the
setting of the Maryland competition before me—but a twisted
intimation of the events leading up to the gruesome finale of
San Francisco seemed to be playing out again on that stage.

University police were running down the hallway toward
the doors to the main hall. I, and other pianists drawn into
the hall by the din, followed them and various late-night
school custodial workers on to the wings of the stage. The
massive hall was still lighted, and the many pianos—set there
for selection by the competitors for the forthcoming concerto
rounds—were sitting all about the concert platform, closed
and shiny and portentous. As I made my way out among the
pianos to the center and front of the stage—where a small
group of university police was gathering and looking down to
the front row of the orchestra, to where the judges' tables had
been placed—I noticed one old custodial worker holding
another who was enrapt in sobs and tears. The old crier could
not be consoled, and she looked from time to time to the edge
of the stage where all the university police were now standing
and peering down to some transfixing sight.

I and another pianist whom I did not know were the only onlookers who got close enough to the scene to see what was below the stage before the university police led all bystanders out of the auditorium.

As I observed before, the stage—which was infamous for its slight downhill tilt toward the audience—was filled with pianos. One of the competition's sponsors had been exceedingly generous this year and had loaned an unprecedented number of instruments for the competitors' selection and for the other recital and concert festivities offered by the competition. There had been ten concert grand pianos assembled for use in this large hall. But only nine were on the stage. The missing piano could be seen lying at the foot of the stage—in remarkably good condition, it seemed, considering the fall. It had crushed a full table and chairs from the long row set out for the judges. Apparently its wheels had not been locked, and it had suddenly crept ever so slowly to the end of the slightly inclined stage and had fallen a full four or five feet to the top of the table. Its legs were broken, but the piano still lay in an otherwise flat and normal position. From below its edges protruded bits of its broken legs, fragments of the table and chairs, and scattered papers and collections of musical scores. Yet the dryness of this mess was soon tainted by evident streams of blood that followed the counter-pitch of the house floor. And if one looked long enough, one could see the leg of one man and both legs of another extending from underneath the crushing combination of wood and metal. Rather like some specialized animals, rather like sea stars of the deep, the piano upon suffering the loss of its limbs, appeared to be growing new ones—in defiance of the most violent vicissitude, and in a thieving ascendancy over its superior but fragile and finite-limbed competitor, Man.

CHAPTER XIV

SEVENTH LETTER

Dear Aunt Elizabeth:

I feel foolish somehow, now, for having plagued you with so much so soon—without our even readjusting to the routines of common intimacy yet. Will you please—and I ask this very seriously—destroy all that I have written to you? It embarrasses me. Why? Because you are not a real letter writer yourself, it seems, and when one does not receive answers as a letter writer one begins to suspect that they are burdening another with requests of discussions that the other is not accustomed to or willing to give. Let's start again upon my return. Again, I ask you to please get rid of my last six or seven letters—all of them, that is. This request itself may seem like another eccentric importunity. But I really beg you to do it, so that I can start with some peace of mind when I arrive in New York in August—can start with only the experiences that we share together.

I don't want you to feel burdened by my strange expectations for the competition this fall. What I hope for cannot perhaps be realized. Please destroy those letters. I do not yet

193

know what the ultimate outcome of the competition in Maryland was. I left before the finals commenced, as I was not advanced to them. I know that Matthewson and Krepps were advanced. But I don't know how the finals have gone or how they may still be going. I only know that there was an assembly on the morning after the terrible accident in Maryland.

My hopes were not met by what was said at this assembly, of course. There had been only a slight glimmer that my hopes were going to be met even before the accident, but I never gave up feeling that I might have a chance of losing on my terms. There had been a sort of chance that this might occur in Maryland—what with the rumors that there was dissension in the jury so early. I was indeed voted out of the competition as of the semi-finals. The assembly on the morning after the great accident only announced the plan of a memorial service to be sponsored by the competition and the intention of the competition to believe that the deceased jurors would have wished that the competition continue, the world of the piano continue, Music and the music of young people continue despite their deaths—and despite the precedent set by the events and the consequences of the competition in December. The finalists were announced and the assembly disbanded. The competition directors had opted to abide by the new majority, and I was free to go, for the new majority had no qualms about their selections. Thus the rumors were true about the undecided judges, I suppose—for since it was rumored that there were still those who wanted me to advance after the semi-finals were complete, support for my advancement seemed to vanish instantly with the death of these two unfortunate judges.

My hopes were not met by this competition. But my hopes have been raised, for despite the maudlin aftershocks of the deaths of two of their own, the jury, the remaining majority held firm—and I was compelled to walk away in mid-battle as the indisputably strongest man. They knew something; they saw something; they heard something, this majority. And they would not let the fear of ritual and mass sentiment stop them from obeying their fear of something infinitely more promising, potent, yet unsettling. But, alas, they were driven more by a realization that fostered fear than a realization that prompted reform. But I was given hope by this, for they remained strong, and thus, Aunt Elizabeth, they were *for* me, if you take my meaning.

CHAPTER XV

DEATH

After I finished reading Boston's last letter, it must have been nearly two-thirty in the morning. I suddenly realized that I had been standing, leaning against my closed piano the entire time I had been reading his letters. My cousin had guessed correctly that his long narratives and musings had begun to fall— or had always fallen, perhaps—on someone (my Aunt Elizabeth) not in direct sympathy with him. But I do not mean to say that she was against him; she was merely too indifferent and too lazy and too sweetly cloudy to follow such efforts as my cousin was willing to make. She had ignored his plea for his letters to be destroyed as she had not even opened the last letters. She must have placed them in her box for his letters when they came and then forgot about them as Boston's short, practical notes began to arrive. There were about three or four of these notes in the box—giving terse details and updates concerning his move back to New York. And there was one more letter.

As always, my sense of identification with Boston was diminished and confused when I thought of the intense pianistic power that supported the angles of his storytelling and provided the springboard for his speculations. And I felt too tired to begin to imagine what Boston might mean exactly by his stories of last December and last May. I slowly began to put the letters into their respective envelopes when I looked up and out the window. The room that I suspected was still Lana's was aglow with lamplight. And at that very same moment the phone rang. With excited, foolish, hope I lunged around the end of the piano and reached for the extension that was on the window seat. I had been standing so long, so perfectly transfixed in one position by Boston's cryptic narrative, that my legs nearly gave way when I took my first step. But without too much of a crash, I made it to the phone before it was all the way through its second ring.

"Port?"

"Yeah?" I said with eagerness and friendliness—as if it were quite common for one to find me awake at that hour.

"It's Lana. I wasn't wrong, then! It was you standing there. It looked like you were writing for the longest time. But I couldn't understand what I was seeing exactly. You looked too high up to be sitting at a desk."

"I've been reading some of—I mean I was reading while leaning against the top of the piano."

"Oh, I'm glad I'm right! I'd look from time to time, and your silhouette just would not move. So after awhile I thought I wasn't really seeing what I thought. Then I thought I saw you move just now."

"No, I'm glad you called, Lana."

"You are?" she laughed. "Glad that I'm calling your house like some psycho-girl going on three in the morning? Glad that I probably almost woke your aunt? And probably even the dead down on the first floor of your house?"

"Yes."

"Thank you for tonight, Port," she began, and I could hear her smile across the line, and she continued with a warm, sleepy, remembering talk that was magnificent to me. It was not magnificent to me for what it recalled—for in hearing it I could tell that I remembered the past with greater clarity than she—but magnificent for the low, whispered tone of it. It ushered in an intimacy, and a contented, secure, yet sultry repetition like a vamp from an old popular song.

For a very long time, perhaps as long as an hour, Lana and I spoke in the night like neighboring playmates or innocent sweethearts, children speaking from house to house with toy telephones of cups and string—and spoke with a connection of spirit that was nearly as tenuous.

"When did we last see each other, Port? I mean before today—before yesterday, now, I mean."

"The funeral of my Aunt Maryland and Uncle William. The last day of April of our senior year," I said.

"Then?"

"Well, it was the last time I knew that I'd get to see you in some sort of sure way. I wasn't brave enough then to initiate anything on my own. Couldn't ask you to the prom or anything like that."

"Oh, God, the prom!" Lana moaned.

"Of course I saw you from afar every day at school until the end. And I had glimpses of you nearly every day that summer until you left just a little before me for college. You left only a day after that Denise girl left. But she was living in her own house across town by then."

"Oh, God! Denise Wick! I forgot about her. Why did you have to remind me of her?"

"I hope you don't think this is too terrible of me, Lana, but I actually looked forward to that funeral because I knew you'd be there and at the reception."

"Oh, my God! So did I! But I thought you might think it was some kind of desecration if I mentioned that—or if I mentioned it first. But before I forget, while you have me remembering it, I told Denise that she didn't have to go to that—shouldn't go to that funeral. I mean, she, like, broke up with your cousin and never mentioned him again until that funeral came up. And why she then thought it was 'the right thing to do' seemed so dumb to me."

"Well, I can tell you it didn't matter. He told me literally everything at that point in our lives, and he didn't mention it."

Lana then lapsed into a long narrative of what she could remember of that day. It was interesting to me as I had not thought of the whole sequence of events in nearly a decade. Her story was interspersed with allusions to the constancy of the appearance of our home street—and when she would say such things, I could see her pull back her blind a bit and look out. She also made asides alluding to her more-or-less lost twelve years since high school. It was not altogether clear to me what was the main substance of her loss, but at times it seemed to lean toward the flattering possibility that she was hinting at twelve lost years of connection to me. But I was neither bold nor sure enough of myself to press this, and so she lapsed into her memories of the night of the double funeral—held in the main house for my Aunt Maryland and Uncle William.

I knew more than Lana, of course—not only because I was in the family circle, but, again, simply because I was learning that my memory was stronger than the beautiful Miss Paw's.

Late in April of my last year of high school, late on a Saturday night, Boston was playing for me in the living room of his old home. This night became uncommon when our Aunt Maryland entered the room just as Boston was about to begin the final movement of his most recently-learned sonata. She was holding a heavy basket of laundry.

"You both sound really beautiful tonight, boys. I know the windows aren't open yet and that no one else can really hear us here. But would you both be too angry if I said that just for once

I would really be grateful for quiet—for just a little pause in our life, the endless concert? It isn't your playing that bothers me. I just want to hear the quiet."

"Sure, Aunt Maryland," we both said.

"Can I just finish the last movement for Port?" added Boston suddenly.

"Okay. I'll be downstairs putting this heap into the machine for a little while anyway."

"I'll be quick about it, Aunt Maryland," said Boston, and he started to play even before our aunt had gotten halfway down the basement steps.

My cousin played, as always—but somehow, then, even beyond his always—with a steely perfection that awed me. As the movement drove on and on—the mighty team whipped into greater speeds and power by Boston's confident driving—I thought twice that I heard what sounded rather like a cat moaning in the distance. Not a cat's meow or its hiss—or the wiry squeal that they give out if one steps inadvertently upon their tails. This was as the low, almost growl-like, hollow, sustained sounding that a cat can make when it is standing ground against another cat. But then came a lull in the piece, and I heard nothing outside of the music besides Boston's pumping of the piano's damper pedal.

As my cousin swirled the work to its end, the piano seemed compliant, willing to abet him by seeming passive so that Boston could serve it to perfection. The sound roared from the piano, but Boston was silent. Uncle William suddenly passed through the room when the piece was no more than a minute from its conclusion. My uncle jogged down the stairs to the basement, and my attention then returned to Boston until the piece came to an end.

When the last chord was no longer the loudest thing in the house, a sound that had commenced before the music's final chord finished out its separate call. It was Uncle William's voice, and it sounded like he said, "—ton!" Then both Boston and I listened in the full silence until we heard the full call without the music in the way: "Boston!"

When we reached the basement, we found Uncle William kneeling over Aunt Maryland's lifeless body. Soon Boston and I were both back upstairs calling for an ambulance. When we returned to the basement, Aunt Maryland still lay in silence, flat on the cold concrete—but Uncle William was slumped over the basket of laundry.

The ambulance arrived with speed and took both Uncle William and Aunt Maryland to Huntington hospital. Boston went with them, but neither my aunt nor my uncle were ever permanently resuscitated in the basement, in the ambulance, or at the hospital. My Aunt Maryland died of a stroke, and my Uncle William died of a sort of massive, sympathetic heart attack.

Lana said she remembered seeing the ambulance, and she remembered seeing me walk back to the main house after it had left.

She remembered the basic details of the viewings and funerals that followed. But I remembered more. On the night of the first viewing, Aunt Elizabeth and Uncle Harry had both my late aunt and uncle arranged in open caskets in the south slumber room. Their caskets were aligned against the east wall, one of the windows to the woods behind the main house clearly visible between the two large wooden boxes. Along the south wall, my uncle had pushed the new grand piano, with its lid propped all the way up— thus the two caskets and the piano formed a sort of semicircle or unbroken line against these two perpendicular walls.

Aunt Elizabeth had asked Boston if he wanted to speak at the funeral. A number of men from the town (friends, clients, fellow attorneys) were going to speak about these two fallen Gourds. Boston said he really did not want to speak. Anticipating her next request before it came, Boston also told her that he did not wish to play the piano at the service either.

More than anything else about this time and about this doubly weighted and doubly intimate funeral, the nature of Boston's initial reluctance to play—or in any way make himself pronouncedly seen at his guardians' funeral—must be noted. Granted, on the night of their deaths, and three of the four days preceding the funeral, Boston was aggrieved. But even on the first night he never appeared or gave evidence that even internally he was truly distraught. Certainly, there were a few mild tears when we took our midnight walk through the woods and to the beach after he returned from the hospital. Yet after we parted that night (he declined my aunt's insistence that he stay with us), I walked a little bit longer. When I returned to the street from walking in town, I could hear Boston working away quite cleanly and freely at the piano—even taking quiet pauses to make adjustments in subtle things, and I could see his silhouette through the blinds as he leaned forward, pencil in hand, to make small notations in his score. Before I went back to the main house for the final time that night, I could not help but feel that Boston's already preternatural abilities sounded yet still more powerful than before—as if yet another well of refinement atop refinement and infallibility had met with a sort of shocking and grand manumission.

I put this out of my mind—for Boston's nearly supernatural advancements at his instrument hardly seemed supernatural to me at that point anymore—and I retired for the night. It was during the afternoon of the next day, when Boston came over after my Uncle Harry brought the bodies of Aunt Maryland and Uncle William into the basement, that I felt I noticed what was so odd about my cousin during this interval and during all that time that followed, until the end of the school year and his departure for college, really: my cousin, who practiced relentlessly during those last months he spent in New York, did not seem to be consulting the piano and his inscrutable metaphoric connection with its matter and suggestiveness for any kind of compensation or support

202

through grief. It was as if he was going to it now with the last of some never-to-be articulated handicap dispensed with for all time. He was at liberty to be with something that had called to him so relentlessly for untold numbers of years, and there was then nothing to impede his response. He kept no curfew for himself now, and he was with that ineffable something—whether it was the piano or what was somehow in the piano or whether it was music or what was somehow in music—with that mysterious master for all the time that his health would now allow.

Uncle Harry disappeared with his assistants down into the basement with the two bodies. Of course, he did not ask Boston and me to help in any way on this occasion. Instead, my Aunt Elizabeth called us upstairs and we three had tea and coffee and rolls together. It was then that I could tell that whatever there had been of grief in Boston—the manifest kind, at least—had passed. He agreed, somewhat reluctantly, to watch a movie with my aunt and me after dinner. Then my aunt refused to let him sleep back at the old house any longer. She made up a room for him, and he consented to bide his remaining days in New York with us in the main house. But even on that night, he went back to the old house after the movie and practiced early into the morning—slipping back to the main house for sleep and then out for school in the morning with little sign of wear upon his spirits.

On the second day of this new routine I would say that Boston's grief—both internal and external—had been altogether ameliorated by his consultation with his mysterious bonds, and then obviated by the joys with which he now contemplated his new liberties. I do not mean that he was not mindful of his duties. Nor do I mean that he could not be drawn into long, lachrymose episodes with my Aunt Elizabeth. No, I mean that there was a discreet part of him so overwhelmed—not by the universe's demonstration of fragility and flux because of this loss, but by some hidden testament of its security and (for him) benign stasis—that

I could tell he was more concerned about giving others concern because of his extreme equanimity than with any other consideration for himself. Thus, I could see him tempering himself, like a man trying to conceal good fortune in the face of another's time of loss—notwithstanding that he was the man most directly influenced by the loss. Again, his love for Aunt Maryland and Uncle William was real and as unbounded as any other full-hearted son's. He was struggling with an opposite, coincidental joy that seemed not unexpected to him—but perhaps unexpected in the extent of its power.

On the third day of this new routine—the day of the first viewing—Boston was quite himself. But he kept this to himself, so to speak, and he continued to practice. On the eve of the funeral, Aunt Elizabeth and Uncle Harry took him into the office, for he was not quite able to hide his equanimity altogether from them. Thus, they asked him a second time if he would be willing to play the piano at the service. They thought playing would be a fitting gesture, if he still preferred not to speak. I did not hear the exchange between my aunt, uncle, and cousin, but I could see them conversing with ease and speed behind the milky glass of the office door, and they soon emerged with the unconcealed equanimity of my cousin and his easy readiness to participate. They had not had to urge him at all.

On the night before the funeral, Boston and I took our usual walk through the woods, across the old baseball diamond, and down to the Sound. I continued to study his good spirits, which seemed to emerge naturally from his almost supernatural ability to improve in the area of his calling. Therefore, thinking that I too would be filled more with an affection for the promise of Nature and experience than with resentment for its random blows if I too could so increasingly tap into the powers of sound, I gave little more thought to Boston's good spirits—for in addition to my respect for his skills (which would seem a fit compensation for anyone's griefs), I saw enough fitful moments of true melancholy and endearingly rightful nostalgia to distract me on that night walk, and during the last months before Boston and I parted ways for good when we both left for school in late summer.

The morning funeral was very crowded. Not only did my aunt and uncle have the family double funeral in progress in the south slumber room, but there was the start of a new viewing going on in the north room, as well. The funeral service was particularly crowded because of Uncle William's many connections with innumerable families and businesses of Long Island. Aunt Maryland was responsible for only a small part of the group, I think. And she had few, if any, relatives from her side of the family still living.

I remember listening to eulogies from many men and women of Pauktaug and Long Island, and I remember admiring Lana and Denise in dresses that seemed as flattering to them and as fascinating to me as if this had not been a melancholy party for which they had to dress. Of course, I recall thinking myself somewhat shameful for looking at Lana for the better part of the service. My grief for Uncle William and Aunt Maryland would come in fitful, unexpected bursts, not then but ever after—and come in poignant, finely shaped vignettes, in self-composed, silently recited short stories that I would conjure during pretty nights when there would be something suggestive from the rain or the cold. Then I would conjure powerful, imagined, understated tales of them, based on real images—of when I saw them from afar with affectionate indifference, and did not count the hours, and saw one of them kneel down before their house, pick up a stray leaf, perhaps, and rise to their front porch in the silence created by the street's length.

I looked at Lana's living beauty (and Denise's), and then I felt remorse and confusion over my resentment of everything about the clergyman. And then Boston made his way to the piano and began, as the minister had said he would, to play for the memory of the man and woman who had made him their son.

I do not know whether I knew as much then—but it was clear to me that Boston did not play for the memory of any pair of mortal souls, for any human life. He played for something immortal. But I could not say precisely what it was, not then—when I was eighteen—or years later, even, when I was talking to Lana on the phone. Again, his playing was no monument to an individual or individuals. It was not a glorification of self, even—and yet it was, but it was not the self that the ego loves. He seemed to be playing in service of something, with the kind of joy that only the most obsequious of slaves can feel when his powers, his great powers, are sure to be seen by his master and please him or it. This master? Who was this? I do not mean any sort of personifiable god or spirit. It was as some sort of natural law. It was as if Boston played only to show that his person, his mind, his heart, could be used to such a high level, to such an as-yet unapproached summit using only mortal hands and mind, and yet still only serve that law of nature—because Boston used *it* (that law) in his efforts to exceed its boundaries. The closer he came to surpassing the range of this law by his ever-increasing powers, the more he seemed to confirm still its invincibility. Yet he was still young enough at that time to enjoy the benefits of his loyal services.

Placed next to my Uncle Harry's slavish attempts to pitifully preserve the bodies of two human beings for a brief period, Boston's labors before his own, long, coffin-like box—it filled with the bones of trees and elephants—was electrifying. He pronounced benedictions over that strange law, strange immortality, giving it power that I, perhaps no one, had yet seen to such an extent in the history of the world—granting all to it, then, without yet hope of ascendancy or compensation. And that law just took and took and breathed wider than it had ever breathed. It was as if gravity had discovered its hold to be much more than it had ever expected, and even bits of dust and light came racing down to it like stones. It was as if gravity had found a man who fell harder and faster than all before him—and could lead innumerable others, a race, to fall in the same way—yet that man, for the time being was happy to fall harder and faster and be nothing but a sort of splattered, performing monkey, crashing upon the invisible surface of this mysterious law's face time and time again.

It was in this spirit that Boston played and practiced the piano until the time he left Pauktaug—and I believe that it was in this spirit that he sprinted through his life until he reached the times of which he wrote about to my Aunt Elizabeth in his letters.

The freedom that he gained from the deaths of his guardians grew until it freed him from his other aunt and uncle, as well—and me. Thus, when Boston left Pauktaug, his communications quickly dissolved and then altogether vanished, and it was if I had no cousin at all. His victorious competitions and concerts meant less and less to us when we heard no more from him, and soon it was almost as much a surprise to me as to anyone else when they learned that the unstoppable Boston Gourd was the childhood best friend and cousin of Portsmouth Gourd, of Pauktaug Village, Long Island.

Boston finished his piece. He had not selected a quiet work. He played a relentless, fast, long, pyrotechnical etude of the highest difficulty—something that he had learned over the preceding two nights. He played it to perfection (in such a way that I can say I have never heard another, live or on record, even touch its infallibility of rendering). The mourners became an audience, and there almost seemed an urge to fall off the precipice of the silence he left behind after the closing of his piece with an uproar of applause—with a roar for this new level of ostensibly continuing life.

Little did anyone there know, however, not even Boston, that one day he would feel that his was the coffin with the most death within it—that behind, soaked in embalming fluids and caked with powders and chemicals, my Aunt Maryland lived on latently, would live on in my mind and in Boston's as symbol of the life that had once questioned the worth of even the highest of known gifts for one of the world's truly speculative boys. She had thought that maybe she had wanted more for her boy, her speculator—her perhaps bastard, wandering, mad but loving and good little questioner. Perhaps there should be more for this baby and boy. Perhaps there should be more for Man. Yet even she relented to the good, to the celebrated and approved rattle in the end.

So it was that when Boston was playing, most of the men and women who were over in the north slumber room to observe the small freedom won by some other stranger that my Uncle Harry had recently prepared, were drawn to the doorway of the south slumber room—and there they listened at the door that was slightly ajar, like meek, pitiful house slaves listening to the Master praise a chattel foreman for a new record yield, a new bumper crop.

CHAPTER XVI

RETURN

I woke early the morning after the night of the Silver concert— very much in love with Lana Paw. At the end of our long after midnight telephone talk, we agreed to a Friday night date. Only my age gave me enough discipline to defer proposing a sooner second meeting. I had my first day of school the next day (Thursday), and she had job interviews for the rest of the week in the city. It also took some discipline for me not to suggest the idea of our riding into the city on the train together. But I held back, and I was proud of myself.

I had to go into the city briefly that day before school, as well, as I had received my yearly note from the school—saying that I had not turned in my immunization forms. I had, indeed, turned them in, but each year the school either called or wrote to say that they did not have them. And each year I turned in another photo-copy of my paperwork.

I practiced diligently for two hours that morning, then I trav-eled into the city on the train and turned in the forms—during which task I was warned by a rather rude office worker that I was only a few minutes and a computer click away from having had my registration cancelled.

On passing Neil Silver's studio, I was amazed to find the door open. I cautiously looked inside and was surprised to see Neil Silver himself actually present at the school where he was said to teach—and clustered about him was a group of five or six students of the school (not just pianists) fawning over his appearance on television the night before. I was about to pull away and leave when Silver surprised me with a hail. I thought he hadn't seen me.

"Hey, stranger! You guys ready for the new semester? Ready for that competition?"

I almost looked behind myself to see who the other of the two guys might be when I realized that Silver meant Boston. I didn't bother to go into the room any farther or to explain that I hardly knew if Boston would ever arrive at all. I just said with as much busy friendliness as I could, because I did not want to linger: "Yeah, I think so. See you tomorrow, Mr. Silver."

On my way out to the street I ran into my old roommate. He was desperate to find a roommate for his new apartment. I thanked him for the offer, but I had no interest in returning to any such living situation.

I wandered about the city for awhile in the afternoon—going to several record and bookstores, all the while wondering in which of the great buildings Lana might be taking an interview. I had pledged to myself that this would be a day of rest, but my sense of schedule suddenly overtook me—so I went back to the school and luxuriated in the rows of empty practice rooms that could still be found before the formal beginning of the semester. However, my practice session was brief. I had told Aunt Elizabeth that I planned to be home for dinner by six, so I caught a train back east at around four-thirty. At about ten to six I found myself walking through the fading light of Pauktaug's gnarled, ancient trees.

I looked for Lana's car as I came onto the street, but it wasn't there. Because the Paws had a very small driveway, I thought perhaps that maybe she had had to park in the street, so I surveyed the dozens of cars that were then crowding the dead-end because of a viewing that was in progress. I kept looking back from time to time until I had to pass around to the back of the house to go in. My aunt was in the kitchen, smiling.

"Someone is here to see you!"

"Who?"

"You really don't know? You didn't see the car?"

"No, to both questions. Who's here?"

My aunt only continued to smile in silence.

"Wait, you don't mean—"

"Yes."

"Where is he?" I smiled.

"He's out walking and waiting in the woods for you. He's stretching his legs after the long car ride. Where are you going?"

"I'll be right down in just a second," I called as I jogged lightly out of the kitchen. "I just have to run to the bathroom for a quick second first."

I ran up to my room and retrieved Boston's letters. I made sure that they all seemed to be in order and neatly arranged in the box as I had found them, and then I returned them to the shelf in the hall where I had originally come across the box. I was even able to find the slight dust ring that had framed the spot where the box had sat, and I placed it precisely in that place.

I passed by my aunt again on the way out the back of the house.

"Sarah's with Boston, Port. Don't forget to bring her back. And we'll all go to a late dinner just after nine in celebration of Boston's return—if you can hold out and not eat before then."

"I think I can make it. Is there a big crowd downstairs?"

"Yes, but I'll make sure that Uncle Harry has them out by a little after nine. Be ready to go just after that."

I went out into the back and crossed into the woods. I thought of how impressive they must have looked to Boston when he had crossed the tree line by himself before me. Not only had my aunt and uncle never not sold off the land, but the trees were even larger, darker, and more indented with nooks and crags than in the times when Boston and I had haunted them as little boys.

I went first by instinct to the center of our little wilderness, to the grassy, vestigial baseball diamond. The paths between the bases were still evident, but now there was an oversized team of young trees standing in the field. Boston was not there, and so something drew me next to the old house foundation to the south. I made my way through the crowded outfield and to the path that led to the dark, little hollow area where the old house's stones still thrust up from the black soil. But Boston wasn't there either. I walked, then, back across the field and down the sloping path to the Sound. When I was halfway down the slope, I could see out onto the water and caught a glimpse of Sarah, swimming back to the still unseen shore with a stick in her mouth. But when I got down the slope a little farther and made my way around the boulders that concealed a small stretch of the sand, there was my cousin, Boston Gourd— standing quite plain and clear where the beginning of the deeps teased the delicate shoreline with a gentle lapping.

"Boston!"

"Port! Really! Really, it's great to see you again! It's—it's hard for me to say how good it is to be here again."

Then he fell silent and placed both his hands on my shoulders and shook me with affection.

We both took to a separate boulder and talked for several hours as the sunlight slowly gave way. For the first hour, Sarah continued to swim out and back after the same stick that Boston had first found for her—no matter how many times we tossed it into the water. But she suddenly became tired, and finally chose a long flat rock—still warm from the heat of the August day—and went to sleep between Boston and me.

After a time Boston felt it was necessary to begin to dwell on the silence he had maintained for so long—to try to apologize for it. He sounded as if he did indeed have sincere remorse for some aspect of the dissolution of our connection, but he did not seem to give any evidence to me that he really wished it had been any other way. Rather than become irritated, I tossed aside all my rights to pride for the evening and deferred this discussion before he advanced very far with it by distracting him with tales of Lana, and he laughed hard to hear my self-deprecating stories of immediate ardor.

I studied him while he laughed. Because I had developed an image for him in my head as I read his letters, I was amazed how little my mental sketching matched what I saw before me. To begin with—outside of CD covers and magazine photographs—his letters were the first extended evidence of him that I had had for nearly twelve years, so on reading them I had consciously tried, at first, to simply age him in my imagination according to what I guessed conservatively the years might do. As I had progressed with the letter reading, however, I also felt compelled to add, for some reason, an increasingly wan and haggard appearance to the face and figure that I suspected was scribbling out such strange letters to my aunt. But his actual appearance neither provided nor suggested any of these qualities. Save for a few subtle lines about the eyes and an evident absence of any last trace elements of baby-skin smoothness in his face, he looked rather like the Boston I knew in my last year of high school—no, even the Boston of the time slightly before that.

I told him that he looked well.

"Oh, Port, you should have seen me last month! That's why I decided to spend away the last bit of money that I had in my so-called expendable file with a surprise vacation at the campsite in Pennsylvania. People there say I came in looking tired and too thin, but that after weeks of walking, eating, and sleeping in the woods there I looked like a renewed man. I feel the same inside."

I wondered how precisely he meant his last line. But he was

rather neutral in its delivery, so I do not think he was implying that he could not get rid of something on the inside as he had on the outside. Yet I was amazed that part of my imagined image for him from my letter reading had turned out to be more or less accurate—when he confessed he had thinned out for awhile.

"No, I am the same man on the inside that I've been for awhile. The outside got a little tired of being asked to serve the inside, so I went somewhere where my outside could rest because the inside couldn't realize most of its ideas."

"You went where there weren't any pianos!" I laughed.

"Right, Port! Right. It's good to be back. It really is. I'd forgotten how much you could understand. You know—and forgive me for saying this—and I don't why, but I had imagined Aunt Elizabeth somewhat differently over the years. And even just seeing her for a little while before I came out here to meet you made me laugh to think how, well—"

"You can say it, Boston. I won't be mad. I think I know what you're going to say."

"No, I can't. Because another thing that I did forget was how really and truly kind she is. I believe that—that in her is, more or less, a slightly sad but otherwise altogether pure kindness. She just surprised me a little."

"By seeming a bit, well, dense? A bit foggy?" I suggested gently so that he could feel forgiven before taking the risk of saying so himself.

"Yes, that's it, Port. That's it exactly. Somehow I had slowly, and recently, painted a picture of her in my head as a quiet, now elderly woman, but of considerable power, hidden behind a satisfaction to remain otherwise taken for a quiet, sweet-natured caretaker. But I only see the latter right now."

"Well, there is a power there, Boston. Sometimes I think the goodness you describe is so well-formed that it translates into hidden power at times."

"Right, Port. Right. Hey, I'm sorry if it's me that is the one that really seems foggy right now. I drove a long way today, and I was up late last night watching a really trying concert that was on television."

"It wasn't the Neil Silver concert, was it?"

"That's it! Is that man as foolish as he sounds? Or do you think someone wrote all that stuff out for him?"

"If anyone wrote it out for him—though I think he was speaking off the cuff—I think it was him," I laughed.

"Well, you've been working under him. You should know. Did Aunt Elizabeth tell you that I'm registered at your school? Can you take having an old school buddy again?"

"Of course I can! I'd like nothing better."

"I think I'm in this Silver's studio."

"You are. I know. He's looking forward to it."

We both laughed at this. Then I asked him what route he had taken on his drive home from Pennsylvania.

"Oh," he said quietly. And then he got up from his rock and leaped to another one, closer to the water, and stood there looking out on the fading light and the mild waves, and to the rising lights of the towns on the opposite shore of the Sound, in Connecticut.

"I couldn't bear the thought of returning to Pauktaug by way of the city, Port. So I drove out of northern Pennsylvania very early this morning, and I meandered on county roads—even a few dirt roads—through the upstate (of New York, I mean) and then I finally descended into Connecticut and went to Bridgeport for the ferry across."

"You took the ferry to Port Jefferson?" I asked, forcing him into a redundant answer before he could continue.

"Yeah, I did. But it was wonderful, Port."

And then I knew he was alluding to our curious origins and the deaths of our parents—something I had hardly, if ever, heard him do save on one or two occasions in our entire lives. He looked again to the lights of Connecticut, which looked then like the distant rim of a disc-shaped galaxy, viewed from its thin, brittle, speckled side—and then he looked back to the maturing second growth woods. They were a magnificent sight of total blackness. Though my eyes had been adjusting to the fading light, they were still not able to see anything in the total, wild, darkness presented by that benighted set of trees.

"It was a wonderful ride, Port. I rode outside the whole way."

Boston and I started then to walk slowly back to the main house.

"But I made it across, Port. I'm going to make it across."

As nine o'clock approached we walked back to the hill that sloped away from the north face of the house, and I looked back and called to Sarah before I went into the trees. She raised herself from her post-swim stupor and caught up quickly. She and Boston managed the hill with speed, and I followed.

The crowd for the viewing must have dissipated a bit by the time we reached the outskirts of the yard, for there were few cars in the gravel driveway on the north side of the house and few cars parked in the street. We hosed Sarah, dried her off, and then secured her in the kitchen. There were still several lingerers downstairs until well past nine, so I went down and told Aunt Elizabeth that Boston and I would be waiting on the front porch. There Boston and I sat in the shadows on a pair of airy whicker chairs and watched as the mourners ambled off into the darkness—they mainly couples. There were a few trios, that combination usually two younger people flanking an elderly man or woman. And there were a few lone mourners, who left unaccompanied and with swiftness.

Suddenly Boston broke in on my easy relation of stories of intermittent and trying piano lessons under Neil Silver and asked me how my playing was going.

"Well, let me tell you, Boston, Portsmouth Gourd is never

going to catch—never, ever, going to be able to approximate—Boston Gourd. I can tell you that."

"I don't know, Port. I always thought you would—that you were—the same as my insides, ultimately. But you've had over ten years to catch me on the outside—with your fingers, I mean. I'll bet you're closer to me than you think in your fingers now. You're probably a match for me now. You were always a match for me on the inside. And you were always good enough that I knew you'd catch me on the outside one day. It was inevitable. That's what I've always wanted, Port, really—someone (especially someone like you that I've known all of my life), someone who I could trust on the inside and the outside, have real exchanges with about the inside and the outside. Now that we've had time by ourselves for so long, we can see for sure how close the work you've done on your fingers, on your outside, lets us match each other on the inside. We'll see just how close the match really might be."

"Oh, come on, Boston. I've heard your recordings, and I've read the—"

I almost said that I had read his letters. But I coughed instead to cover myself, then. He looked at me with interest. I continued: "I've read the newspaper and magazine articles. Boston Gourd is invincible."

"Boston Gourd is invincible!" he repeated with good-humored self-mockery.

"But, again, Port, what about you? What's been going on with your outside, your fingers? What have you been working on? I know that you worked your way into the studio of Neil Silver so that you could go to graduate school here."

"And so did you recently! Without hardly any effort."

"Yeah, yeah! That was more because I have a reputation and he had heard of me before. You, Port, really had to play for your spot. But I'm not even sure that I have the time or interest to try to go to school and prepare for this new competition at the same time."

"Well, you might as well try it, Boston," I smiled.

"Oh, yeah? Why is that, Port?"

"Because I'm going to."

"You are? Wait, you mean that you're in this competition, too?"

"Yes."

"Well, we really will see what kind of matches we are."

I laughed. "I'll hardly make it very far. But I'm looking forward to it anyway."

"Well, we'll see, Port," Boston mused quietly as he looked at the last of the mourners gathering in the walkway in the middle of the lawn.

"We'll see, Port, if you really can enjoy such a thing. Still, there is a lot that can be gained from such a venue, such a display. Don't you think?"

Boston looked to me when he asked this, and he was somewhat cryptic in his tone.

"Yeah, I'm sure there is. But, again, remember, Boston, I've never been in a competition that is so—"

Boston did not let me finish.

"I'm sorry, Port. I'm just a bit tired. I hope you do well. I really do. We'll work together so that you can win this—"

"Boston!"

"No, I mean it. I think you'll do well. I'm sure you're ready."

Then he smiled and looked a bit cryptic again:

"And your old cousin will try to play in such a way that it seems like he is—or is, really—playing his hardest, but you'll win anyway. I'll try to throw this one."

"Now, Boston, let's just be clear from right now. You're going to play like you always do."

"But I do always play as I always do—"

"And you're not throwing anything because of me," and I smiled a bit, then—just in case I sounded a bit too earnest too soon and sounded foolish.

Boston went from his cryptic voice to a dead, but untargeted seriousness, which he aimed away from me and out onto the night air.

"Don't worry. I won't be throwing anything on your account. You just stand to gain from my common course. It will only be coincidence if you gain from what I do. I throw all my competitions, you see."

I took a deep breath so that I could laugh at this and break what I thought would be a silence after a joke that I did not quite get. But I checked myself when I could hear Aunt Elizabeth calling for us from the back of the porch.

I got up and asked Boston if he was ready to go. He got up, as well, and looked over the railing of the porch and down onto the last of the mourners milling about in the front.

"Sure, Port. I'm ready."

I took a step to go but noticed that Boston was still lingering, still looking down into the yard at the quiet men and women in suits and dark dresses—and on a late floral arrangement that was delivered up the front walk by a courier.

"Boston?"

"Oh, yeah. Sorry, Port. It just looks like the end of a concert down there."

I went back to his side and looked down on the mourners.

"Yes, it does. Doesn't it?"

Soon, after a brisk walk, Boston, Aunt Elizabeth, Uncle Harry, and I were in one of the nicer restaurants on the west side of Pauktaug's Main Street—just opposite to the theater, in fact, where Boston and I had shared the bill during our last year in high school.

We had a long, quiet, warm, celebratory dinner in view of the harbor and of Long Island Sound.

Aunt Elizabeth suddenly interrupted our talk with questions about Boston's social life in Los Angeles. I excused myself at this point so as to visit the restroom. On my return, Boston was trying to humor my aunt.

"No, it's okay if you didn't read them. Actually, I'm glad if you didn't."

"But I did read them. And I enjoyed them all. I just didn't get to them all yet. You wrote a lot. I wanted to give it all my equal attention."

"Of course!" laughed Boston.

"Really. I just didn't get to the last few yet. I didn't even get a chance to open them up yet."

Boston laughed a bit more. Then he said: "I think it's more than just the last few, or you'd know that I haven't been with that girl since last year!"

"Oh, I knew!" insisted my Aunt Elizabeth.

Boston stopped this exchange when I settled in next to him on the inside of our booth again, but he added before it ceased altogether, "But they're on the shelf in the third floor hall?"

"Now, Boston! Leave them for me to finish. I want to read them all before you take them away!"

"No. Too late, Aunt Elizabeth," smiled my cousin, as my aunt continued to remonstrate with him.

Uncle Harry, tired of this particular topic, interrupted at this point.

"Boston, I hope you find your piano all right. You might want to have it tuned by a professional tuner, but I've been toying with it since it came, and I think you'll find it in pretty good shape. It actually held its tune really well, I think, during the trip across country."

"I believe you. I've moved it a couple of times after I left Pauktaug—even had to have it in storage when I couldn't find an apartment for awhile—but it always held pretty firm. I could never really rationalize getting a new one."

"Why would you? It's been yours for so long. It still looks

good, and it plays as strong as ever. But, Boston, even though Port's allowed me to learn a lot from some experimentation on his piano, I'm no expert. So you still may want to have someone else look at it."

"No, I'm sure it's fine, Uncle Harry. I appreciate it."

"But, oh, Boston. This I can tell you with sureness. Port and I watched the movers set it up when it came, and we both felt that the third—the outer leg—didn't look quite right."

"Yeah, I know about that. There's something wrong with the bolts that hold it to the actual body of the piano."

"It's not just that," inserted my uncle with some excitement. "Someone put in a poor replacement for the bolts at some point."

"Yeah. That happened during one of the moves. I didn't notice it until someone pointed out that the leg looked like it was at an angle. It makes the piano look like it might even fall over. Anyway, by the time it was brought to my attention I wasn't sure how long it had been like that and after which move the funny replacement bolts were put in."

"Well you can say that again—that it makes the piano look like it is going to fall over. I've ordered new bolts for you, Boston. In the meantime, I came up with something that I found and machined just a bit in the basement that'll hold it should you want to move the piano just a little. But I wouldn't move that piano a lot!"

"I saw the piano. It's fine where it is. I really appreciate all the work you've put into the piano, and I'm—"

At this juncture Mrs. Paw (Lana's grandmother), who must have, unseen to us, been eating at another place in the restaurant, appeared before our booth and leaped into our conversation.

"Oh, my! Hello, everyone! Oh, my! Port, Lana told me I might find another Gourd among you when I saw you all together again! And I think that was true! This is Boston, here again, isn't it?"

"That's him all right!" I smiled.

"Well, I really didn't even have to ask, Port. You and Boston look so much alike. I didn't see it as much when you were both boys and in high school. But now I really see it. You could almost be brothers."

I looked to Boston for a moment—who was on my left and on my side of the booth—and he seemed to look back at me with a subtle reaction. He seemed to give me a brief, searching, questioning gaze.

Lana's grandmother squeezed onto the edge of the seat next to my aunt, and there she talked quietly with her for a few minutes while Uncle Harry, Boston, and I lapsed back into talk of pianos. We soon expended ourselves on that topic, and my uncle gave me the money for the dinner and asked me to go settle the bill. I was happy to leave, then, for Mrs. Paw and my aunt had progressed into a conversation that necessitated intermittent looks in my direction—thus it was clear that they were discussing my recent date with Lana.

When I returned, Mrs. Paw had disappeared back to the booth from which she had emerged, and we all walked home in the late August darkness. Boston and I spent the next hour slowly unloading his car of boxes and other items from his cross-country move. Each time I went past his box of letters on the shelves in the third floor hallway, I wondered if Boston would take note of them or finally repossess the box. He never did. He continued to talk light-heartedly of his recent time hiking and resting at the campsite in Pennsylvania as we continued to go back and forth between his room and the car.

When we were done, we put the last of the boxes—things he did not need to unpack right away—underneath the piano, and went downstairs to tea with Aunt Elizabeth and Uncle Harry. There Boston listened to one last reprimand from Aunt Elizabeth concerning his tardiness and his failure to do more than just check in with the answering machine during the entire month of August.

She relented after he took a few charming oaths to be a perfect resident from then on.

Boston said that he thought it would be best if he skipped the first day of school and got himself in order and unpacked. Though I was still planning to go into school the next day, I proposed one last walk through the woods and on the beach before bed, and Boston cheerfully consented. Sarah went with us, and we three crossed the old diamond, went amidst the gnarled bass-clef trees surrounding the old house foundation and then went back down to the water's edge.

We talked for quite awhile there, and we skipped stones against the still water until well after midnight. The moonlight gave me a fundamental view of Boston's face as he vigorously continued our stone skipping. It was then that I could finally answer, to myself, the question that Boston seemed to have posed to me in silence when Mrs. Paw was first hovering over our table.

Yes, I think we do look like brothers, I said to myself.

Boston looked at me as I was studying him, and then he just smiled.

"You getting tired, Port?"

"Yeah, I think I am," I answered.

"Why don't you go back now. I just feel like lingering here for awhile. I feel like taking it all in again. I'll keep Sarah with me."

"You sure?"

"Yeah, I'll be fine," said Boston as I started to walk away from him.

Then he looked to the very light waves that had started up in the mild surf of the Sound, and he said, "The waves, the water, look like the scrolls of violins unfolding, don't they? But don't worry. I'm not going in tonight."

"Sarah might if you don't watch her."

"I will. I won't go in until you do."

"I don't think I'm going swimming anymore this year."

"Good. See you tomorrow, Port."

I left Boston there by the water's edge and went to bed. Early the next morning—before anyone else was up—I left for my first day of school and my first lesson of the semester with Neil Silver. After I was out the back door and onto the porch, I remembered something that I had left behind in my room. I went back and got it, and it was when I was leaving my room again that I looked to the shelves once more in the hallway and took note that the box of letters was gone.

CHAPTER XVII

REHEARSAL

My first day of school was the start of a wearying routine that would last until the competition in late October. Though I had become accustomed to Neil Silver's frequent cancellation of lessons during the previous school year, I was still surprised to find that he was not there for my first lesson of the semester. The cancellation notice on his door that first time claimed illness. During all of September and early October the notice excused Neil Silver for a tour of Australia and Japan. As I was long past being surprised at Neil Silver's habits of professorial absence, I was only surprised to discover that the school did not think it odd that at best I—and any other Silver students—only received about three lessons a semester.

When Neil Silver finally returned to New York in mid October, he was absorbed with preparations and business for the first running of his Manhattoes Competition. He would call me frantically from time to time and insist that he wanted to hear me in my material. But the times he offered were usually late at night or at some odd weekend hour—never at the original lesson time. I had complied with such demands in the past—when I had lived in the city and such treks were not too much of a bother for me—but as the competition neared I preferred to skip the long train ride into New York in favor of long, quiet, uninterrupted hours of practice. It amused me to find that Silver felt annoyed when I declined his offers. But with Boston in the house, I felt that I had an overqualified set of ears at hand to offer a critique if I needed one. Silver seemed useless to me.

Of course, Silver also tried to contact Boston—as Boston was, indeed, listed on Silver's studio roster. But Boston would not take or return Silver's calls. Boston, in fact, would have nothing to do with school.

His routine, as was mine, was set to start on that first Thursday of school. As I had only one other class besides my lesson, I was able to leave the city early that day and arrive home in the late afternoon. Boston and my aunt and uncle were just sitting down to dinner when I arrived, and Boston was laughing at a letter that was in his hand.

"Here's Port. Port, you got one of these, too. Didn't you?"

"Oh, yes. A warning about not being immunized. Well, I am. And I keep giving them the proof of it."

"Well, I sent them the proof of it, as well. But they say that I haven't."

"They say that every year. Just go with me to the health office tomorrow and—"

Then my Aunt Elizabeth jumped in: "Boston says he won't be going in with you this semester." She raised her eyebrows in mild disapproval and looked down at her plate as she said this.

"Aunt Elizabeth, I never promised anything—never promised that I'd be in school."

"Maybe not, but it would be so good for you—to be out and meet other people. And then you'd be on your way to your degrees so that you could teach at a college someday if everything doesn't go as you plan."

"This competition is going to be my last, I hope, Aunt Elizabeth. I know that Silver is vain enough that he'd hold a place for me in his studio even if I don't go to school this semester. And in this competition I think things are going to go my way, and I won't need these contests anymore."

I was amazed when Uncle Harry interrupted at this point and gave weight to Boston's decision.

"Elizabeth, things can be—and should be—a little different for Boston. He's on a level that is so high, that even I think he should be left alone to follow this competition path till he is too old to try anymore with that. School is always there. And I think— I suspect—that he'll have enough of a reputation to get a teaching position at a college even without the higher degrees. Most can't nowadays, but Boston does have some extreme exceptions on his side."

"All right!" sighed my aunt, with a vehemence that made me suspect that this exchange had been going on well before I had come in on them at the dinner table.

Boston closed the topic with a smile:

"Besides, I sent them all my paper work, and the school still says I can't attend classes because I'm not immunized!"

The rest of the dinner was rather quiet, and I tried to amuse everyone with mock complaints about my lengthy, laborious day. We were close to clearing off the table when the phone rang. My uncle answered. The call was from Lana, and it was for me. She must have held her composure for my uncle, for he did not seem at all disturbed by their brief exchange. When I took the phone, it was difficult to understand her at all at first, for she was rambling and crying—and angry with frustration. I asked Lana to start over after a few seconds had passed.

"Port, I came home from the city—I was supposed to have dinner out with my grandmother—I'm here at her house now—she's awake and talking and everything but she doesn't quite make sense and I think she can't move herself. She won't let me call anyone about it and—"

"I'll be over there in two or three minutes through the woods. Your car is there?"

"Yes."

"No, forget that idea. Just call an ambulance. I'll be right there."

I told everyone at home what was happening, and then I crossed the woods on foot and was in Mrs. Paw's backyard in under a few minutes. Mrs. Paw was still where Lana had found her on the couch in the living room. I was not conversant with such things, but I was pretty sure that her grandmother had had or was having some kind of stroke. There were moments when she was completely lucid, and she could then also move about in her seat as if nothing afflicted her. But then moments would come when one could tell that she was not there, that she was not seeing out of her eyes.

Lana would just stand back and cry when this would happen and repeat my name.

"Did you call the ambulance?"

"Yes," she sobbed.

Soon the paramedics arrived, and they moved Mrs. Paw from the house and into the ambulance. Lana and I followed them in her car all the way to Huntington Hospital.

After about an hour, Lana's parents arrived, and she went with them to talk with a doctor. I thumbed through magazines until they returned a few minutes later. They did not know much more about Mrs. Paw's condition, but I had been right in my guess that she had had some kind of stroke.

As we all settled down in the emergency room waiting area, I remember at first feeling guilty that it had occurred to me that Lana and I probably would not have our planned Friday night date. And then I felt further guilt when I felt regret that I was no longer alone with Lana in attendance of her grandmother—felt a bit jealous of her family and wished that I felt comfortable and in a sort of established place with them at that point. But this guilt was suddenly assuaged by a slight embarrassment when Lana favored me for company over her parents. There seemed to be no rift or anger that I could perceive between them. She just came over to where I was sitting after her parents settled in close by the nurse's station. My embarrassment changed back to guilt when I realized that I looked forward to the prospect of keeping a vigil with Lana for as long as she liked. And then I felt guilty for thinking again and again that she was a girl who handsomely and prettily survived the tear-smudging of her own makeup. Some compact attractive women only seem attractive to me when they aesthetically stay within the lines, but Lana endured blurring. And I told myself that she seemed less brittle and fragile to me because of it, even if the opposite was most likely true. She was still wearing the red silk blouse and black skirt from her day of interviewing in Manhattan. I admired all of this.

There were intervals when I would shuffle over, however, and talk to Mr. Paw. Then there were times when Mrs. Paw (Lana's mother) would come over to Lana and me and take a seat—and whisper to us hoarsely over the din from a television set that blared from the wall above our heads.

Finally during one of Mrs. Paw's visits, she came over and suggested that this ordeal of Lana's grandmother's was not something that was likely to resolve that night. She suggested that we drive back to Pauktaug—and that she and Mr. Paw would stay a little while longer. Lana started to cry again at this, but I was surprised and flattered to find that she also got up and readied herself to go with me.

I drove her car home, though it was something of an affected gesture, for she seemed quite composed, in a way, despite her crying. Without seeming indifferent to her grandmother, she kissed me when we were about to part and said that she still wanted to see me for our appointed Friday night—if not for our original plan, then for something during which we could be together and be close to home so as to listen for news of her grandmother's condition.

I went back home and found my uncle and aunt in the office on the first floor of the house. I gave them a summary of the evening, and then I went out to the woods and beach looking for Boston and Sarah. I found them by the water—Boston throwing a piece of driftwood; Sarah swimming out and retrieving it time and time again. After I gave the summary of my evening with Lana Paw one last time, Boston and I lapsed into one of our Sound-side conversations in the darkness.

"I thought I might find you practicing when I got back. We only have about a month and a half to get ready now."

"I'll be ready. I don't mean to sound conceited. But I'm ready. I'm already ready. I don't practice much anymore, Port."

"Really?"

"Yeah. I'm not really dependent on tactile contact with the instrument very much anymore. Oh, of course, I'll practice with you in those last weeks, just to be sure. But I don't learn much at the piano anymore, really. I just read from the score at a desk or while sitting on my bed—places like that."

"I've heard of such things. But I've never met anyone who could really do it."

"I didn't really reach that level till sometime around last fall, I think. Yes, that's when it was."

"I've made a sudden improvement, myself," I suddenly volunteered.

"Really? I'm looking forward to hearing it."

Then Boston looked at me with a probing but brief examination—rather like he had at the booth in the restaurant the night before. But it soon passed.

Boston threw the stick out on the water again, and Sarah followed.

"You're going to do fine in the competition, Port. Remember, you're the one who is going to win this time. I want to play as well as I can, but I want to lose. But no favoritism here. This isn't for your sake, understand?"

He laughed a bit then and looked at Sarah paddling back to shore. He did not think I would answer.

"Yes, I think I do understand."

I said this plainly, and it surprised me. But it raised the ante of Boston's probing look of response to a slight inner shock on his part, and he looked away from me. But I could tell he was thinking intently on something though he continued to affect to watch Sarah with serenity.

"Yeah, I don't practice too much anymore—hardly at all. Of course, I don't learn new pieces as fast that way, but my repertoire is more or less static now. It doesn't make a difference anyhow. All the good pieces are the same anyway."

I held myself back from answering this. Boston looked at me this time, and he knew I understood this last assertion just as much as I had understood his last question. This fascinated or disturbed him. I could not tell which. He remained silent, afraid (perhaps for the first time), that he was not alone—afraid that someone might be sympathetic to him beyond the realm of affection or the realm of his piano playing.

He was right. I was sympathetic. But he could not tell to what degree. I could not tell myself either. And I remained silent, too—afraid (more embarrassed than afraid) that Boston was sure that I had read his peculiar but merely speculative and narrative letters, letters that he had intended only for my aunt, or perhaps for anyone to whom he could disburden himself without being understood. It was then—though I did not know what to make of it—that I suspected he might never have thought my aunt a likely party to ever read or fully understand his letters. I suspected, then, that letters meant merely to placate a long neglected aunt and soon-to-be affectionate overseer had accidentally grown into something he wished he could have retracted. But I did not ponder this long—as Boston continued to speak after he hurtled the stick back onto the water yet again.

"So, do you know exactly what it is you're going to play in all the rounds for this contest?"

"Yes, I think so. This is one of those competitions that dictates almost everything."

"Yeah, a lot of the really newer competitions are trying to go back to that sort of thing—'so the competitor can be tested under less than optimum circumstances'—all that sort of stuff."

"I really feel like I should be playing more twentieth-century music than I am—and more really recent pieces. But I'm not."

"What difference does it make?" Boston said. "I almost never play anything anymore that isn't a part of the most hackneyed, established, popular, central repertoire. Again, what difference does it make? I only play the pieces that please everyone's grandma! Some people think—everyone thinks—that the public is 'resistant to the new and experimental.' Hardly. They're resistant to the potential, to the promise, of Man—to the threat of the artificial. In music from any period of the twentieth-century's so-called avant-garde, what one hears is self-sufficient Man driving away from the aged Natural Laws that dominated all music before it—and driving closer and closer upon systems, upon the orderings of Man. The audiences aren't really disconcerted by the new sounds. They're disturbed to hear their old Music, their old guardian, challenged. But there isn't enough challenge in this new music even for me. Therefore I like to challenge the old public, challenge them and their old master where they suspect—feel sure, rather—that he is strongest. Know what I mean, Port?"

I felt that I did know what he meant, but I said nothing. I just smiled, and then he just smiled back.

"Sorry you had to spend all that time at the hospital tonight, Port—even if Lana is such a hot number. I haven't been to a hospital since they made some of us at school play for some charity program. What a waste! How backward!"

When midnight neared, Boston, Sarah, and I walked back to the main house. On the way up the slope from the beach, Boston asked me about the list of competitors for the October competition. Uncle Harry had told him about it. Boston volunteered to give Sarah a quick bath with the hose, and I volunteered to get the list to read to him while he worked off the salt from Sarah.

When he was done, and while Sarah shook off the final rinse from her bath, I finished reading the names from the competition's roster.

"That's an unusual field of players," Boston muttered rather indifferently as he pulled his sleeves back down.

"Why is that?" I asked.

"Because I've been in so many of these things, I usually know a lot of the competitors. There are a lot of new people on that list—new to me, anyway. I don't know any of the men on that list—and maybe only one or two of the girls. I just know you, really—and me, of course."

After we dried Sarah off as much as we could, we went inside and locked Sarah in the kitchen for the night. Before we parted ways, I questioned Boston in a friendly tone.

"If you aren't going to go to school, and you don't practice much anymore, what are you going to do with yourself?"

Boston answered quite soberly, as if the answer should have been clear to me from the unspeaking probes we had exchanged since his return.

"I'm going to think about what it is we should do next, Port. I'll see you in the morning."

I spent some time in my room hovering over my closed piano in silence, leaning against its side and reading from a score that lay on top of the flat lid. At about a quarter to one I looked out my window over to Lana's house. Lana's car was still alone in the driveway, so I imagined that Mr. and Mrs. Paw were still at the hospital. Lana's bedroom light was on as it had been on the night of our first date two days before. And just as it had two days before, the phone suddenly rang, and I was able to pick it up even before the first ring was done. Lana and I talked for a very long time, even though I had to go into school the next day and had a practice schedule that I knew I would not fail to observe.

Starting with that night's call, I commenced what has been the most intense romantic connection in my life thus far. It escalated with a fervor that was entirely unexpected by me. Yet I hardly needed to protect my piano playing from this living passion—for the advance in my skills that I had discovered only days before expanded, developed, itself escalated beyond my most boyish hopes of the long past and beyond the range of my complete involvement with Lana Paw—a girl who looked a match, even a metronome notch better than even the most alluring sights in a magazine.

CHAPTER XVIII

PERFORMANCE

T he weeks passed, and a rich, cold, autumn framed my many trips into the city for school by day and my many evenings of practice and my walks with Boston by midnight. My renewed connection with Lana—though not my first adult romantic relationship—blossomed into what I feel compelled to call my first affair, in the premarital sense of the word— for there was such a speed and power to it. Suddenly, my poor aunt—who was not one to bear evolution very well—thought that maybe I was spending too much time with Lana, what with school and the imminent competition. But as she was the one who had originally hoped that I might pair off with Lana, and as even she could tell that my piano playing was taking on some heretofore undiscovered power and indefatigable security, she questioned and vetoed herself within the course of the very same conversation she had designed for her warning.

But I did spend all my Friday, Saturday, and Sunday evenings with Lana. And we took dinner together whenever we could during the week—and occasional lunches in the city when she was on her job search. Things were not going well for her along that line—and she was unwilling to take anything less than what she had had back in Chicago to start with. As well, her grandmother never recovered from her stroke or strokes, and the Paw family was more or less resigned to sit vigil for a woman who had been given very little time left to live.

All this while, as I prepared for the competition, and even as it began in October, my playing continued to rise to levels I had never imagined for myself. I felt I was enjoying a power that music, that Nature herself was said alone to enjoy—power without remorse or conscience.

I was free of the piano, free of music—that is how well I could play. Even I could detect how evident this was, for I progressed to the finals of the competition with ease and certainty. My sudden, almost preternatural advance in skills made it seem natural to me, and not a flattering shock, that by the time the last round was reached, the concerto round, the press and media followed "A war of cousins—A war between two Gourds!"

Perhaps I felt so little for music at the time because I was feeling so much for Lana. Indeed, as far as romantic, sexual love is concerned, I felt it then for Lana Paw—felt it overpower me, though other parts of myself were operating beyond my wildest expectations for their capacity. It overpowered me as an orchestra can sometimes overpower one in a concerto—there are times when one cannot hear one's self. I argued that maybe I could not hear myself in those excitedly maddened months because of the crash of Lana's hair, which hissed across the air like mallet-struck platinum cymbals with each toss of her head.

There was also the ever-present suggestion and presence of my cousin, Boston Gourd—always there to remind me of how far one could truly go with the piano. As the weeks of that autumn unfolded, I discovered that he indeed no longer possessed a tactile dependency upon the instrument. I never heard him practice; I never heard him play the piano for his own or for anyone's amusement. Instead, he seemed to take pleasure in alleviating my aunt and uncle of certain tasks. He would work on the grounds or go on drives for my uncle or aunt, and as October approached, he even started to work during many of the services.

Though Boston was a Gourd, a family member, he carried with him enough suggestion of worldliness and minor celebrity that my aunt and uncle dropped even a sense of probationary monitoring of his habits. They were pleased that he was pleased to be at the house. And they were not conversant enough with the history, abilities, and work habits of an ultra-accomplished pianist to ever question his routines. (And when the competition commenced, and they went to as many of the rounds as they could— and saw the others on public television—they felt confirmed that Boston was best left alone.)

But I did hear him play on a few occasions at home.

His mere presence in the house added a pressure and self-awareness to my practicing—even with all of its advances—that even the most challenging of recitals or master classes could not provide. But there were a few nights when I would seek him out— find him in his room reading, or find him in the woods or on the beach with Sarah—and then bring him in and play things through for him.

On these occasions, my playing seemed to remind him of something—jolt him into a recollection that he would have to attend to practicality at some point. Thus, without any comment upon my own playing—which he now acknowledged in a way that was both flattering and threateningly puzzling to me (with a probing look and silence)—he would sit down and repeat for himself whatever work I had just played for him. It was always at a level that was shockingly good—as respects the outward sound of emotional involvement, technical perfection, and interpretative command. Yet when he rose from the bench, he had the air of an unchallenged proprietor who merely returned to his home one last time before a trip to make sure all the windows and doors were secure. Everything was always secure for Boston.

The last time I played for Boston in this way was on the night before the competition's first preliminary. When I was done and when he was done, we went for a slow midnight walk into town and around the docks of Pauktaug Harbor. We rested on the end of one of the longest docks, and he turned to look at me there. It was the second-to-last time that he would look at me with his increasingly probing, but oblique examinations. I had not said anything this time to make him look at me this way. As in the case of the other two times that I had played for him, he was reacting to something that my mind and my newly empowered fingers had silently said through my playing. Again, I was flattered and disturbed by his silent scrutiny, and then he suddenly spoke.

"You know, Port, I never talk about this. I don't think we've talked about this more than once or twice in our entire lives. But I do think we may be brothers—real brothers—after all."

"Maybe we are," I answered as I looked out onto the water, and then I looked at Boston and could tell that he wasn't concerned with the scene.

"Maybe we could have some sort of blood test and see what the case really is. What do you think?"

"Maybe," he shrugged. "But I don't think so. I think I know the answer anyway."

Boston and I walked back to the house, and I went to bed on the eve of my first exposure to a major international piano competition.

During the two weeks that unfolded with the competition, I rarely stood outside of myself—or felt the need to—so as to objectively study this seemingly unstoppable advance in my playing. With each rise in my strange indifference came yet new triumphs of external accolade from the results of each round of the contest. My uncle and aunt were elated, and for the first time in over a decade, the old main house became an ostensible symbol to all in Pauktaug of a kind of striving, ascending, continuing, life instead of a pleasantly manicured emblem of the penultimate portal of the dead before burial.

Boston was unstoppable, invincible from the very start. It is often said that one needs nerves of steel to play at the highest levels time and again under the critical eye and ear of the modern world of classical music. But when Boston played then, it was not as if nerves of steel were meeting the steel and copper strings of that world. It was as if a complete form of steel was meeting its challenger—no, it was like he served himself as iron against the trembling strings and brassy pedals. And never during the entire course of affairs—even on the extremely well-advertised final round afternoon when Boston and I and a few others went against one another in our chosen concertos—did my cousin ever eye me or any other pianist with the look of one competitor for another. He seemed altogether indifferent to the other pianists, but there was a sense that he was inwardly regarding something about me at all times.

I played my concerto, and my newfound command carried me through with an inexorable, indefatigable, power. But that newfound command also brought with it a rather mild response in my soul when I met with an acclaim roaring from the hall—and even the orchestra and the podium itself—when I raised my hand away from the keyboard after the last pounded chord of my concerto. After my curtain calls were through, my indifference drove me to the back of the hall where I was free to observe and satisfy the only care and fascination that ran through me as the competition progressed—what it was I might finally understand in Boston from watching him play.

Boston and the conductor took their places. For an extra moment I watched the timpani player place his hands and an ear onto one of the drums' heads and listen—almost as one would when they place an ear next to someone's chest to see if a heart-beat can be heard. Then the conductor began to beat time, and there was a long roll from that same drum—then Boston and the orchestra began to play.

I thought Boston's performance might reveal something to me. But I felt so close to what I heard, and it told me nothing. And there was the added irritation of a man sitting next to me who fell asleep during the last two movements.

Boston's concerto performance was the meeting of his iron against the vulnerable steel yet again, and the audience roared and roared when it was through—and held him to the stage much longer than they had held me. The stage was besieged with flowers at the end.

It was not until early evening that Boston and I were able to go home to Pauktaug. He left on an earlier train than I did, for I was supposed to wait for Lana for a dinner date in the city. I knew that she couldn't make the concerto round because she was visiting her grandmother in the hospital back on Long Island. But when I went to the restaurant and she did not appear after twenty minutes past our meeting time, I called her house. Mrs. Paw, Lana's mother, was there, and she said that Lana was still at the hospital, but that she had left word that she wanted to meet that evening when I came home.

After Mrs. Paw gave me a perfunctory reading of Lana's message she asked about the competition. Then she sighed and told me that Lana was upset and that her grandmother had not survived the afternoon.

"I guess she just wants to talk to you about that, Port."

I changed out of my tuxedo in the restaurant's bathroom, and soon I was on the railroad heading home to Pauktaug. As far as the competition was concerned, both Boston and I had nothing to do but to wait for the closing ceremonies and the announcement of the winners that would come the next evening. I didn't think too much about it during the train ride, and I fell asleep after I had to change trains at Jamaica Station. It was nearly dark when I arrived at Pauktaug Station. By the time I rounded the bend onto our street the night was full, clear, and starry black.

Lana called out to me from her porch, and I went to her. Her was face was entirely spent from crying, yet she looked beautiful just the same. She was dressed in stringent black exercise tights and a top of the same material that exposed her middle, and her hair was wet from a shower. But she had a jacket over all of this. We sat on a close little porch glider—close like on a piano bench when one is playing a duet, four hands at one piano. All that follows she whispered to me in a controlled, resigned tone, as if she had been rehearsing it for some time:

"I just took a shower even though I knew I was just about to go to the gym. That was kind of dumb, wasn't it?"

Her blonde hair was darkened into thick-stringed sections from the wetness. She tried to finger-out the dampness as she continued to speak.

"Port, I think you know my grandma died this afternoon. Your aunt and uncle are the sweetest people. They've already volunteered to take care of everything, and I just love them. And, Port, I—you must know that, in a different way, I think I'm in love with you, too. But, Port, things haven't gone the way I saw things going here, and my husband—my ex-husband—called today, too, and I don't think I can live with myself if I don't try again to make things work with him. He's going to come to the funeral."

She was set in her conclusion, but I am almost sure that she expected—and thought it her due—that I would either contest this or show a great deal of grief.

"Look, Lana, why don't you rest for now? We can keep talking as much as you like as long as you're here. I'll make sure that we do everything right by your grandmother."

I had heard a teacher consoling an eliminated student during the semi-finals of the competition. He assured her that all was just beginning for her—that she had a lifetime ahead of her with the piano. I almost felt like I was paraphrasing or alluding to that counsel as I continued with Lana.

"And I'll always be your friend here in Pauktaug who you can call when you feel you need to look backward and into the past. I'll always be your friend, you know."

"Oh—" she began, and then she found more inside of her that could still cry. She leaned against me. I kissed the side of her head (into her damp coils of hair) and then held her for awhile and felt silly, in a way. I looked at her rigid, tense form, and with her black, curved clothes, she still resembled a fine, indefatigably maintained, instrument. But she had feminine, fragile legs, that could bear very little.

I walked home—consumed with my thoughts as to how this loss would color, augment, or eradicate my growing, mighty indifferences. I felt a backward, perverse, elation when I went into the back of the house. Both my aunt and uncle were there to meet me.

"Is Lana all right?" my Aunt Elizabeth began.

I smiled. "Yeah, I think she's all right."

Then there was a long silence, and then my aunt and uncle rushed toward me and squeezed me with pride. I could feel the breath and laughter of their simple joy when they were so close that I could not see their eyes. My aunt broke away to put tea and a little concerto celebration treat before me on the table.

"Where's Boston?" I asked.

"Oh, he's asleep up in his room. I don't know how he even walked back after the work he went through this afternoon," said my aunt.

My uncle took a seat then and beamed to me.

"I've got both of you on the tape from PBS that your aunt and I watched as soon as we could come upstairs from the service today. Can I put it on again now?"

"Oh, thanks, Uncle Harry," I sighed—as if it were paired to the first full breath I had drawn since the afternoon's performance. "I'm not ready to watch it yet. But it did go pretty well, didn't it?"

"Pretty well!" laughed my aunt.

"Pretty well?" shouted my Uncle Harry with an endearing disbelief. "I've lived to see my little Port—and little Boston—on their way to becoming the world's greatest and most famous pianists and one of them here still isn't sure about it! You're a good boy, Port. I've always loved you for it."

I warmly studied my aunt and uncle during a placid lull in our talk as we all began our tea. As I looked to each of their faces through an endearing, mellowing, distancing wisp of steam from my teacup, the phone rang.

My uncle picked it up, heard a few words, then covered the mouthpiece with his hand.

"It's Neil Silver for Boston—as if he thinks there's really any reason for either of you to talk to him now!" my Uncle Harry laughed.

"I guess I should go tell Boston anyway," I said as I got up. "Tell him to hold on for a second."

I went up to Boston's room, but he wasn't there—but I did, for the first time in a while catch a glimpse of his box of letters. The letter box lay neatly atop some unpacked moving boxes stored under the piano. I looked in my room, as well, but he wasn't there or anywhere on the third floor. I remembered that I hadn't seen Sarah since my return, so I was pretty sure then that Boston wasn't even in the house. I decided to pick up the extension in my room and tell Silver yet again that Boston was not in at the moment—though this time, unlike all the other instances, it was perfectly true.

"Boston's still not there! He's never there!" Silver paused for a moment; then he laughed good-naturedly. "Does he really even live there? Anyway, Portsmouth, what can I say? You boys pulled it off. You really pulled it off. It's kind of embarrassing, really. I've been getting all this praise all day from everyone for my teaching—but I haven't heard you all semester. And I've never had a lesson with Boston, ever! But you both did what you did, did what you had to do."

The latent criticism in his last lines irked me, but I remained silent.

"Listen, Port. This thing's really all over, so I'm going to allow myself to commit a really big faux-pas. I wouldn't do this—or leave such a message with you if I thought I could reach Boston—but I don't know if I'll have a chance to counsel either of you guys for awhile after tomorrow night. I'll be in Russia and China till January. Anyway, this is a real faux-pas to tell you this. But I'm going to anyway. I couldn't cast votes for either of you guys because you're under me as students, but the jury has asked for a tie-breaker's input now at the end. To put it as discreetly as I can, tell Boston to expect good news after I deliver my decisions to the jury tomorrow afternoon. I'd really like to see him before I leave."

Silver continued without breath or pause.

"The day after tomorrow I leave, and I won't be able to see him or you till next semester—and I won't have a spare moment at all tomorrow night during the closing ceremonies. I feel like I should give both you guys at least some business counsel—if I can't give you musical counsel. I wish I could hint that you're both going to have equally good news, but I can say that I think you'll still be pretty happy tomorrow night, too, Port."

"Well, I'll certainly tell Boston as soon as I see him," I inserted.

"Wait. Wait a second. I haven't given you the message yet. Tell Boston that I'll be in the hall—where you both just played today and where we'll have the ceremonies tomorrow night, of course—till the wee hours tonight. And I'll be there from ten in the morning till one in the afternoon tomorrow. You both don't have to come at the same time, but I want you both to come at some time during one of those periods so we can discuss what's ahead for you both."

"Oh, all right. I guess I'll come tomorrow around noon. Is that all right?"

I heard him write down and mutter *noon* to himself.

"That's fine, Port. What about your cousin?"

"Well, I'll tell him the times, and at the very least I'll try to get him to come with me tomorrow."

"Good. Good. I'll be in the main hall at those times—right on the stage. And tell Boston that I'll be there tonight to two, three— who knows what o'clock in the morning! I've got to practice, too, you know, so I might as well do it there when there is still such a wealth and variety of pianos lying around!"

I told him again, then, that I would be at the hall the next day at noon.

"All right. All right. Good work, Port. Stellar work today, Port."

I went downstairs and finished my tea and celebration cake with Uncle Harry and Aunt Elizabeth. Soon they had to go back down to the office to monitor a viewing, and I went out into the woods to look for Boston.

I found him by the shore, as I had found him many times before that fall, engaged in playing near the water with Sarah. When I reached him, Sarah brought the stick to me, and Boston sat down on his usual rock as I took to throwing for Sarah's swimming game.

Boston leaned back and looked up at the sky in silence for a time, then he let out a mild sigh to mark the closing of the day's hard combat.

I broke the silence and told him first about Lana's grandmother passing away. He said nothing in response to that. Then I told him what Lana had told me through her sobs and tears on the porch only about an hour before. He was almost silent to this, almost indifferent. But when I held to silence myself, then, and continued on with nothing but throwing Sarah's stick, he finally asked me, "So, what do you think about that?"

"About what Lana told me?"

"Right."

I thought about it for a moment, and then a large grin and a strange, almost perverse but sincere laugh came from me:

"I don't really care."

Boston smiled and laughed, as well, but then he stopped and rose up from his rock. Sarah was slowly swimming back to me as he did this.

He slowly shuffled closer to me, then stopped short from me at about two or three paces.

"What?" I asked him, and my own smile and laugh faded away altogether. I was not sure what I felt at that moment. I did not feel clearly threatened in any discernable way—nor did I feel comfortable. I took one pace backward involuntarily, and then Boston subtly made up the ground. Sarah emerged from the water at that point. A moment later I had her large stick of driftwood in my hand—and I slowly patted my free left hand with its end, like one might do to confirm the feel and power of a billy club.

Boston looked out onto the water with a strange indifference, then. But soon I could tell he was studying me—and this is the last time that he did this—with his probing, inscrutable eye. He was looking for something in me just one last time, and he felt he knew it was there.

I broke in on this latest silence with a report of Silver's call, and with weary accuracy I listed all the time options that Neil Silver had offered. Boston suddenly looked at his watch. And then he asked me, "Really? That's what he said?"

I just muttered an assent to this, looked to Boston, and then gave into Sarah's request that I throw the stick out onto the gentle Sound once more. She went in after it.

Boston started to head back to the house, but before he was out of range he looked back to me and said, "Port. That was telling playing from you today—very telling."

I wasn't sure what to say to that exactly. And then I thanked him.

"Well, I'll see you tomorrow, Port. I'm off to bed."

Soon my cousin was far up the west end of the beach, and the darkness of his outline melded with the darkness of the night as he took to the trees and ascended the slope.

When I finally returned to the house, I bathed Sarah quickly and then went up to my room. My aunt and uncle were still downstairs—and I looked down to the front walkway of the business to see pairs and groups of mourners coming and going from our house. They moved with the swift quiet of latecomers to a concert.

I lay down for a time. I was very tired, but then I quietly rose from my bed and went to Boston's room. I knocked, then looked in. He was gone.

I crawled underneath the piano and leaned against the back wall—feeling safe in that little cave-like darkness. I looked through the box of ordered letters and found the last, still unopened envelope. The old clipping from the *Pauktaug Press* was stuck to it, and I peeled it off. In the comprehensive silence, I neatly slit the letter open using a credit card and began to read.

CHAPTER XIX

LAST LETTER

Dear Aunt Elizabeth:

After all that I wrote in my last letter, you may find it odd that I should write to you again—outside of brief notes about my upcoming trip back to New York. Yet I still mean what I wrote in my last letter. I ask you to get rid of—if not destroy—all of the letters I have written to you. Not a one of them, and not the whole collection considered together, even approximates an expression of the idea I was chasing in my wandering writing. Strangely, I feel compelled to try to summarize what I was after just one more time—and then to see this letter off to join the set. But I still want whatever this turns out like to be destroyed, as well. I crave a sort of peculiar completeness—the set complete with one more effort from me; the set complete with a mutual fate of fire or trash bin. I know now—I think I know—that you are not a correspondent at heart. But please give me some word next time you send me one of your little notes or cards saying that you have indeed destroyed my letters. Don't keep them.

    I don't know why I plagued you with them—and couched what I wanted to say in such a long series of tedious narratives. I think, now, that my only goal should have been to let you know that I am well and happy—that I will be bringing a fellow who is well and happy—and clearer in his mind about the arrangements of things generally—back to Pauktaug this summer.

I would not want you to worry if I seem quiet to you now— quiet in a social way and in a musical way. Due to some great fortune of biology or mind or skill, I have discovered that I am not dependent on tactile contact with the piano in order to practice. So please do not think that the silence I bring home is brought on by sadness or frustration. So many people in this world go about claiming that they can't even hear themselves think. I was like all those people, Aunt Elizabeth. And then getting better and better at the piano made it worse. But now things are clear to me, and I can hear myself.

Why did I pick you for my reader, Aunt Elizabeth? I have told you some of my reasons. But I think they are faulty now. I think now that I picked you because you are one of the only people I still know of and can imagine whom I might trust who was an adult when my Aunt Maryland was still living.

She was a great lady, a great woman—a great man, if you take my meaning. I fought her as child. But as a man I've come to think nothing but what I suspect she thought. Even on that first day you and Aunt Maryland took us for our first piano lessons (you probably think I couldn't remember this), she thought that there might, that there should, be something even better that could be offered me. Even then she thought this. How did she know? I cannot say. It took me nearly thirty years to realize it for myself. But she knew it then.

Indeed, Aunt Elizabeth, there should have been something better offered me than merely the piano and its mere music. There should be something better offered and taken by all Man. My aunt knew. She knew even on that first day of lessons—

There is a part of Man—a part of the soul—called Reason. It is that part of him that is not altered by tuition. That Reason, that great intuition of Man, is always touted as the better part of himself, the force behind his individuality. It keeps him above the paltry sway of style. But that Reason, that intuition of Man is also a part of a greater Intuition: the will of the Universe, of Nature (this is, at first, both a boon and a yoke upon his individuality). All this, taken together, is called Reason. It is linked with, it is the laws of Nature. And one of these laws is as all the other laws—interconnected, eternal, ostensibly without flaw. Man is connected to this Eternal through his sliver, his string of Reason.

If we take, then, but one of these laws as representative of all the other laws—take Music, Sound, as a law—and still contend that the laws of the Universe, Nature, are connected to Man through his link, this link, this comprehensive tendon called Reason—then Reason makes Man, through that part of him that is Reason, eternal.

But what if Music is proven flawed—Music one of the laws standing, again, for all the laws? Then if Man rejects and ejects Music from himself, and thereby rejects Reason, his Reason, and therefore all Reason, then he is left only with his mortal self. He is the survivor. Thus, he is superior.

There was a time when my public, the public, began to see this through me. But they were too cowardly, at last, to do anything but slip back into being *for* Music again. They only chose to become filled with terror at the suggestion of their never-to-be-tapped, infinitely mortal and limitless selves. Gravity is an illusion. We only choose to give into it. Those who died—those judges—were only too happy to join their bones with the shards of elephant tusks and the splinters of soundboard pine.

But why did Man originally point the way for me to see so much in myself? And now that I see for myself my own power, why don't they assist me in the final blow to Music?

Why resist? If only I could have seen it myself when there was a consensus from them, as well. But they dismissed me, then, perhaps, because I was unknowing—for that I could forgive them. But now I cannot forgive them. And now they cannot forgive me for reminding them so potently of all the work that lies ahead for Man.

Competitions are a slow process by which flaws, weaknesses, are culled. Any true judge, any true judge for Man, cannot rest now when there is still a pianist left standing. All these must be eliminated—for there is a silence, a newness, that must now be heard. The piano must lose. Music must lose. Nature, Reason—they must lose.

Man does not win—but he begins.

CHAPTER XX

PIANO

When I reached this point in Boston's last letter, I stretched my leg out—part of a wakefulness coming over me—and I pushed against the third leg of Boston's piano. I could hear it creak for a moment, and then I could just barely see that the brass wheel was in motion and that the piano was going to fall.

I rolled out just as the leg gave way and the piano's nose answered the tug of gravity and pounded into the floor near the spot where I had been reading and had found the box of letters. I got up and stood in the stillness and listened to the piano's strings vibrating with a gentle zing from the impact. And then I looked inadvertently about the room in my daze, and my eyes fixed upon a familiar sight. Sitting discreetly between a stack of scores were the temporary, distinctive looking bolts that my Uncle Harry had placed into the piano's third leg so as to keep it from falling.

I left the house immediately and didn't say a thing to anyone. Somehow, it seems, no one had heard the fall of the piano—even though a small hole had been created through the floor and ceiling separating the third and second floor.

I ran to the station and waited for the next train to New York. I waited for a tense five minutes, for an exasperating local train that would stop at every station along the course west. I stood on the platform and watched the train come in.

Surely there had been, somewhere, sometime, trains (maybe old trains) that had collapsed of their own accord—when some unfortunate mechanic had been beneath some critical rusted axle at some crucial rusted moment. Perhaps catastrophes were even caused by well-maintained, off-duty trains—sliding out of gear and rolling along to crush some unsuspecting person on the tracks. But usually it was the train in service that killed—and it was the driver, the man behind the personifiable eye of the front window of the lead car, who could not stop the train and its great weight in time. There was almost always a person behind the engine's window—unable to stop the train; or unable to stop himself with that weight at his command (that weight that he also deplored); or happy to barrel on, to clear the tracks and the future by a mad and mighty, clean force.

I somehow endured the train ride. The cars vibrated westward along the lines of tracks until they vanished under the river to coil and wrap around the tall pegs of skyscrapers. And soon I was in the blare of Penn Station. I remember the crass wail of a saxophone player standing on the subway platform as I waited for the *1* train. People watched him warily, but one man threw a coin into the musician's hat.

Soon the subway arrived, and most of the men and women on the platform covered their ears as the train's squealing brakes brought its equally raucous bulk to a halt.

When I reached the hall, I actually found the lobby and the adjoining restaurants and shops quite busy and crowded. I slipped past a roped-off entrance to a stairway that led to the various tiers of the hall. For nearly a quarter of an hour I tried door after door, yet not a one of them was open. I felt foolish for not having gone right away to the back of the building and the stage door. And having reached the top of the building I decided to go back down, outside, and around to that entrance. But before I descended I tried one last peculiar looking door. I pressed my ears against it softly before attempting to open it, and I could hear the sounds of piano playing rumbling behind it softly but rather plainly.

I opened the door and discovered that I was in a control room at the back of the hall, above the top balcony. I could see the lighted stage and the darkened hall before me.

The stage was covered with pianos from the competition—and still riddled with the chairs and stands from the orchestral seating from the concerto rounds.

Neil Silver sat before one of the instruments at the center of the stage. He played a passage or two and then stopped. Boston stood behind Silver, and he pointed down to the pedal housing of the instrument.

Even after all that just happened that evening, I stood there and watched as Boston stood straight, tall, and removed from the precinct of the piano. Silver continued to make demonstrations at the instrument—with all his trademark contortions and histrionics on the bench. Though Silver looked healthy, strong, and young when I had seen him standing at other times, he looked at the piano then as he always did—controlled, broken, hunchbacked, even beaten. The music rose up to me with strength as I watched Silver's repugnant ministrations over the keyboard.

Then he paused and turned on the bench so as to talk to Boston once more—seemingly in a relaxed, informal way. I could not make out their conversation. Boston remained stationary, quiet, and standing.

I felt, suddenly, that I might almost be able to summon the primitive remembrance that had haunted me at the Silver concert I had seen in August in the company of Lana—but which I could not fully realize or seize. But I let go of the effort to remember—

even though I stood there feeling an uncontrollable and sober admiration for Boston. Despite all that had just happened, I stood there silent, possessed by complicity.

Silver rose from the concert bench and followed Boston underneath the enormous instrument. There they seemed to be examining the pedals and its appendages that rose up and into the undersides of the piano above them.

I leaned against the sliding window that was before me at the front of the booth. It had been left ajar, and that is how I had faintly heard Silver's playing through the door a minute or two before.

I opened the window all the way and gently called out Boston's name in the resounding acoustics of the great room—finally called out and allowed my voice to leap over the edge into a necessary fratricide. My voice fell down the balcony and into the orchestra with a suicidal plunge.

There was a motion from under the piano. Boston, who appeared to be closer to the edge of the stage, seemed to begin to roll from underneath the heavy black monster toward its outer front leg. Then that leg gave way, then the other two. The piano fell flat to the floor of the stage, and after the reverberation of the crash had ended, there was silence.

I ran down to the lobby and out into the street. I made my way to the stage door and ran past a familiar guard who only waved and smiled when I passed. When I reached the doors to the concert platform, there was a piano technician on his way into the wings.

"Wow! Portsmouth Gourd! Concert's over, fellow. Take a rest! You deserve it."

"I think Boston Gourd and Neil Silver are in there!" I hissed, out of breath.

I followed the piano technician as we made our way onto the dim stage.

"Yeah," he whispered in answer, "even with all these pianos,

Neil Silver asked me to set up another one for his use for tomorrow night's ceremonies. Can you believe that guy? I was just in here an hour ago for the set-up. Now I'm here to tune it."

Then the floored piano came into view.

The technician dropped his bag. He ran toward the piano, then halted.

"We didn't secure the bolts? What? We didn't secure the bolts? What? What? Didn't we secure the bolts? Didn't we secure the bolts? But this piano's been up all evening—and been rolled around the stage!"

I lingered over the piano for a moment. The dim light made the blood look black as it ran slowly down the delicate pitch of the stage toward the orchestra seats.

The technician stumbled back against one of the other pianos and began to vomit.

I looked to him and said, "I'm sure you secured them." But I don't know if that was ever of any use to him. And I avoided the articles that came out later which speculated about what may have happened.

In the seconds of quiet that followed, I walked around to the front of the piano. Something possessed me to open the lid and look inside. There was nothing to see there but the instrument's shiny strings and new felt hammers. I closed the lid and walked to the front of the piano.

In the half-minute that it took for the piano technician to leave and reach the security guard at the stage door, I delicately opened the key cover at the piano's front. I depressed one key. The tone sounded clear and true all the way to the last seat at the back of the hall, and then wafted back with clarity to the point of its origin.

Much later, I called my aunt and uncle and told them where I was. Somehow, I told them what had happened. My aunt just began to cry and my uncle took over. He told me to come home as soon as I could.

"And, Port, if your aunt asks you to play for his service I don't think you should fight her. You should do it. I think you should do it."

"I will, Uncle Harry. I promise."

I went to the train after I told the police again how I had seen the piano fall. I really couldn't tell them anything else for sure. And I couldn't think of a reason to then.

Boston had used an instrument of music to spearhead his attack on Music—and an instrument of music, as well, I suspected, to eradicate, crush, the unsympathetic. But the wild black coach he commanded drove against itself at last, turned back into a pumpkin even for him and smashed down on Boston. I was left, then, according to the story, either the last of the Gourds—or just simply alone, if, then, there were no more Gourds. Either way, all were unrelated who remained back home.

This I knew for sure—

I walked out into the noisy streets and headed toward the subway. Though the traffic and the city continued to sing, it was the air I noticed. I passed the piano moving trucks that were parked near the hall (prepared to carry off the competition pianos), and I recalled that the Indian Spring that had arrived with the return of Boston's piano had long passed. After that air had come a few more hot days—and then a long stretch of bracing autumn weeks; then a brief Indian Summer. But I thought of the air of my own breath, then; something was escaping with it. And I would carry on a lingerer for just a little while in the blare of Manhattan as I waited for the eastbound train at Penn Station—I a sort of fading Indian Boston.

I rode the train home in the darkness after midnight. The noise of the city slowly dissolved until there was nothing but the sound of the train coiling and shaking eastward. I looked across the aisle to a man sleeping in his seat. He had on a pair of head-phones, and I thought it would have been nice to have my tape player with me—to have something to listen to during the long ride home.

Then I thought of the labors that my uncle and aunt had before them—particularly what my uncle had before him. Not only did he have Mrs. Paw's body to contend with, but now he would also have my cousin's. It would take all his reconstructive and cosmetic skills to present Boston's body for a funeral. My aunt and uncle always encouraged open casket funerals.

I didn't go home right away that night, but walked for a long time around the streets west of the village, then along Main Street and the docks, then along the shore behind our house, and then finally in our woods. I wanted to let the ring of the train ride fade from my ears before I went inside. But even after that sound passed away, the sound of the frost-fearing crickets took its place.

I started to walk home. Then the thought grazed my mind that the results of the competition were still undecided. But it didn't matter, I thought. I would never play as well as I had just played ever again. And then I reminded myself, that if things didn't go so well for me along those lines after awhile, I could always go into the family business.

Printed in Great Britain
by Amazon.co.uk, Ltd.,
Marston Gate.